"Something's wrong between us and it's getting worse all the time!"

Polly turned so she was looking straight at him. "I want to talk about us, Michael. I've been putting it off, waiting for the right moment, but it never comes."

He began to protest, but she put a finger on his lips, silencing him.

"We don't communicate anymore. I hardly ever see you. You come to bed after I'm asleep and you're gone when I get up. We don't make love. I...I actually feel at times as if you're avoiding me. *Are* you avoiding me, Michael?"

"Don't be ridiculous, Polly." He could feel the tension flood through his body. He was irritated with her, and his voice reflected it....

Dear Reader,

Family Practice is one of the most difficult stories I've ever attempted.

Like all romances it is about hearts that break and, through the magical alchemy of love, mend again. The inspiration for it came from brave and dear friends who said, "This happened to us, use whatever part of our experience you find useful. We'd like it to be helpful to someone, somewhere."

I'm humbly grateful to them for their generosity, and constantly in awe of their courage. Of course, this book is not their story. Like all fiction, this is about imaginary people in an imaginary world, but fiction and reality do meet in the domain of emotion.

I hope this story touches your soul as their story touched mine, and that you remember love is the most potent of medicines, the magical element that heals when all others fail. May it heal your wounds and fill your hearts with peace and joy.

Bobby Hutchinson

FAMILY PRACTICE
Bobby Hutchinson

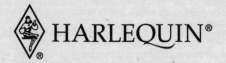

HARLEQUIN®

TORONTO • NEW YORK • LONDON
AMSTERDAM • PARIS • SYDNEY • HAMBURG
STOCKHOLM • ATHENS • TOKYO • MILAN • MADRID
PRAGUE • WARSAW • BUDAPEST • AUCKLAND

ISBN 0-373-70844-0

FAMILY PRACTICE

Copyright © 1999 by Bobby Hutchinson.

Look us up on-line at: http://www.romance.net

Printed in U.S.A.

FAMILY PRACTICE

For

Thomas McCloskey
June 17, 1979 - March 28, 1993

Thank you, thank you, to Terri Kessler, M.O.A.,
Lynn Archibald, Morgan Price
and especially, Lois and Greg.

PROLOGUE

IT WAS A WET Vancouver morning.

Dr. Michael Forsythe burst through the entrance doors to Emergency at St. Joseph's Hospital, black raincoat flapping around his tall, powerful frame like crows' wings. His curly, coal-dark hair was damp from the dreary February drizzle. His heart was pounding and his stomach knotted with dread.

"Where is she, Leslie?" The triage nurse stood behind the desk. She was the one who'd called his office with the urgent message.

Years of experience and an iron control during medical emergencies ensured that Michael's voice was calm, reasonable. It revealed nothing of the turmoil inside him.

"This way, doctor." Leslie led him to a private treatment room.

Michael paused for a moment, hand on the door. "Thanks, Leslie. Has she been seen by anyone?"

"Dr. Duncan spoke with her when she arrived, and she called in the psych resident, Dr. Keeler, when it became obvious Mrs. Forsythe was in crisis. He was with her until just a few moments ago. He's seeing another patient at the moment, but he'll be around if you wish to speak with him. Mrs. Forsythe asked us to call you immediately when she arrived, and of course we've put in a call to her general practitioner, Dr. Hudson.''

The nurse was far too professional to share her own feelings, but Michael recognized warmth and compassion in her tone and was grateful.

''Thank you, Leslie.'' He waited until she'd walked away, then he took a deep breath and opened the door.

''Polly? It's me, sweetheart,'' he said in a soothing tone, moving toward the slight figure huddled on the bed.

She lay with her back to the door, curled into a fetal knot, arms locked around her knees. Her long tawny hair was caught in a single thick braid. She was wearing brown tights and a loose, matching sweater, twisted now around her painfully thin body.

Michael approached slowly, then reached out a tentative hand to stroke the vulnerable curve of his wife's fragile back. He kept his voice soft, reassuring, forcing his own despair back into the dark corner of his soul where he'd managed, only barely, to contain it.

''Polly? Can you talk to me, my love?''

She was trembling. He could feel the faint vibrations rippling down her spine. She rocked her head, and he could hear her rapid breathing. Her eyes were closed, long dark lashes fanned against pale clear skin that pulled too tight across elegant high cheekbones. She'd lost a frightening amount of weight during the five months of Susannah's illness. As a result, she looked almost childlike, much younger than her thirty-five years.

"Valerie told me you tried to reach me at the office this morning, Pol. I'm sorry I wasn't there. I had an emergency—one of my patients at the Spalding nursing home fell and broke her hip— and I left in a hurry, without my cell phone."

She nodded just once, and Michael felt immense relief. At least she was responding to him, however faintly.

"Do you want me to hold you?" He realized that he would never have asked before. He would have just gathered her into his arms and cradled her. Now, however, there was this distance between them that he couldn't seem to bridge.

She shook her head and he flinched, trying to withstand the pain her rejection created in him.

"Can you sit up, then, darling, and talk to me?"

"I…can't. I already talked to the other doctors. I told them how it is. I can't go over it all again, Michael—it hurts my heart. I can't stand feeling this way anymore." Her voice was suddenly shrill. "I need…I need to be sedated. I want to be taken up to the psych ward. Please, Michael. You tell them I want to be taken to the psych ward. I want them to give me something, to knock me out so I can't feel." She was pleading now. "Just for a while, Michael. For a few days, a week. They said no, but you can make them do that for me, can't you, Michael? You're a doctor—you can sign an order or something.''

''Polly. Oh, sweetheart. Listen to me, love. That's not the answer. You know it's not.''

''Shut up.''

Her voice became a shriek, and in a single sinuous motion she was sitting, startling amber eyes huge and crazed, features twisted with rage.

''Just shut up. Don't you *ever* dare tell me what the answer is for me. You don't know. You can't know. You…you're never there. Nobody's ever there, I'm alone all day. I can't stand being alone. I can't…I can't…''

She started to cry, that awful keening that signaled utter agony. ''I want my baby. I want Susannah back. Oh, God, I want my little girl.''

The words reverberated in his chest so intensely, so hurtfully, he thought his heart would literally tear apart. It was now eleven days since their nine-year-old daughter, Susannah, had died here at St. Joe's, upstairs in Room 314, at 2:45 a.m. on a Sunday morning.

Michael had brought her in earlier that night after she'd lapsed into a coma, knowing as he hurried through the Emergency entrance that his beloved daughter would never leave this place alive.

And each night since then he'd come out of exhausted sleep—if sleep came at all—feeling the light, still weight of her as she rested against his chest; feeling the desperation, the agony, of knowing he could do nothing more except bring her here to die.

"It hurts, Daddy," she'd said to him earlier that day. "It hurts me. Make it go away...."

He couldn't think of that, couldn't allow himself to think of that.

"I want my baby, I want my baby..."

Polly's awful wailing echoed in his head, and he reached out and took her shoulders in his hands, fingers tightening on her.

"Listen to me, Polly. Stop this now." His voice was harsh because there was no other way he could deal with this. "If you really want to be signed into the psych ward, of course someone will do it. But we both know it's not the answer."

"Then what is, Michael?" Along with entreaty, a hard, unforgiving anger glittered in her eyes. "What can I do to stop the hurting? The pills you gave me don't help. I can't sleep—I'm awake all night."

He knew she was, because he was, too, but somehow they couldn't comfort each other.

"I don't want to feel anymore. I just want to be sedated so I can sleep, so the pain...goes...away."

"They won't do that, Polly. They must have told you they won't do that. Sure they'll give you meds temporarily, but they'll also insist you talk to someone, just as I've been begging you to do."

He'd set up an appointment with a grief counselor, but at the last moment Polly had refused to go.

"I can't spill my guts to a stranger. I never have and I shouldn't have to now," she'd insisted. "You're not doing that—why should I? And we've got each other, Michael. I want you with me. I want you to take a few weeks off and just be with me. Please."

"I can't, Polly. I have patients relying on me." His working had created a terrible chasm between them, but he couldn't do what she asked. He could control his agony only when he saw one patient after another, putting every ounce of concentration into his job, doing so until he was exhausted.

He'd instructed his office nurse, Valerie, to increase his patient load, to accept the new patients they'd formerly referred to other physicians, so that every moment of his day and most of his evenings he was frenetically busy.

"Will you at least meet with the staff social worker?" he pleaded. "Will you let her come here and see you if I can arrange it? She'll also suggest you see someone who does grief counseling, but for now maybe she can help. Then, after you talk to her, if you still feel you want to be admitted, I'll see to it."

Polly slid back on the bed and braced her shoulders against the pillows, wrapping her arms once again around her drawn-up legs. She dropped her head until it rested on her knees; her voice was muffled and passive. ''If that's what I have to do, Michael, okay, I'll do it. Send for whoever you like. I don't care anymore.''

He looked down at her, this passionate, unpredictable woman he'd been married to for thirteen years, this exotic, broken butterfly he adored, and for a moment, more than anything in the world, he longed to bridge the abyss that yawned between them.

He took a tentative half step toward the bed, but then he turned abruptly and quickly left the room. Frannie Sullivan would know someone who could help Polly, he assured himself. He walked to the desk, praying that Frannie was in her office and that by some miracle she'd have time to come to Emerg to deal with his wife, because he couldn't.

He had patients who worshipped him, who brought him gifts and wrote him letters and told him he'd saved their lives or their marriage or their sanity.

And yet for Polly he could do nothing.

''MRS. FORSYTHE? How do you do? My name is Frannie Sullivan.''

Polly lifted her head. The tall young woman who'd come into the room smiled at her, but it wasn't her beauty or her friendly countenance Polly noticed first. It was her very pregnant belly.

Polly was instantly choked with anger. How

could Michael do this to her? This promise of new life was the worst sort of betrayal.

"I've spoken to Dr. Keeler and to your husband, Mrs. Forsythe. You're having a rough time, aren't you?"

"I wouldn't be here—would I?—if my life was hunky-dory."

Polly's sarcasm revealed her anger, but Frannie ignored it. Instead, she smiled again. "Gosh, I haven't heard that expression since I was a kid. Hunky-dory—my father used to use it."

Polly suddenly remembered her own father vividly, and for the first time in years she longed for him. Dylan Rafferty, her huge, flamboyant Papa, was long dead. She remembered him best for bellowing at the three of them—Polly, her sister, Norah, and their mother, Isabelle. "Get in the car, my girlies. We're going home and everything's gonna be hunky-dory from now on."

And for a month, or maybe six months or even ten, it was hunky-dory until her parents' next massive fight. Then her mother would pack the huge brown suitcase once again and, dragging her sobbing daughters behind her, board a Greyhound bus. They'd get off in some nondescript little town and her mother would find a place for the three of them to live. Then she'd find a job—usually waitressing at the local greasy spoon. Polly and Norah would enroll in the local school, and for an indeterminate time they'd survive the terrifying interval it took for their papa to find them, make peace with Isabelle and bring them home.

Yeah, it was hunky-dory, all right.

Polly dragged her attention back to the hospital room because Frannie Sullivan was speaking again, asking the questions that seemed like litanies around this place.

"Can you tell me how you're feeling right now, Mrs. Forsythe?"

Suicidal. Desperate. Sick, frightened, hopeless. Polly searched fruitlessly for a single word to describe all of it.

"Awful. I feel awful. That's why I came here."

"Can you tell me what particular thing you feel awful about?"

Didn't she know? Of course she did. Surely everyone in this entire hospital knew Dr. Forsythe's daughter had died. So what was the point of making Polly verbalize it? Did this stupid woman think she needed to be reminded? The terrible rage that overwhelmed her at unexpected moments surged up like a firebomb inside Polly, and she screwed her face into a parody of concern.

"Oh, gosh, didn't anybody mention it to you? My kid died of brain cancer eleven days ago." Polly used the snippiest tone she could muster. "I know around here death isn't any big deal—you all just get used to it—but for me it was sort of traumatic, you understand."

Then the rage supporting her suddenly fizzled

and the pain in her chest expanded again until it engulfed her.

"Oh, shit, oh, shit, oh, shit." Polly wrapped her arms around her legs and rocked, utter misery overwhelming her.

Frannie's voice barely penetrated. "Mrs. Forsythe, are you wanting to kill yourself?"

The question didn't bother Polly because it was exactly what she'd planned for today, before the inexplicable impulse came over her to drive to St. Joe's and stagger through the door. She'd been heading for the Lion's Gate Bridge. From there she'd thought to make her way through West Vancouver and onto the Squamish Highway. It was twisting and treacherous, high above the ocean. To go faster and faster, then miss a turn and fly off into blessed oblivion that dark February morning would have been so simple.

Polly had lied to the psych resident when he'd asked the same question, but she didn't have the energy for lies now, so she told Frannie Sullivan the truth.

"Yeah. I planned it. I was going to do it today. Because I can't go on. Don't you understand, I don't want to go on?"

Frannie's manner may have been gentle, but she was direct. "It's been eleven days since your daughter's death. What's kept you safe until now?"

Michael? Michael was her safety net—or so

she'd always believed. She'd waited so patiently through the endless days, waited for him to understand that she needed more than the few hours at night when he was there to hold her close; when, with the help of the medications he provided, she could sleep. She'd believed he.would come to understand that she needed him more than his patients did, needed him to stay with her, that she was in a dangerous and terrible place. But this morning when she'd struggled up out of drugged sleep and he was gone again, when she'd called his office and he wasn't there, she'd stopped waiting. She'd finally understood that Michael wasn't going to be there for her, wasn't going to help. He was going to walk out the door, leaving her alone to face the empty hours, the empty house, the empty room at the top of the stairs.

"Who do you have as support, Mrs. Forsythe? Who can you call on to help you through this? Is your mother alive—can you call on her? Do you have a sister you're close to?"

"My mother's alive, but she's no help." Frannie Sullivan obviously had no idea how utterly ridiculous it was to suggest Isabelle lend support to her daughter. Polly's mother was and always had been so thoroughly self-absorbed she had nothing to offer anyone.

As for Polly's sister, Norah... Anger once again blazed inside her, the familiar anger of betrayal.

"My sister's busy with her own life." The truth

was, Norah didn't have much of a life, no family, no husband, just her job as a nurse here at St. Joe's—which made it so much worse that Norah had deserted Polly.

Right after the funeral, Norah had left. For four days she hadn't answered her phone or called to find out how Polly was. Then, when she came back from wherever she'd gone, she, too, went back to work. Oh, she'd phoned during the past few days, asking if Polly needed anything, but she wasn't available, not really. Polly knew Norah had adored her niece, that she was grieving also, but Norah couldn't comfort her. She obviously didn't have any idea how to even begin.

The fact was, Norah didn't really know her sister at all, Polly concluded with bitterness. They were and always had been opposites in everything.

"Do you have close friends, Mrs. Forsythe?"

Friends? There were women she knew, other doctors' wives, the mothers of Susannah's friends, but Polly had never bothered to pursue female friendships. Her life had been busy; she'd had Michael, her daughter, her art, her beautiful home. She'd been one of the special ones, the blessed ones. She had—used to have—such a perfect life.

"No close friends. Nobody. Just my husband. And he's..." She couldn't betray Michael, even now. "He's very busy—he's a doctor. You know how that is."

"I see." Frannie nodded. "So what I'm hearing

is that you're feeling alone and very disturbed, and you'd feel safer and more supported if you were admitted to hospital. Is that what you're saying, Mrs. Forsythe?''

"Yeah." It was a relief to be heard. "*Yes,* that's what I'm saying. I've been saying it over and over again. Doesn't anybody listen around here? *I want to be admitted.*"

"Okay, I hear you. And I firmly believe we all know what's best for ourselves. Under the circumstances, a short stay is probably a really good idea, Mrs. Forsythe. I'll speak to Dr. Keeler. And there are several grief therapists who are excellent. I'll make some calls and find out which of them has an opening."

Polly looked up at the other woman, and her eyes slid helplessly to the woman's rounded belly. "When is your baby coming?"

"Six weeks." Frannie stroked the mound beneath her navy shirtwaist. "I lost my first baby when I was five months pregnant. I'm just now starting to hope that this time we'll be okay."

Now it was Polly who nodded, and something shifted a bit inside her. "I miscarried before Susannah was born." She'd blotted out the memory over the years, but now it came back and she heard herself saying, "I don't want a grief counselor. If I have to talk to someone, I'd like it to be you."

Frannie hesitated, looking into Polly's eyes for

a long moment. They were calm and very blue, Polly noted.

"I'm not an expert in this field, you understand, Mrs. Forsythe. Perhaps someone else would be more helpful."

Polly shook her head. "I won't talk to anyone else."

There was silence while Frannie considered.

"Okay, then." She held out a hand, like a businessperson sealing a word-of-mouth agreement. "If that's what you want. But I'll ask you to make me a promise."

Polly waited.

"I want you to give me a no-harm commitment, a promise that you won't attempt suicide during the time we work together. Your word of honor."

Polly thought it over. In the five months that Susannah was sick, Polly had gradually turned against her church, her minister, even her belief in God. She'd tested each and found each lacking. None had made her daughter better or eased the pain of her death. And today, Polly had lost faith in her husband. She certainly had no reason to trust herself. She'd lost hope in every foundation that had held up her world.

"In return," Frannie said, "I promise you I'll do my very best to help you through this. You have *my* word of honor."

The woman's words sounded like a sacred oath, and Polly wanted so very much to believe them.

"Okay. I promise. No suicide." She took Frannie's extended hand and held it for a moment. It was a long-fingered hand, warm and surprisingly strong.

"Then I'll set up appointments for us starting tomorrow, Mrs. Forsythe."

"I guess you'd better call me 'Polly.'"

Frannie's smile showed she was pleased. "I'd like that—if you'll call me 'Frannie.' Now, I'll go and talk to the resident about your admission. Do you want me to send your husband in to be with you?"

The agony had eased somewhat while Frannie was there, but now it came back. Michael couldn't make it go away. Wearily, Polly shook her head. "He needs to get back to his office. He'll have patients waiting."

"Okay. I'll see you tomorrow, then," Frannie confirmed.

The door sighed shut, and once again Polly was alone. She looked at her watch. She'd been at the hospital almost two hours now. Time was passing.

Time. Half the well-meaning people at the funeral had muttered platitudes to her about time healing all wounds, and it had been all she could do not to scream and strike out at them. How could they talk about a future? All that mattered was the moment, and getting through it somehow to the next without Susannah.

CHAPTER ONE

Fourteen months later,
Seattle, Washington

"MICHAEL. It's Michael Forsythe, isn't it?"

Michael paused in the hallway outside the meeting room and waited until the short, robust man with the graying hair caught up to him.

"Good to see you again, Michael."

The man smiled and stuck out a hand, which Michael shook as he combed his memory for the other doctor's name and came up empty.

"Ralph Stern, from Pasadena. Internal medicine. We met three years ago at that conference in Vancouver. How've you been?"

"Fine, thank you." Michael summoned a smile, still trying to place Stern.

Fortunately, the other man was a talker.

"I spotted you at the presentation yesterday afternoon. Wanted to say hello then and there, but I promised my wife I'd take her out for dinner and then shopping right after the seminar. It went lots longer than I figured, so I had to leave before it ended." He winked. "Mary was put out with me as it was. You know how women are about things like that. Your wife with you?''

"Not this time." Michael vaguely remembered meeting Stern, but again no details sprang to mind.

Stern didn't have the same problem. "You still living in Vancouver? G.P., I seem to recall, with your own practice. Am I right?''

Michael nodded. "You have a good memory, Ralph. Better than mine, I'm ashamed to admit.''

Stern leaned close and whispered, "Ginkgo biloba." His breath smelled of garlic. "Swear by the stuff. Couldn't remember my own phone number before I started taking it. Not approved by the American Medical Association, but hey, whatever works, is my policy.''

"And mine. I've heard of ginkgo. I'll try it—if I can remember to get some." Michael smiled at his own weak joke, and Stern grinned appreciatively.

"You're still too young to need it. Speaking of memory loss, I see Griffon's giving a presentation on Alzheimer's this afternoon. Should be interesting. You staying for the dinner tonight?''

Michael shook his head. "I want to get home early. I have a meeting to attend tonight. I'm leaving right after lunch.''

"Smart idea…beat the traffic. What is it—about a three-hour drive from Seattle to Vancouver?''

"If you avoid rush hour and get lucky at the border. Did you drive up from Pasadena?''

"Yeah, and we're not going back until Sunday. We don't get to Seattle often. Might as well take advantage while we're here. Mary's mother's supervising the kids. It's a chance for us to kick back and relax, enjoy some time alone together. You have a family, Michael?"

Michael's stomach clenched the way it always did when he was forced to speak of Susannah, but his voice remained calm and matter-of-fact. "One daughter. We lost her fourteen months ago. She was nine years old. Astrocytoma."

Shock played across Stern's face, and Michael felt the immediate emotional distancing that occurred with a lot of people whenever he spoke of Susannah's death from brain cancer. They didn't know how to respond, and it made them pull away.

"God, I'm really sorry."

Stern's face turned magenta, as if he'd committed a social blunder of the very worst type. It was a reaction that had become familiar to Michael over the past months. He'd learned that doctors, who dealt with death all the time, were just as awkward as anyone else when death became personal.

"What a helluva thing to have happen."

Michael had never managed to formulate the right reply to that. He nodded and remained silent.

Stern reached out and gripped Michael's forearm in a wordless attempt at condolence. "Well, guess we'd better get in there if we're going," he said in a hearty tone. "Good to have met you again."

Michael let the other man precede him through the doors to the conference room, sensing that Stern was relieved to get away. For a moment he stood with his hand on the knob, considering, then he turned and strode down the hall to the elevators.

Up in his room he went straight to the phone and punched in his calling-card information. Then he dialed his home number, knowing even as the phone rang that Polly wouldn't be there. If he'd really wanted to talk to her, he would have used the number of the cell phone she always carried in her handbag.

He didn't want to talk. He just wanted to listen. Calling his home number was a ritual he'd performed for months now, and he'd stopped feeling foolish about it.

After the third ring the answering machine picked up. His wife's husky voice, with its undertones of energy and animation, said, "I've gone shopping, big surprise. Leave your name and number and I'll call you back."

Just the sound of her voice was enough. The ache in his gut, the tension in his body, eased somewhat, and he hung up before the beep.

He gathered up his shaving kit, stuffed several soiled shirts into the side compartment of his sports bag and bent over the bed as he packed his gray suit and tweed sportcoat in the suitcase.

Straightening, he caught sight of himself in the mirror on the opposite wall. He noticed the strain on his face, the grimness of his expression.

"Smile, Forsythe, smile," Polly used to tease, pushing up the corners of his mouth with her fingers. "You gotta learn to smile more—you're gonna scare your patients. Practice, now. One, two, you can do it. That's the ticket—feel the burn."

She hadn't done that in a very long time.

He gave the room a last careful check, then shouldered his bags and made his way down to the desk—a tall, powerful man with perpetually tousled, curly black hair, tanned skin and an intense manner. He was entirely unaware of the appreciative glances of several well-dressed women in the lobby.

Ten minutes later he was in his car, winding his way through Seattle's noon-hour traffic toward the freeway. It was a sunny, warm April day, but he rolled the windows up and turned on the air-conditioning. Then he slid a tape of classical music into the player and turned up the volume until he could feel the sound permeating every cell in his body.

This, too, had become a ritual. He'd learned that if the music was loud enough, he could lose himself in it. He thought for a wistful moment of Polly, wondering where she was and what she was doing, and then he let the music overwhelm him.

POLLY WAS THINKING about buying the skirt and vest she'd just tried on in Brambles, one of her favorite small boutiques on Vancouver's trendy Robson Street.

"That's striking on you, Mrs. Forsythe. I knew it was you as soon as I saw it. You've gotta be really slim to wear that cut, and the color's great with your hair—I love it short, by the way."

"Thanks, Dana. It's a good fit, isn't it?" Polly stroked a hand down the aubergine silk vest, turning in front of the three-way mirror to check the back view. The bias-cut skirt clung to her hips and thighs, then flared provocatively to midcalf length. The vest was good even with the simple navy T-shirt she had on; buttoned up, the vest could go it alone for evening wear.

And it would work with other things in her wardrobe, she assured herself. Which was a ridiculous rationalization, because she had so many clothes that inevitably something was bound to go with something else. She glanced at the tag, raised her eyebrows and whistled.

"It's pricey, but it's a designer label," Dana said. "The quality's there—full lining, finest silk."

"What the heck, I'll take it." Polly went into the dressing room and slipped off the outfit, then handed it over the top of the door along with her charge card. "Do this for me while I change, will you, Dana? I'm late—I'm meeting my sister for lunch—it's her birthday."

She quickly wriggled into her slim paisley skirt and matching jacket, then settled the gold chains she'd looped around her neck and ran restless fingers through her wheat-colored hair, encouraging it to stand on end just the way Louie had when he cut it yesterday afternoon.

She leaned in close to the mirror and applied color the shade of ripe strawberries to her full mouth, then fumbled in her bag for the amber shadow that matched her eyes. She brushed some on, found her small round sunglasses in her purse and put them on, then burst out of the change cubicle.

Dana already had Polly's purchases folded in tissue inside one of Bramble's distinctive black shopping bags. Polly scribbled her signature on the charge-card receipt without even looking at the total, waved a cheery goodbye and hurried out to her car. She and Norah hardly ever met for lunch, and now she was going to be at least fifteen minutes late, she realized, squealing the tires as she pulled into traffic.

She knew Norah was always ten minutes early, which drove Polly nuts. It made her feel inadequate. Why did so many things make her feel inadequate lately? Or was it just one big thing—her marriage—that made her feel that way?

She shoved the thought out of her head and concentrated on driving. There was a parking space right in front of the café. She breathed a prayer of

thankfulness and wheeled into it. After grabbing
the present from the seat beside her, she shoved
change into the meter, then sprinted into the restaurant, deliberately ignoring the sign that indicated the parking spot had a thirty-minute limit.

She saw Norah right away, in a long, loose,
printed beige dress that didn't do a thing for her.
How could *her* sister have been born without any
sense of style? Polly wondered in despair.

Norah was sitting at one of the wrought-iron ta-
bles in the garden area under the skylight, sipping
iced tea. Polly plunked herself on the empty chair
across from her, blew out a huge breath and
handed over the birthday gift. "Sorry I'm late.
Happy thirty-fourth, baby sister."

Norah smiled the hesitant one-sided smile that
was one of her greatest charms. She stroked the
small box with a forefinger. "Look at this wrapping paper. I hate to even open it it's so wonderful."

Polly grinned with pleasure. She'd spent hours
the night before designing the wrapping paper and
the card, painting tiny roses all over crumpled
brown paper, figuring out a card that was mean-
ingful.

Norah carefully undid the card from the intricately knotted twine and slid it out of its envelope.
Polly had found a childhood picture of the two of
them and glued it onto a folded piece of ragpaper.
Polly was about eight, Norah six. They were sitting

on the steps of their parents' house, squinting into the sun, arms wound tightly around each other, knees bare and scabby. Their mother had taken the picture—taking pictures had been Isabelle's hobby. She must have told them to smile, because they both had huge phony grins on their faces. Norah was missing two top teeth right in the front.

Inside the card Polly had printed: "With or without teeth, you'll always be the sister of my heart. Happy birthday, dear Norah."

Norah's hazel eyes filled with tears, and she gave Polly a quavery grin. "Thanks so much, Pol. Your cards always make me cry. How can you figure out exactly the right thing to say?" She unwrapped the gift, then folded the paper into a meticulous, tidy square before she took the lid off the small jewelry box.

Norah's exclamation of shocked delight was exactly what Polly had hoped for. She watched as her sister lifted the antique oversize gold watch on its long, heavy chain out of the nest of cotton wool. The intricately scrolled case glowed in the muted sunlight that poured through the skylight above them.

"Oh, this is too much. Oh, Polly, it's exquisite. But it must have cost the earth."

"Try it on." Polly bounded to her feet, took the watch and slipped it over Norah's dark, silky head, settling it on the front of her nondescript dress.

The watch made a statement, just as Polly had

known it would. Norah was tall, five-seven to Polly's five-four, and her height meant she could wear such an important piece.

"Oh, Polly." Norah's eyes were troubled. "It's far too expensive. You can't spend this kind of money on me."

"Phooey. It's perfect on you. I saw it and just knew you had to have it. Pretend it's a family heirloom."

"That's a whopping big pretend. Our family runs more to plastic than gold." Norah cradled the watch in her hand. "I'm very grateful—don't think that I'm not—but I still think it cost way too much."

"Stop worrying and just enjoy, okay?"

The waiter appeared, and Polly grabbed the menu and studied it, then made an instant decision. "Cauliflower soup and a vegetarian bagel on sesame, loaded."

Norah took much longer, asking questions about the daily soup and the types of salad dressing before she finally ordered. Then, still cradling the watch in her palm, she tipped her head to one side, eyeing Polly. "When did you get your hair cut?"

"Yesterday afternoon. I got tired of it long. You like?"

Norah considered and then nodded. "You got it streaked, too, right? I definitely like it, but I thought you said once that Michael liked your hair long."

Polly felt a stab of irritation. It was hard to tell anymore what Michael liked, and she didn't appreciate Norah's reminding her of it. She waved her hand airily.

"Nothing like a change. It's a surprise. He hasn't seen it yet. He's in Seattle at some medical conference."

"How come you didn't go along? I thought you loved Seattle."

Polly shrugged. "I didn't feel like it this time." And Michael hadn't asked her. She really didn't want to talk about Michael right now.

"Why don't you get your hair cut, too, Norah? This new guy I found is a genius. His name's Louie. He's in a salon on Granville. You could get it lightened a couple of shades—I bet it'd turn a rich oak color." She squinted at Norah. If anyone was guessing, they'd probably assume Norah was the older sister, with her straight, brown, no-nonsense, shoulder-length bob and her frumpy dress. Although the watch really helped. No doubt about it.

"I like my hair this way. It's easy to pin up into a bun for work, and I don't have to fuss about getting it cut all the time."

Polly had had enough similar conversations to know that Norah wouldn't change her mind, so she gave up. "How's work going? Lotsa babies?" Norah was an obstetrical nurse at St. Joe's. She'd never married, and work was her whole life, as far as Polly could figure.

"An avalanche of them. Must be the full moon. Yesterday we delivered the cutest twins you ever saw, a boy and a girl, both with curly red hair. The parents already have four other kids and the dad's out of a job, so this is gonna be a real stretch for them. The pregnancy was an accident." Norah rolled her eyes. "Listen to the moms and it sounds like three out of every five kids are unplanned. Makes you wonder what people're thinking about. Not birth control—that's for sure."

Polly nodded and smiled and did her best to look interested, while inside her heart kicked painfully against her ribs just as the child she longed to carry would have, the child Michael refused to let her conceive, the child who would fill the aching void Susannah had left behind.

CHAPTER TWO

POLLY OFTEN IMAGINED the child she would have. It would be round-cheeked and beautiful. Its downy head would nuzzle her breast as a rosebud mouth closed greedily around her nipple. One tiny hand would curl around her finger, relaxing as her milk soothed the hunger pangs...

She should trick him, get pregnant without his consent, sabotage the condoms, the spermicidal cream. It wasn't the first time she'd considered it. After all, she'd tell him, accidents happened all the time, just ask Norah.

Except she couldn't. It would be a betrayal of everything in their marriage.

Not that Michael didn't want another child; she knew that. It was because of that first miscarriage; and then Susannah's birth had been difficult, so difficult he wouldn't let her try again.

But it was her body, damn it. It was her life. She'd screamed those very facts at him only days ago. He'd said, in that quiet, deliberate *doctor* tone that drove her nutty, that although her body was hers, he refused to risk her life with *his* child.

"Cauliflower soup? And the Caesar for you,

ma'am. Enjoy.'' The waiter placed their food on the table, and Polly concentrated on it, willing herself to taste, to swallow, to comment on how good everything was, even though she wasn't hungry in the slightest.

"You talked to Mom recently?'' Norah buttered a hot roll.

Polly shook her head. Here was still another subject she'd rather not get into. "Not since that last argument I had with her over the yard. You?''

Norah nodded. "She called this morning. Wants me to go over there for supper tonight to celebrate my birthday. I thought maybe she'd invited you and Michael.''

"Nope. I guess she's still mad at me for telling her the place looks like the city dump.''

"It does, but you *were* kind of hard on her.'' Norah tore pieces off the roll and lined them up in a row on her plate. "Losing your temper doesn't get you anywhere with Mom—you should know that by now. It just makes her mad, and then she gets more stubborn than ever.''

Polly put her spoon down and gave her sister a look. "*Me,* hard on *her?* Try that the other way around. That woman doesn't give a moment's thought to anyone but herself. She never did. And you can't deny that yard of hers is a pigsty, to say nothing of the house. Have you gone into her bedroom lately?'' Polly shuddered. "Cartons piled halfway to the ceiling, clothes everywhere. And the basement, vegetables going rotten, old furniture, all those boxes of old magazines. God. All I was doing was suggesting she let us hire somebody to clean it up. Is that so bad?''

''I know. I know what mom's like. Let's not argue about it, okay?'' Norah gave Polly a placating smile. ''I just go insane sometimes and actually think we could all get together and have a nice meal, the way normal families do.''

Polly shook her head. ''Not in this lifetime. Not with our mother. She's anything but normal.''

''And what's normal anyway, right?'' Norah couldn't stand discord; Polly knew that.

''Right.'' Polly relented. After all, it was her sister's birthday. They shouldn't rehash old grievances over a celebratory lunch. ''Certainly nobody I know even comes close.''

But even as she tossed off the flippant words, Polly knew they weren't true. At dusk, after the stores had closed and there was nothing to do and nowhere to go but home, she searched for normal families as she drove slowly down quiet streets, up back alleys.

In summer they were gathered around barbecues, swimming in backyard pools, tossing balls in parks, walking aimlessly with a dog on a leash, a baby in a backpack, an older kid on a tricycle. In winter they sat around a fireplace, making popcorn, watching rented videos.

They were everywhere—mothers, fathers, children, happy families doing everyday things. And the worst of all for Polly was that she remembered exactly how it felt to have a normal family of her own.

Stay focused on the present. Wasn't that what Frannie had always recommended? Polly faked a grin and said, ''So what's happening on the relationship front, Sis? Any action I should know about?''

Norah smiled and shook her head. ''None. I haven't been out on a date in months.''

Polly felt familiar irritation flare at Norah's passiveness. If it were *her,* if she were single and lonely, as she suspected Norah was, she'd darned well find a way to meet someone. Vancouver was a big city; there had to be attractive, available men out there.

''No cute single guys at the hospital?'' It seemed to Polly a logical place for meeting men.

''Obstetrics isn't exactly the best place to meet single guys. The patients are all female, remember,'' Norah pointed out with a grimace. ''And besides, it's not very romantic to date someone who spends his entire working life examining vaginas. Who wants to date someone who knows more about your private parts than you do yourself?''

Polly had to laugh. Norah could be funny sometimes.

''Maybe you oughta try a younger version of those dances Mom goes to. She never seems to

have any shortage of guys hanging around.''
Polly's tone was acerbic.

"I guess I missed out on whatever genes Mom
has that makes her irresistible to men.'' Norah concentrated on her salad. "And at her age, it's innocent—there's probably no sex involved. I read a
report in a medical journal that said about seventy
percent of men over the age of sixty are impotent
for one reason or another.''

"Impotent I couldn't care less about,'' Polly
said. "It's just too bad none of them are clean
freaks who'd tidy up that yard of hers.''

Norah gave her a pained look, and Polly held up
her hands, palms out, and said, "Sorry, sorry, not
another word about Mom's place, I promise.''

It was an easy vow to keep, because the waiters
arrived just then with the chocolate-layer cake
Polly had special-ordered when she'd made their
reservation.

Candles ablaze on the cake, the staff grouped
around the table and sang "Happy Birthday,'' and
although Norah was embarrassed by the attention
they attracted from the other patrons, Polly sensed
that her sister was pleased. They ate slabs of cake
with ice cream, and it was after three by the time
Polly waved a cheery goodbye to Norah outside
the restaurant.

There was a parking violation tucked under the
windshield wiper of her car. Unperturbed, Polly
extracted it and shoved it in the glove compart-

ment, along with the other two she'd recently accumulated.

She must remember to give them to Michael. His business manager, Raymond Stokes, took care of such things.

Before she started the car Polly sat for a moment, deliberating over where to go for the rest of the afternoon. She extracted her cell phone from her handbag and dialed home for messages.

Modern Accents had called, saying the china she'd special-ordered had arrived; this pleased her. Next there were several hang-ups, and several messages asking that Michael call his bank manager, which Polly ignored. Then the machine beeped again, and her mother's loud, irritated voice came on the line.

"Polly, you know how I hate talking on these things…you're never home anymore. Anyway, I'm calling because I want you and Michael to come to supper tonight. It's Norah's birthday, you know. Come at five. I like to eat early. And call me so I know you heard this, okay?"

Polly's mouth thinned with anger and exasperation and she drummed her manicured fingers on the steering wheel. So Isabelle had decided at the last minute that she'd invite them, had she? And trust her mother to just assume they didn't have a thing to do except race over there, slavering with delight.

Well, Isabelle could just think again.

Polly turned the key and the motor roared to life.

Michael was in Seattle, and she was going to pretend she hadn't gotten the message in time. She'd already celebrated Norah's birthday; she wouldn't be letting her sister down.

To hell with Isabelle.

Darting from lane to lane in the heavy afternoon traffic, Polly headed over to Pacific Center to pick up the china. Then, she decided, she'd go and sit in a quiet café somewhere and drink Perrier water and lime juice for an hour or so. By the time she got home her mother's invitation would be ancient history.

IT WAS LATE AFTERNOON when Michael parked in the circular driveway in front of the house; he'd be leaving again in a few moments so there was no point putting the car in the garage. He wanted to check on several of his hospital patients, then drop by the office for the list of the house calls Valerie would have lined up for him for this evening.

He slid out of the car and stretched cramped muscles, breathing in the smell of bark mulch and newly turned earth from the flower beds. The gardeners had come by today, Michael noted. The rosebushes were pruned and bedding-out plants were arranged in careful patterns in the flower beds and along the slate path leading to the front door.

Inside, sunlight streamed through the skylight in

the living room, and the smell of lemon oil and pine cleaner signaled that the cleaning service had also come by recently.

"Polly?" Michael's voice echoed through the large, airy rooms and up the wide stairwell, even though he knew she was out. Her car wasn't in the driveway, and the house had a different feeling when Polly was in, as if her energy charged the very air.

He made his way into the kitchen and opened the fridge. A pitcher of orange juice sat on the top shelf. He poured himself a glass, programmed the answering machine to replay today's messages and drank the juice as he listened. He was surprised when the third urgent request from Arthur Berina, his bank manager, contained the man's home number.

What was up with Berina? Why wasn't he contacting Raymond if something financial had been overlooked?

The next message, from Polly's mother, indicated to Michael where his wife probably was. He glanced at the clock, and decided he could at least make an appearance at Isabelle's before he was due at the meeting that night. Also, with luck, he could reach Berina before he left the bank for the day.

He punched in Berina's number and exchanged pleasantries with the clerk who answered. Her father was one of Michael's patients. In a moment Berina came on the line.

"Michael, thank you for returning my calls." Berina's voice was strained. "There's a problem with your accounts, which I'm certain is easily remedied. I'll just call things up on my computer so I can be accurate here. Ah, there we are. Are you aware that both your business and your personal checking accounts are overdrawn?"

Michael scowled. He wasn't, and Berina was making him feel like a kid called up in front of the principal. This was exactly why he had a business manager. Raymond must have screwed up somehow.

"Today your direct debit deductions took both accounts well beyond your overdraft limit," Berina added. "I authorized the payments, of course, but I'd appreciate it if you would cover them at your earliest convenience."

Now Michael was shocked and puzzled as well as annoyed. "You're quite certain both accounts are overdrawn?"

"Absolutely certain. I have the balance sheet here in front of me." Alarm sifted through Michael as Berina read off staggering amounts. He frowned, trying to figure out how such a thing could possibly have happened. Raymond was meticulous; he'd never made a mistake like this before.

"But I deposited several generous checks to

each account only a week ago,'' he said after a moment's thought. ''The deposits must have somehow gotten screwed up.''

''I have a record here of two deposits, one to your business account and one to your personal account.'' The manager read off the dates and the amounts; both seemed correct. ''However, two debits went through that same afternoon, for more than the deposits.''

Michael knew he hadn't authorized Raymond to withdraw such large amounts. ''Look, Arthur, I'm terribly sorry about this. As you know, my business manager, Raymond Stokes, handles my financial affairs. I'm going to call him right now and find out what's going on. Certainly either he or I will be in first thing tomorrow to straighten this out.''

A long, pregnant silence followed, and Michael waited impatiently, wondering what on earth Arthur expected him to do beyond that.

''I hate to be the one to break this to you, Michael,'' Arthur finally said dolefully. ''I was afraid of this when I found your accounts were overdrawn. I was notified by the R.C.M.P. just this afternoon that Stokes has disappeared, along with sizable amounts of his clients' money. It appears two other clients of ours also used him as their business manager. There's a warrant out for his arrest.''

CHAPTER THREE

MICHAEL SHOOK HIS HEAD in shock and denial. "That can't be right, Arthur. It must be a different Stokes. I've known Raymond for years. He's absolutely honest. He's been my business manager for five years. It has to be a different man."

"I've got the information from the police right here in front of me," Berina said. "It was actually Mrs. Stokes who notified the police. She thought her husband was away on a business trip, but after a few days she realized that all the money in their personal accounts was missing."

He read off Raymond's business address and phone number. With a sinking feeling inside, Michael recognized them; they were Raymond's.

"When the police checked Stokes's office, they found it stripped," Berina reported. "Apparently his partner, Ms. Coombs, is missing, too. The police suspect they left together. Several of his clients realized that their accounts were empty, and that's when it became obvious people's money and some of their investments were gone along with Mr. Stokes and Ms. Coombs. I hope this isn't going to affect you too seriously, Michael."

Berina paused expectantly, but Michael didn't respond. He felt as if he'd taken a hard punch in the gut.

"I suggest you call this Constable Roper I spoke with today."

Berina gave the number, and Michael scribbled it on the pad beside the telephone. Then he slowly replaced the handset, trying to stay calm to determine how serious the situation was, but knowing already that it could be financially disastrous.

Over the years as his medical practice had become larger and his business affairs more complex, he'd gradually turned over control of almost all his financial dealings to Raymond. Raymond's office paid all his monthly bills, both personal and business related. They managed his investments, calculated his income tax, kept track of his expenses. He wouldn't know for certain until tomorrow, but certainly Raymond had access to far more than his checking accounts.

Michael swore, and icy foreboding ran down his spine. He stuffed his hands into the pockets of his trousers and strode blindly through the gleaming, artistically decorated rooms of his house, cursing his own stupidity at giving such control to someone else.

Mentally he went over what he could remember of his investment portfolio. There were mutual funds, stocks, various diversified investments Raymond had recommended over the years. The man would have had to forge Michael's signature to cash them in, but that wouldn't have posed a problem. Michael had authorized Raymond to sign Michael's name numerous times, when some niggling piece of paper needed his signature immediately and Michael had been too busy to break away.

Feeling sick, Michael acknowledged he'd been trusting and increasingly careless, believing Raymond to be an honest man.

Michael's practice earned him a generous income, but expenses were correspondingly high. The house was mortgaged fairly heavily; he and Polly had moved to this upscale neighborhood only four years before from the modest bungalow they'd lived in since early in their marriage. They'd done extensive, very expensive, renovations—rewiring, adding the pool in the back and a studio for Polly's art, putting in another full bathroom on the main floor. The changes had necessitated a hefty second mortgage.

Also, he'd bought new office furniture and several pieces of expensive medical equipment in the past year. And he'd given Polly the new car for her birthday last November. Plus there was the steady stream of household bills, the staggering amounts Polly charged to her cards every month. She'd become a profligate shopper some months after Susannah died, and Michael had never discouraged her; if it brought her some measure of happiness, it was worth it, he reasoned. It was one positive thing he could do for her, he'd told himself bitterly, and he could afford it. After all, he'd safeguarded their future well with wise investments.

Now it was probable those investments were gone.

A terrible sense of loneliness and failure overwhelmed him. He went to the phone and dialed Isabelle's number.

When his mother-in-law answered, Michael greeted her and then asked for Polly.

"Why, she's not here, Michael. And I must say, she didn't even bother calling to say the two of you couldn't make it. I had the table all set and everything," Isabelle said in an aggrieved tone. "The very least she could have done was let me know that the two of you were too busy to come to her own sister's birthday dinner."

Michael tightened his hand on the receiver, but his voice remained calm and pleasant. "I'm sorry, Isabelle. We're not very organized. Polly's not home and I've just arrived back from Seattle. I heard your invitation on the machine just now and assumed Polly was with you, but if she's not it's because she didn't get the message. I apologize for both of us."

His mother-in-law went on for several moments about Polly's never being home and the fact that she'd cooked all afternoon. Finally Michael interrupted. "Could you let me speak to Norah for a moment, please? I want to wish her a happy birthday."

He actually didn't want to talk to anyone but Polly, but it seemed the fastest way out of this mess. Isabelle would say the same things in fifteen different ways for the next twenty minutes if he allowed it.

He greeted his sister-in-law and passed on his wishes for a wonderful birthday, apologizing again for not getting home in time for the dinner.

"That's okay, Michael, I knew you were out of town because I saw Polly earlier today. We had a nice lunch," Norah volunteered. She raised her voice a little, making sure Isabelle would overhear. "I told Mom that when I saw Polly this afternoon she didn't know anything about the invitation to come over here."

Sweet Norah, Michael thought wearily. She was always trying to make peace between her mother and her sister.

"Do you have any idea where Polly was headed after lunch, Norah?"

"I really don't. She didn't say."

"Well, I'm sure she'll be home any minute now. Thanks, and happy birthday again."

When Michael hung up, he glanced at the clock. He'd better hurry if he was going to be on time for that meeting. He took the stairs two at a time. In the ensuite bathroom, he peeled off his shirt and paused for a moment, inhaling the faint but distinctive scent of Polly's light perfume. It clung to the towels she'd used, the blouse and tights she'd casually tossed on the top of the hamper, the white velour housecoat hanging on the back of the door. He took a fistful of the fabric in his hand and brought it to his nose.

Polly. He'd have to tell Polly about the loss of their money and, if worse came to worst, the fact that their investments were gone, as well.

His heart sank. Susannah was gone, and now it looked as if their financial future was in jeopardy.

The sessions with Frannie Sullivan had helped Polly. She'd seen Frannie regularly for the first six months, but then she'd stopped going. She'd said it was because she was feeling stronger, but Michael knew all too well she was still emotionally fragile. It was just at the time she'd stopped seeing Frannie that Polly had started spending money recklessly.

He'd have to tell her about Raymond. Undoubtedly, the media would broadcast the facts behind Stokes's disappearance tomorrow morning anyway. He'd have to talk to Polly about it tonight. He dreaded it.

As he washed, shaved, then hurriedly pulled on a fresh shirt, Michael thought it over and reasoned that if their financial situation was as critical as he suspected, he wouldn't burden Polly with all the sordid details right away. She'd always relied on him to manage their finances, so she wouldn't suspect how devastating this could be for them.

He'd tell her some of the facts, of course; just not all of them immediately. Somehow, someway, he'd get them through this latest catastrophe without upsetting her any more than was absolutely necessary.

It was only money, he reminded himself bitterly. He could make more. Money wasn't even in the same league as brain cancer, was it?

Before he left the house, he scribbled Polly a note:

Sorry I missed you, my love.
Got home early but have to go to this meeting, hope your day's been good. See you after nine...

M.

AT 9:20 THAT EVENING, Polly was sitting on a high stool at the kitchen counter, flipping through a decorating magazine and having a cup of tea, when she heard Michael's car drive into the attached garage.

She looked expectantly toward the connecting door, and a moment later he came into the kitchen. He smiled when he saw her, then stared as he shrugged out of his coat.

"What've you done to your hair?"

"Had it cut. You like?"

He came over and stood beside her, and for a moment she was nervous. On one level, she knew she'd cut her hair to force him to look at her, to really see her again. She wanted him to want her, the way he used to. But he'd loved her long hair. Had she also been punishing him?

"It suits you very well." He leaned over and kissed her, the lightest brush of his lips across hers.

Not much of a greeting, some inner voice taunted her, *for a man who hasn't seen his woman for two whole days. And here you thought a haircut might change things.*

"Got any more of that tea in the pot?"

He sounded determinedly cheerful, but she was aware of the weariness in his eyes, the lines of strain around his mouth, and her heart twisted. She loved him so very much. She wanted things to be good between them, but somehow she didn't know how to make them that way anymore.

"Lots. It's chamomile."

He took a cup from the rack and poured from the huge blue teapot, then leaned back against the counter as he sipped it. His long, strong body had always been elegantly beautiful to her artist's eye, and it was still. His lean face, with its clean-cut planes and determined mouth and chin, had been reproduced in feminine perfection in their daughter. Susannah's head had been shaped with the same leonine grace as Michael's, covered with the same coal black, unruly crop of curls. The only feature she'd inherited from Polly was her amber eyes, startling and arrestingly beautiful with such dusky hair.

Susannah would have grown into a breathtakingly beautiful woman. Even as a little girl, she'd loved clothes and had an eye for what suited her.

Michael, too, wore clothes well, Polly mused. He was a sexy man, although sex had become one more area in their marriage that wasn't working all that well.

Stay focused. Stay in the present. Don't get mired in regrets... Frannie's suggestions were like a soothing voice in her head.

"So, how was Seattle?"

"Sunny, for a change. The drive back was good, not too much traffic."

"And your meeting tonight? Was this the group you were doing a presentation for?"

He nodded. "It went okay. Same old stuff. I talked for a while—they asked questions."

She knew he'd spoken about new treatments for cancer. She'd never attended one of the numerous lectures Michael had given since Susannah's death, but Polly was aware through a casual conversation with another physician that Michael was now regarded as an expert in the treatment of the disease. He combined conventional treatment with any alternative form of medicine that showed promise, just as he'd urged the doctors to do with Susannah.

However, he didn't discuss this part of his work with Polly.

True to form, he changed the subject now.

"I spoke to Norah this afternoon, wished her a happy birthday. She said you'd had lunch together. Did you know your mother invited us for dinner tonight?"

"Yeah, I knew. I didn't want to go. And she didn't ask us until the last minute anyway." She realized she sounded defensive. Michael believed she was too hard on her mother.

"I told Isabelle I was sure you hadn't gotten the message, and Norah said the same thing, so it might be a good idea to stick to that story."

His tone was mellow, and he smiled at her and winked; for a moment she glimpsed the old Michael, unguarded and open.

Polly smiled back. "Okay, I will." She acknowledged she should at least have called her mother to refuse the invitation. She waited to see if he'd say something more about it, but he didn't, and the intimacy was gone as quickly as it had arrived. Silence fell.

Polly watched him, wondering if this tension that stretched between them would ever disappear, if there would come a time again when they could argue, even fight, the way they had before, knowing their marriage was secure.

At one time, she thought with an ache in her heart, Michael would have swept her into a bear hug after getting home after a trip, swung her off her feet, kissed her breathless, whispered what he planned to do to her later...

With Susannah giggling at her parents' foolishness...

Stay in the now. Again Polly could hear Frannie's voice emphasizing the words that had become almost a mantra. And Polly managed to do it more often than not these days, which was a small miracle.

Michael was saying something, and she realized she'd missed part of it.

"...you remember I mentioned once that I thought maybe Raymond was having an affair with her? Well, apparently they've both disappeared, along with everyone's money. Arthur Berina told me. I'm afraid Raymond cleaned out our checking accounts. I'll go to the bank in the morning and straighten out the matter."

It took a moment for Polly to understand that Michael was, incredibly, talking about Raymond Stokes. She set the cup she was holding down and stared at him in shock and horror. "Raymond? Raymond Stokes has run off with that woman from his office? Carol, Clara—what was her name?"

"Clarissa Coombs."

"But...but she's lots older than he. And she's an accountant, I thought you said."

Michael's parody of a smile came and went. "Guilty, Your Honor, on both counts. Apparently

her age and ability to add and subtract must have
turned Raymond on.''

Polly was aghast. ''So he's taken off with her
and he's *stolen our money?* I can't believe this.
How much money, Michael?''

He hesitated and then shrugged. ''I'm not entirely certain, but I'll find out tomorrow morning.''

''But surely the police…'' Polly trailed off.

''They're on it, but he's had a head start. He's
undoubtedly left Canada, and I don't suppose the
R.C.M.P. will treat this as a major international
crime. Of course, there's always a chance they'll
catch him and recover what he's stolen, but they'll
have to find him first. And Raymond has always
been a very smart man, so I suspect he's planned
this out pretty carefully.''

Polly watched her husband, trying to gauge how
upset he was over this unbelievable turn of events,
and realized there was no way she could tell. In
the past months Michael had perfected a calm, un-
ruffled persona that prevented anyone, most of all
her, from guessing what was really going on with
him. He'd put up a wall against emotion, and she
couldn't get past it.

His lack of honest reaction infuriated her, and
she suddenly banged a fist on the counter and hollered at him—something she hadn't done in a long
time.

''For God's sake, Michael, don't just stand there
and pretend this doesn't matter. This is terrible.

Surely you're angry or worried or…or desperate or something.''

A grimace flashed across his handsome features, then disappeared as quickly as it had appeared. ''I'm not overjoyed about it, but I don't see that getting crazy will solve anything. And there's no point worrying until I find out the extent of the damage, is there?''

She wanted to scream at him, beat him with her fists, somehow find a way to break through the wall that divided them and liberate the passion she knew was trapped there. But she'd done all those things at different times in the past months, trying to elicit some honest reaction, and nothing worked.

The man she'd known for more than a dozen years, husband, lover, friend, father to her beloved daughter, was gone, replaced by this automaton, this man who looked like Michael and sounded like Michael, even smelled like Michael, but wasn't him at all. Whatever this thing was between them, it was killing their marriage as surely as the tumor had killed her daughter.

She gave up. ''Okay. I guess there's nothing anyone can do right at this moment anyway. I'm tired, Michael.''

It was all too true. A bone-deep weariness had rolled over and through her. ''I'm going up to bed. Coming?''

''In a while, love. I have some charts to do, letters to write.''

The faint hope that had lingered in her faded. She knew it would be hours before he came to lie beside her, if he did at all. Some nights—all too many nights—he slept in the spare bedroom, always with the excuse that he'd had to work late and he knew how difficult it was for her to get to sleep so he didn't want to disturb her.

They rarely ate dinner together because he was always working late. If she so much as mentioned their daughter's name, he got up and left the room. It had been three weeks since they'd made love, if that's what the joyless coupling she'd instigated could be called.

She'd insisted Frannie give her the statistics on marriage breakdown after the loss of a child, and the high percentage hadn't surprised her in the least.

Up in their bedroom, she poured a glass of water and gratefully swallowed the tablets that would bring oblivion.

CHAPTER FOUR

JUST AS MICHAEL SUSPECTED, the next morning's newspaper reported Stokes's disappearance and the plight of the clients he'd defrauded, but because of a major airline disaster in India, the story was relegated to page four.

All the same, Valerie had read it before Michael arrived at the office, and she'd folded the page neatly and placed it squarely on his desk blotter.

"I guess he stole your money along with everyone else's, huh, Doctor?" She shoved her glasses up her nose and sniffed in disgust. "I can't really say I ever liked Raymond Stokes, but I can't believe he'd pull something like this," she fumed, jerking her chin at the article as she set a brimming cup of coffee and a fat bran muffin in front of him.

Valerie Lamb had been Michael's office nurse since he'd first set up practice, and he often thought she was like the sister he'd never had. But then, Valerie was everyone's sister, taking the neediest of his patients under her wing and doing whatever she could to help them. He'd watched her use her lunch hour to drive elderly patients to physio so they wouldn't have to take the bus. She baby-sat two-year-olds so their mothers could talk quietly to Michael about their problems. She comforted anyone in want of comforting, young or old. It was a wonder such a tiny, stubbornly thin frame could contain such an immense heart.

For months now she'd been bringing Michael home-baked muffins each morning. She knew he left the house at six to do hospital rounds, and that he usually didn't bother taking time to eat.

"Raymond did all our accounts, didn't he?"

Her voice was troubled, and Michael thought she was probably worried about her check, which was due this Friday. Valerie was a single parent, with two out-of-control teenage sons and an invalid mother who lived with her and whom she supported. Her job as Michael's office nurse was the financial glue that kept the family housed and fed. Of course he'd make certain none of this affected her.

But that wasn't it at all. "I just want you to know that if things are tight, you can put off paying me for a while. I've got a nest egg that'll see me through."

Michael had to swallow a sudden lump in his throat before he could smile and reassure her.

"Thanks, Val, but that won't be necessary. I'll have to take over the bookkeeping for a while, but certainly this won't affect you or the practice in any way."

The truth was, Raymond's duplicity could affect

every aspect of Michael's life, because he now knew the accountant had all but cleaned him out. Up since dawn, Michael had called investment companies in the East, and his worst fears had been realized.

The final tally wasn't in because the companies needed time to gather all the details, but it appeared that Stokes had, over the past few weeks, cleverly liquefied a sizable portion of Michael's investments. A few he hadn't been able to touch, but they were insignificant compared with the mammoth amounts he'd filched.

Raymond had been extremely clever. He'd paid some of the bills for the month, but only the ones that might have alerted Michael to what was happening. Most of the monthly bills were still outstanding, with no cash to cover them. Michael had had to swallow his pride and negotiate a sizable loan from the bank to meet his immediate expenses at home and at the office.

His stomach churned at the memory. In light of what Stokes had taken and the staggering amount of Michael's unpaid accounts and monthly expenses, Arthur Berina was very reluctant to extend the already substantial line of credit; it had taken a great deal of persuasion to convince him to authorize the loan, and the manager had made it clear Michael would have to find another source of credit if any further funds were required.

When Michael asked about extending the mortgages on the house, Berina had cited the drop in real-estate prices in Vancouver. He'd said the mortgages Michael was already carrying were actually more than the assessed value of the property.

Valerie's voice interrupted such troubled thoughts.

"There've been a number of calls this morning—the names and numbers are all here. And you have about twenty minutes before your first appointment. That'll be Mrs. Nikols and her new baby. Here's her chart."

Valerie placed the chart and the neat list of callers at his elbow, and when she left the room, Michael scanned it.

Constable Roper, R.C.M.P., was the first person on the list. Michael grimaced, realizing he would have to talk to the police right away. Also, several representatives from the various investment firms he'd spoken to earlier that morning had already called back.

Three patients requested that he phone immediately.

Next on the list was a social worker, Garth Silvers, who worked for Community Services. He and Michael had met several times regarding a child Michael suspected was being mistreated.

Concern about the little girl made him call the social worker first. He dialed the number, wondering what new catastrophe might have befallen his small patient, but Garth reassured him the child was fine; her grandmother had taken her to stay with her for a time.

Embarrassment tinged Garth's voice as he added, "The reason I called is personal, Doctor. I heard of a complaint the ministry received about property owned by an Isabelle Rafferty, who I believe is your mother-in-law?"

Wondering what was to come next, Michael confirmed the relationship.

"Well, a number of neighbors have signed a petition insisting something be done about the garbage in Ms. Rafferty's yard," Garth reported. "They feel that things have reached the stage where the yard is a fire hazard as well as a potential breeding ground for rats, and they claim that's lowering their own property values. Several of them have indicated that unless the yard is cleaned up promptly, they'll take legal action. I wanted to notify you first and see if something could be done before that happens."

Michael looked at the framed pastoral print on his office wall and wondered what the hell else could possibly go wrong in his life today. "I appreciate your call, Garth, and I promise you I'll take care of this right away," he said with far more confidence than he felt.

Polly and Norah had been trying for months to get Isabelle to do something about her yard, to no avail.

"Assure the neighbors that the garbage will be

gone within a week.'' He hung up and expelled a long, weary breath. Exactly how was he going to manage that? He'd have to talk to Polly to figure out a course of action. She'd be mortified when she heard about the petition.

The police constable was next on his list, and Michael dialed the number, relieved to hear that Constable Roper was out for the morning and would return the call that afternoon. This would give Michael more time to fully assess what Raymond had stolen.

In rapid and efficient order, Michael dealt with the three patient calls. He'd just finished when Valerie tapped on his door and announced that Mrs. Nikols was waiting in examining room one.

Valerie silently pointed at the untouched muffin, and Michael quickly devoured it and gulped the now-lukewarm coffee before he hurried in to the new mother and the baby he'd delivered just days before.

This was the part of his workday he liked the best—office hours with one patient after another requiring his full attention and no time lapses in which to think. Today, however, keeping his mind on his patients was difficult.

He worked steadily, and at twelve-thirty there was a short lull. He hastily ate the sandwich and fruit Valerie put in front of him, then dialed home. Polly often slept past noon, drugged by the sleeping meds she'd become reliant upon. He'd tried to wean her off them, but it hadn't worked.

She picked up on the third ring, and she sounded wide awake. "I'm just reading this article in the paper about Raymond," she said as soon as she knew it was Michael. "It says here that some of his clients have nothing left, that he stole all their investments." Her voice telegraphed her anxiety. "Did that happen to us, Michael?"

He knew he ought to say yes. Instead, he reassured her. "We did lose a substantial portion of our portfolio, but there's no major damage done, Polly. I figure I can make up the shortfall in no time."

And maybe what he was saying wasn't way off the truth. As far as their day-by-day expenses went, he could certainly earn enough to pay what was owing. But now they had no comfortable cushion behind them, no investments to rely on should an emergency arise. *Another* emergency, he thought bleakly. He was relieved when Polly shifted the focus of the conversation away from their situation.

"Why would Raymond Stokes do a thing like this, Michael? Apparently he even took his wife's money," she was saying in a scandalized tone. "It says here that all she's got left is their house, and Raymond even had a large mortgage on that. It must be terribly hurtful for her—his going off with another woman... How could he do those things to the person he was married to?'' It wasn't just a rhetorical question. Polly was honestly puzzled.

"I guess we never really know anyone all that well, Pol.'' Michael saw her in his mind's eye, sitting on a stool at the kitchen counter, wrapped in her white velour robe, coffee and newspaper close at hand. He adjusted the image to include the new hairdo, and felt a pang of regret.

Even the ones we think we know best, he added to himself. "I thought Raymond and I were friends, but this shows I didn't really know him at all.''

"They didn't have kids, did they?''

"Nope, no kids.'' Michael tightened his fingers on the phone. "He said once that his wife didn't want any.'' This subject could be explosive with Polly, and he didn't want to get into it.

She didn't respond for a moment, and when she did he was relieved that she didn't say any more about children. "Did you know Raymond's wife? Jennifer—isn't that her name?''

Michael relaxed. "Jennifer, yes. I was introduced to her at a luncheon Raymond and I were both attending.''

"What's she like?''

"Short, rounded. Pleasant. We didn't talk much. I remember thinking she was a good balance for Raymond, because he talked a lot and she was quiet.''

"Sort of like us.'' There was humor in her tone.

"I talk—you listen. So apart from getting robbed, Doc, how's your day going?"

She was cheerful now, and Michael hated to change that, but he had to tell her about the situation with Isabelle and the neighbors.

He did and, predictably, Polly was upset. Michael knew she also felt humiliated.

"It's horrible having my own mother live this way," she moaned. "Sometimes I swear she does it just to embarrass me. She knows I care what her neighbors think—I grew up in that house."

Michael glanced at his watch. "I know, love. We'll talk it over later and figure something out, but I've got to go now, Pol. My next patient's waiting."

"So is there any point in making dinner?"

Her voice was suddenly brittle, an unnecessary reminder that more often than not, he'd been absent for the evening meal.

He knew it was wrong of him to extend his workday into the evening, but sitting at the dining table alone with Polly was agony. He couldn't bear the empty space at his right, where Susannah had always sat.

So get over it, Forsythe. It's been over a year. You're a man. Your job is to be strong. What the hell's the matter with you?

"I'll be there about six."

"I'm not sure I even remember how to cook."

Polly probably intended the words to be humorous, but they came out snappy, instead, and he felt annoyed at her, as well as guilty for all the dinners he'd canceled or avoided.

But he had no right to be annoyed at Polly, did he? He was the one who'd screwed up.

The call ended and Michael shoved the disturbing issues it raised back into the shadows of his mind as he concentrated on one patient's problems after another.

It was after five and Valerie had just left for the day by the time Michael saw his last patient, a four-year-old girl named Clover Fox. Her father, Jerome, had walked into the office an hour earlier without an appointment, assuring Valerie he'd wait as long as necessary if only Michael would see his daughter. He'd moved to Vancouver from Saskatchewan several months ago and didn't have a family doctor.

Valerie had felt sorry for him and of course Michael had agreed to see the child.

The wan thin girl squirmed on her father's knee, nose and defiant pale-blue eyes red and runny, coughing at intervals from deep in her chest. Michael glanced over the detailed history Valerie had asked Jerome to fill in, then looked up and smiled at the little girl.

"So, Clover, it says here you're not feeling so hot." He winked at her and added, "You're sure a big girl. How old are you, anyhow?"

She gave him a baleful look, then hesitantly held up four fingers.

"Four, huh? Well, four is a really good age to be," Michael said approvingly, turning to the handsome young father and asking him about the child's general health.

"She catches everything going," Jerome Fox reported with a sigh, stroking a big hand across his daughter's fine hair.

Michael noted that Jerome had the tough, scarred hands of someone who did manual labor.

"She coughs at night, and she feels really hot to me. Then this morning she broke out in this rash on her back and chest."

"Is she in day care, Mr. Fox?" It helped to know a child's routine, who she might be in daily contact with.

"No, I'm taking care of her full-time right now."

"Your wife works?"

Jerome shook his blond head, and lines of strain showed around his eyes. "Nope, Tiffany left us. Two weeks ago now. But we're making out okay on our own, right, Clover?"

The girl nodded, then hid her face on her father's chest.

"I see." Michael felt compassion for this man and his sad-eyed little girl. No job, no wife, a sick child…it must be really tough.

"I'm looking for a job, Doctor." Jerome

sounded defensive. "I work on construction as a laborer. I moved out here because a local company hired me, but right after I got here they folded. As soon as I get another job, I'll find good day care for Clover," he assured Michael. His shoulders slumped. "It's just tough to get out and look for work and take good care of her at the same time, especially when she's sick."

"I can imagine." Michael smiled again at the little girl and gestured at the examining table. "How about sitting up on here for a minute, honey, so I can have a look at you and figure out what's making you feel bad?"

Clover scowled, shook her head and clung to her father. He spoke to her in a gentle tone and lifted her firmly up to the examining table. She struggled against him and her mouth bunched as if she was about to cry, but no sound came out.

Michael, familiar with children, took his time, trying to reassure her. He showed Clover the stethoscope and gave her a tongue depressor of her own. When he tried to examine her throat, though, she bit down hard, narrowly missing his fingers. At the same moment, she kicked out her foot in its sturdy little runner, connecting hard with his thigh.

A few inches closer to center and she'd have decked him, Michael reflected. It was obvious Clover was a fighter, and that endeared her to him. It was the passive, quiet children who concerned him.

"She's running a low-grade fever, but her lungs

are clear. A viral infection is causing the rash on her back and tummy.''

Michael watched as Jerome helped his daughter back into her jeans and slipped her faded-purple sweatshirt over her head.

''Does she need a prescription?'' Real anxiety colored Jerome's voice. ''It's just that I'm really short on cash—Tiffany pretty much cleaned out our bank account. I've applied for unemployment insurance, but there's a waiting period.'' Jerome sounded close to desperate. ''I've put my name up in different places, offering to do any odd jobs, but so far nothing's happened.''

Today, Michael understood so well how it felt to have one's bank account cleaned out. ''She doesn't need antibiotics. The virus will run its course. Just keep her warm and make sure she gets lots of rest. Take her off milk—milk creates mucous. Give her lots of clear liquids, vitamin C, echinacea, garlic.'' He rummaged in his desk drawer. ''Here are some vitamin C samples, and some echinacea. And here's a bottle of cough medicine, as well. If she doesn't improve in the next day or two, bring her back.''

''I will. Thanks a lot, Doctor, for seeing us without an appointment. And for all this stuff.'' Jerome stood and carefully put the items in the pocket of his threadbare woolen jacket.

Clover wrapped herself around his leg, glowering up at Michael, who handed her a tiny coloring book and four crayons—one of a number of "prizes" he kept on hand for his youngest patients.

"What do you say, Clover?" Jerome prompted.

"I don't like green," she responded instantly, shoving the offending crayon back at Michael, who laughed.

"She's contrary," Jerome said, with a shake of his head after he'd finally extracted a grudging thank-you from his daughter. A rueful pride edged his tone.

Michael had noted that Jerome was gentle but firm with Clover, and that her clothing, although worn, was clean, as was Jerome's.

An idea had been forming in Michael's head as Jerome reasoned with his daughter. "You mentioned you're interested in doing odd jobs?"

"Absolutely," Jerome replied eagerly. "I'm willing to take on any work at all. I can supply references from my former boss and some of the people I've worked with."

Michael explained about Isabelle's yard, emphasizing that his mother-in-law could be difficult. "The best thing would be for me to take you over there now and introduce you," he decided on the spur of the moment. "You can have a look around and see if you want the job. Then, if she's agreeable, you could start as soon as Clover's feeling better. Do you have transportation?"

"Yeah. I've got the truck parked outside."

"Here's the address. I'll meet you there." Michael scribbled on a sheet torn from a prescription pad.

It took only moments for him to gather the charts he needed to update, set the security system and lock the front door. On the way to Isabelle's, he called Polly on the cellular phone and told her his plan.

"She'll never let you do it, you know." Michael could hear the clatter of plates and the running of water. Polly was obviously making dinner. "But I suppose if anyone can persuade her, you can. The only thing I ever did that my mother totally approved of was marry a doctor."

"Don't be too sure of that," Michael teased. "She told me once that a dentist would have saved her more money. She said she's covered by Medicare and anyhow she hardly ever gets sick, but she's had to spend a bundle on her teeth."

Polly groaned. "That's my mother, hardly the most sensitive of women. Dinner's nearly ready, Michael, so don't let her lure you into sitting around drinking beer with her, okay?"

"Okay. I'll be home soon." He was pulling into Isabelle's driveway, and he looked, really looked, at the house and yard, seeing it as the neighbors must, and feeling sympathy for them.

Isabelle's house was in a residential area off Main Street, one of a block of houses built in the early fifties on generous treed lots. The others on the block had fresh paint or siding, neatly trimmed lawns, tidy hedges and flowerbeds. Isabelle's house stood out like a frowsy drunk at a church social, front lawn weed-choked and decorated with an immense and crumbling cement birdbath. The front porch sagged away from the house, and on it stood an overstuffed chair and two packing boxes, as well as a rolled-up rug that had sat there as long as Michael could remember.

As Michael got out of his car, Jerome stepped out of a battered blue pickup, then unhooked Clover from her child's seat.

"I peed my pants," she announced immediately.

Too late, Michael realized that Isabelle probably wasn't going to appreciate his bringing a kid with wet pants and a virus to visit her, any more than she'd be delighted with the idea of Jerome cleaning up her yard.

The day wasn't improving with age. He led the way to the front door and rang the bell.

CHAPTER FIVE

"MICHAEL, COME ON IN. Who's your friend?" Isabelle was a tall woman, five-ten, and she had a loud, commanding voice and a definite presence.

Michael introduced Jerome, and Isabelle nodded, scrutinizing him from behind her stylish glasses.

"How d'you do, young man. I saw you sitting in my driveway and wondered what you were waiting for. Is this girl yours?" She looked down at Clover without smiling, and the girl looked back at her, her expression grim.

"What's your name, child? What's that rash all over your neck? Better not be measles or something else I could catch." When Clover didn't respond, Isabelle snapped, "Cat's got your tongue, I see."

"I peed my pants," Clover announced in an injured tone.

Isabelle made a disgusted noise. "You're too big a girl to be doing that, aren't you?"

"She told me, but there was nowhere to stop," Jerome said. "Could we please use your bathroom?'' He held out a paper bag. ''I've got dry clothes for her right here.''

Isabelle gestured behind her, along the turquoise hallway. ''Go ahead. Bathroom's right down there.'' As soon as Jerome and Clover were gone, Isabelle said, ''That rash she's got contagious?''

Michael assured her it wasn't.

''Good thing. Come on in the front room and sit down.''

Michael followed her into the claustrophobic living room and sat gingerly on a dingy sofa whose springs had long since retired. It always amazed him that Polly, with her flair for decorating, her artist's eye, her love for order and beauty, was Isabelle's daughter.

Isabelle had no decorating sense at all. She never threw anything away. Instead, she constantly added bits of furniture she bought at yard sales, fitting them in wherever there was space, impervious to clashing colors or designs.

Cardboard boxes littered every room of the house, stacked against walls, tucked under beds, filled with paperbacks, magazines and various items Isabelle had bought and then couldn't find an immediate use for.

She sat in a recliner across from Michael and lit a cigarette. The house smelled strongly of stale smoke.

Michael had long ago given up suggesting Isabelle quit. "Gotta die of something" had been her cheerful response each time he brought it up.

"I'm going dancing over at the Elks hall in an hour," she announced. "But we could have a beer first—there're a couple cold in the fridge."

"Thanks, but I'm heading home for dinner, I'll pass on the beer." Michael was trying to figure out how best to bring up the touchy subject of the yard cleanup, and he figured maybe a little flattery might help.

"Going dancing, huh? You look very pretty, Isabelle." He knew she was vain, but the compliment was sincere. She was an attractive woman, dramatic in both manner and choice of clothing. She was wearing a soft green dress that flared over her generous hips and showed off good legs in dark hose. She had high-heeled black sandals on her feet, and her short hair was tinted a dramatic shining gold and sprayed into a stiff helmet. At sixty-seven she was strong, healthy and proud of the fact that she didn't appear her age.

Here again Michael often puzzled over the vagaries of genetics. Mother and daughter couldn't have been less alike.

"Why'd you bring him over?" She jerked her chin at the bathroom door, where a toilet was flushing noisily.

Michael quickly explained that Clover was his patient, adding that Jerome was a single parent, out of work and needing a job. Now came the tricky part. Mentally, he crossed his fingers.

"I thought, if you were agreeable, I'd hire him to clean up the yard for you. See, Isabelle, I heard today that your neighbors are taking up a petition. They're upset about the piles of rubbish in the back. They've reported you to Social Services."

Michael braced himself for anger and outright rebellion against the neighbors and their petition. Isabelle had a fierce temper, so he was totally taken by surprise when she threw back her head and laughed loudly.

"A petition, huh? Well, good for them. I always figured they had no guts, but people can surprise you. Are they offering to pay for the cleanup?"

Michael grinned. Isabelle was outrageous, and he liked her for it. "No, I'm paying. I have a reputation to uphold and that yard of yours is doing it damage." He said this in a teasing tone. Isabelle knew very well that he didn't care at all about reputation, but both also knew that Polly did.

Neither acknowledged that now. Instead, Isabelle laughed again, a great, raucous belly laugh.

"Well, if you're paying, then go ahead and pay. What's the point of having a rich son-in-law if I never take advantage of him, eh?"

Michael appreciated the irony of her words. His guess was Isabelle had far more in her bank account at this moment than he did.

Jerome and Clover came into the room just then,

and Isabelle repeated her offer of a beer. Jerome accepted and she went off to the kitchen. She returned with two cans and a small box of juice, which she handed to Clover.

"So I understand you're gonna tidy up the yard for me, young fellow."

"If that's okay with you, ma'am. I sure will do my best." Jerome hesitated and then added, "Would you mind if I brought Clover with me? I don't have anyone to leave her with. She won't be any trouble, will you, honey?"

Clover shook her head and sucked loudly on her drink.

Michael stiffened and held his breath; Jerome's request could ruin the entire plan. Polly insisted that Isabelle didn't like kids, that she was never a satisfactory grandmother to Susannah.

But once again, Isabelle was agreeable. "Fine by me. Bring her along, just so she isn't running in and out the house every minute."

Michael could hardly believe it had been so easy.

When he told Polly the good news twenty minutes later, she was pleased but skeptical.

"I can't believe she gave in just like that. What does this Jerome guy look like?"

"Big, healthy, about thirty-five. Strong muscles, good physique. Thick blond hair, tanned skin. Handsome."

"That's what did it," Polly declared. "Mom has

a weakness for good-looking men. When's he starting?''

''Probably day after tomorrow. Clover should be better by then.''

''Clover? Who'd name a poor unsuspecting child 'Clover'?''

''Her mother, probably. She walked out on them a couple weeks ago, Jerome told me.''

Polly shook her head but didn't comment.

Michael was pouring them each a glass of wine. The table looked lovely. Polly had set it with her usual eye for color, selecting a plain buttery-yellow cloth with huge patterned blue-and-yellow napkins that she'd sewn. The centerpiece was a low pottery bowl planted with blooming hyacinths in plum and purple and a rich, deep violet that matched the starkly simple dinnerware.

''Have I seen these plates before?'' Michael picked one up to admire it, surprised at its weight.

''I just got them yesterday. I had them special-ordered from Italy. Each is slightly different because the set is handmade. See the gradations in the color?''

Michael stared at the plate and knew this was the precise moment to tell Polly such extravagances had to end. At least three other full sets of china sat in the tall cupboards lining one entire dining-room wall—china that was seldom used. They rarely entertained, and this was the first dinner the two of them had shared in more than a week.

"They're exquisite, don't you think?" Polly caressed the smooth surface of a plate. "Beautiful things like these give me such pleasure."

Michael looked at her, taking in the delicate lines of her lovely face, which her new haircut emphasized; her smile, so poignant a contrast to the sad vulnerability in her eyes; and he just couldn't say what needed to be said—that they were on the verge of bankruptcy, that she really should pack these blue dishes up and return them to the store because there was a real possibility that he couldn't pay the bill when it came in.

Instead, he sipped his wine, took a seat and, without tasting anything, ate the rich vegetable stew, the fresh crusty bread, the delicate endive salad his wife had prepared.

They sat across from each other at the heavy oak dining table, an Italian tenor's rich, evocative voice flowing from the sound system. The tastefully decorated room filled with shadows as darkness fell outside the wide windows.

Polly had grouped candles around the bowl holding the hyacinths and she lit them now. She was wearing a long blue lacy sweater over dark tights, and with the new short hairstyle, she looked like a young girl in the candlelight, a desirable girl he should scoop up in his arms and passionately love.

But the weight of the house settled around him like a stone; the awful emptiness of the child's bedroom at the top of the curving stairway haunted him; the missing place setting on his right, where Susannah had always sat, filled him with pain. She used to wriggle in her chair, her electric energy lighting up the room. She'd often spilled her milk on the tablecloth and his trousers, and she'd once laughed so hard and long at one of his silly jokes that she'd choked and vomited her dinner all over the cloth. She'd sometimes rested her small foot on his thigh under the table. And she'd giggled, with that special hitch in her voice, when he teased her.

"Oh, Daddy, you're so silly."

Blessedly, the telephone rang.

"Let the machine take it," Polly urged.

But he was already out of his chair. A moment later he stuck his head into the dining room long enough to say, "Sorry, Pol, I've got to go to Emerg. One of my patients was in a car accident."

She didn't protest. Just looked at him and nodded, her expression stony.

Michael felt irritation niggle at him. This was his job, after all; she knew he had no choice when an emergency arose. He found his keys and then went back into the dining room.

"I don't know how long I'll be. Don't wait up for me." He bent to kiss her, but she turned her face and his lips grazed her cheek. He shrugged into a jacket and hurried out the door, ashamed of the relief that surged through him. And as he got into the car and drove away, he turned a tape on full and forced his mind to focus only on the urgent needs of the patient waiting at St. Joe's.

TWO DAYS LATER, Polly drove slowly up the back alley of Isabelle's house and parked alongside the ramshackle picket fence that bordered her mother's property. It was a sunny morning, and she told herself she was there to make peace with Isabelle over the missed dinner invitation, but the truth was, curiosity about Jerome Fox had drawn her.

She slid her sunglasses up over her forehead and sat for several moments, watching the young man working in her mother's backyard.

He hadn't noticed her yet, or if he had, he wasn't paying any attention, and Polly took the opportunity to study him.

He *was* a fine physical specimen, just as Michael had suggested. He wasn't especially tall, but he looked extremely strong, with sharply defined muscles in his arms. His body was lean and tanned. His gray T-shirt was stained at the armpits and down the back with sweat, and his faded, dirty jeans clung to his muscular thighs and hung low on narrow hips. Thick blond hair curled from under the rim of a billed cap, and his features were strong and well-defined. He was lifting rotten boards from a pile and tossing them with ease up and over the rim of the dump bin Michael had had delivered.

Polly slid out of the car and straightened her short denim skirt.

"Hi, there. Wow, it looks better around here already," she called cheerfully. When he turned toward her, she walked over to him and put out her hand, smiling. "I'm Polly Forsythe. How do you do?"

"Jerome Fox. Pleased to meet you, Mrs. Forsythe."

He pulled off his work glove and rubbed it down the side of his pants before he shook her hand. He smiled back at her, his teeth even and very white against his tanned skin. He had brilliant blue eyes.

"You're Doc Forsythe's wife?"

"I am, yes. And please call me 'Polly.' You have no idea how thrilled I am to see this yard getting cleaned up. It's a total disaster area."

He grinned and nodded. "It's a mess, all right."

She had to laugh at his droll tone. "Your little girl's feeling better? Michael said she had a virus."

"He gave us some stuff. She's lots better today, no cough or fever or anything. Your husband's a really good doctor."

"Why, thank you, sir. I'll tell Michael you said so. Well, Mr. Fox, I'll leave you to it."

"Just call me 'Jerome.'"

"Okay, Jerome." She motioned toward the house. "Do you know if my mother's inside?"

"Yeah." He frowned. "Clover's in there, too. She went in to get a drink a while ago and hasn't come out yet. Maybe tell her I want her out here with me? I sure don't want her bugging Mrs. Rafferty."

"I'll tell her." Polly went up the wooden steps to the kitchen door, careful not to lean on the broken railing. She tapped on the screen door and then opened it.

"Mom? Hi, it's me."

"I saw you drive up."

Isabelle was seated at the kitchen table, a cigarette between her fingers and a mug of coffee at her elbow. A small, unattractive little girl sat beside her, boosted to table height by several telephone books. In front of the child was a mug of milky coffee, and between her fingers she had a small piece of paper towel rolled up to resemble a cigarette. She was holding it exactly the way Isabelle held hers, and she had her denim-covered legs crossed at the knee just the way Isabelle did.

"This is Clover. She's Jerome's kid." Isabelle gestured at the child and then at the coffeepot. "You want some? I just made a pot."

Polly went to the cupboard and got a mug, surreptitiously checking to make certain it was clean before she poured coffee into it. Isabelle's cupboards were often infested with bugs, which bothered Polly a whole lot and her mother not at all.

She sat at the table, thinking it was unfortunate

Jerome Fox's daughter hadn't inherited his good looks. Clover was a most unappealing-looking child with her stringy pale hair and watery, narrow eyes. To make up for her critical thoughts, Polly gave the little girl a wide, friendly smile. ''Your daddy said he wants you to come outside with him now,'' she told her in a kind tone.

The girl gave her a suspicious look and didn't smile back or move an inch from her perch. She put her imitation cigarette to her lips and pretended to take a long drag, then she blew as if exhaling smoke. She even squinted at Polly the exact way Isabelle did when she exhaled.

It should have been funny, but Polly was disgusted, instead. Her mother's smoking was something both she and Norah abhorred. They'd tried every ruse to get Isabelle to stop, with no success. Allowing a child to imitate such a dreadful habit was nothing short of criminal in Polly's estimation.

''Leave Clover be. She's not hurting anything.'' Isabelle took a drag on her own cigarette and blew the smoke out through her nose in a long stream.

Irritated, Polly waved a hand in front of her to deflect it. ''This smoke's hurting her, Mom. She's been sick and it's a lot healthier for her to be outside than to sit in here inhaling this poison. You know the studies all say that second-hand smoke is just as bad for you as smoking yourself, and children are particularly vulnerable.''

Why did her mother always bring out her prissy, preachy side? Polly wondered.

"Oh, pooh, you can't believe everything you hear. I've got all the windows open. Don't get your shirttail in a knot." Isabelle tapped ash into the ashtray defiantly and Clover instantly copied her.

Isabelle laughed. "Susie used to pretend to smoke like me, too, when she was small, remember?"

Of course Polly remembered. She'd spent hours talking to Susannah about smoking, telling her how dangerous the habit was, trying her best to walk the fine line between not castigating her own mother while still discouraging her daughter from adopting Isabelle's filthy habit.

And why had Isabelle insisted always on calling her granddaughter "Susie"? Her name is Susannah, Polly had said more times than she could count, to no avail. And it irked her now just the way it always had.

Well, this was typical, Polly thought with disgust. She couldn't be around her mother for two seconds without either lecturing or wanting to scream.

"I'm sorry I didn't get your message about Norah's birthday dinner, Mom," she forced herself to say. "Michael was out of town, and I wasn't home— I spent the afternoon shopping."

"No harm done, I suppose." Isabelle eyed Polly speculatively. "Although how anyone can spend an entire afternoon going from store to store is beyond me. I see you got your hair cut.''

''Do you like it?''

''It takes some getting used to. You haven't had it short like that since you were a teenager. And those streaks are different.''

Why couldn't her mother just say, for once, that she looked nice? Polly mused in despair. And why should it matter so much?

''I needed a change.'' Polly sipped the strong coffee and tried to swallow—along with the brew—the disturbing emotions her mother roused in her.

Clover suddenly picked up her mug and drank with great gulping sounds; then, still holding her make-believe cigarette, she wriggled down from the chair and headed out the door. It slammed behind her.

''She's a queer little duck,'' Isabelle remarked. ''Doesn't smile much. Did the mother just walk out on them, or what? She said her mommy was gone and she and her daddy got along fine.''

This, at least, was safer ground. Polly nodded. ''Apparently she did. A couple weeks ago, Michael said.''

''Some women should never be blessed with kids,'' Isabelle pronounced self-righteously. ''Why, any animal's a better mother than that.''

Polly figured she'd heard her mother say the same thing a million times over the years. Her reaction was always exactly what she felt now: she wanted to confront Isabelle about *her* lack of mothering, point out that she had been anything but perfect, dragging her small daughters all over the province, subjecting them to the constant stress of new schools in whatever town Isabelle landed them in.

Isabelle had never put her daughters first in her life, not really, Polly raged inwardly. She saw only her own needs, her own desires, her own passions, and to hell with her children.

"Michael looked beat last night. He's working too hard. You oughta make him take some time off. The two of you should go to Hawaii or something. God knows you can afford it," Isabelle said.

Again, Polly felt herself having to squelch the automatically angry response her mother's words evoked in her.

"Michael enjoys working hard. I couldn't get him to take time off if I tried." And right now the idea of going on a vacation with her husband terrified Polly.

If they spent long hours in each other's company, the abyss at the center of their marriage might no longer be a place they could avoid.

CHAPTER SIX

POLLY COULDN'T STAND sitting in her mother's messy kitchen another moment, having Isabelle lecture her on things the woman knew nothing about. She picked up her cup and carried it to the sink, rinsed it under the hot tap, set it on the cluttered drain board.

"I've gotta go, Mom. Michael said it might be a good idea to pay Jerome at the end of each day. He probably needs the money." She dug in her handbag and pulled out a checkbook. "Just figure out the hours and fill in the amount." She printed "Jerome Fox" on the check, and then scribbled her signature at the bottom of it.

"I don't mind Michael paying for the yard cleaning—it was his idea—but I want to pay for the painting myself," Isabelle commented as Polly put the check on the table in front of her.

Polly stared at her. "What painting?"

"The outside of the house, silly. Now, don't look so surprised." It was obvious Isabelle was delighted at Polly's shocked reaction. "I decided this morning that the place needs freshening up, and if that young man wants the job, I'm going to go down and choose paint this afternoon.''

Polly was thunderstruck. The appearance of the house had been a thorn in her side for years, and she'd nagged and all but begged Isabelle to attend to it.

''What's made you decide to paint all of a sudden?''

''It's spring. As long as Jerome's here anyhow, I might as well take advantage of him.''

Isabelle's answer only reaffirmed for Polly how impetuous her mother was. Polly decided not to comment, in case Isabelle changed her mind. But if she was going this far, there was a faint possibility Isabelle might agree to a general spring housecleaning, a sorting through of the debris that littered every corner of the old house. And the basement. Polly shuddered just thinking about the basement. *Play it cool and casual so you don't spook her, Polly.*

''Painting's a great idea, Mom.'' She couldn't wait to call Norah. Her sister was not going to believe this.

''What color are you thinking of?''

''Blue. Or maybe turquoise.''

Lordie. Isabelle was capable of turquoise. Polly had to head her off at the pass. ''What about white? With green shutters and trim?'' She held her breath. The last thing she wanted was to discourage Isabelle.

"You think white?"

Isabelle considered it, frowning, then she shook her head and Polly's heart sank.

"White's boring. White's got no pizazz. Maybe painting's not such a good idea after all. It's liable to run into a lot of money, and it would take weeks with one person doing it. Cost me a fortune if he charges by the hour. Besides, I dunno if I could stand somebody around that long."

Polly felt herself beginning to panic. Isabelle couldn't change her mind now; she just couldn't.

Inspiration struck. "You pay for the paint and let Norah and I go together on the labor. It could be your Mother's Day gift."

Isabelle prided herself on practicality, and Polly could see that this idea appealed. But then Isabelle shook her head again. "It's the having somebody hanging around morning noon and night for weeks and weeks that I'm not sure about. I like my privacy."

Polly racked her brain for a solution, and the answer sprang into her head, fully formed. "Look, Mom, I'll come over and help Jerome paint. I enjoy painting, and we'd get it done in half the time." Excitement filled her as she thought about it. Of course this was exactly the right thing to do. She felt giddy anticipation at the idea of having an actual job, something she had to climb out of bed for in the morning. For so long now, she'd been filling in time, getting through the days. This would provide some purpose to her life, at least for a while.

But Isabelle was shaking her head yet again. ''Now, Polly, that's crazy. You're always so busy. You know you're never home.''

The criticism was a familiar one, and it had always made Polly angry and defensive. This time she was simply honest.

''I don't wanna be home, Mom. Being home reminds me of Susannah, and I can't stand it.'' The vehement words tumbled out before Polly could stop them, and she tensed, waiting for Isabelle to reprimand her, remind her what a luxurious home she had and how grateful she ought to be to Michael for providing it.

But Isabelle took a noisy gulp of her coffee and tilted her head to one side. ''So you think white, huh? Well, you always were the artistic one. It might look okay at that, white with a dark-green trim.''

Polly gaped at her mother. Were there really times when Isabelle could be reasonable?

''So you want to go ahead with it?''

Isabelle took another slurp of coffee and nodded. ''I just said so, didn't I? Before we go any further, though, let's go outside and talk to Jerome, see if he even wants the job. And maybe I can talk him into a flat fee—that would save you girls some money.''

Jerome absolutely wanted the job, and he was

perfectly agreeable to a fair amount and to having Polly work with him. The yard should be finished sometime the following afternoon, he estimated. He had several loads to take to the dump. Then he and Polly could begin painting the house.

They eagerly discussed it. They'd rent scaffolding and they'd have to scrape off the worst of the old paint, but it wouldn't be a bad job at all.

"C'mon, Mom." Polly was elated. "I'll drive you to the paint store right now and we'll get what we need."

"Scared I'll change my mind, huh?" Isabelle grinned knowingly at her daughter. "Okay, I just have to put on some lipstick and then we'll go. Clover, you want to come for a ride in Polly's fancy car?"

Polly was annoyed at her mother for inviting the child along. She hoped the little girl would refuse, but instead Clover came trotting over from the dirt pile where she'd been digging with a garden fork. The knees of her pants were dirty, and her face and hands were streaked with grime.

"Better wash up before we go," Polly instructed, wondering why she should feel such aversion to a four-year-old. She'd always liked kids, but this one irritated her. Feeling guilty, she smiled at Jerome. "We'll take good care of her."

"Thanks. It's important for her to be with women. I think she misses her mother."

The unpredictable rage that Polly thought was a

thing of the past suddenly overcame her. The words she'd flung at Frannie so often in those weeks after Susannah's death echoed in her brain. *Why should she have lost her child, when there were women who didn't even want theirs?*

Isabelle was coming down the back steps, Clover close behind her, and the shameful thought couldn't be suppressed as Polly stared at the little girl. *Why couldn't this child have died instead of Susannah? Clover's mother didn't care enough about her to even stick around.*

It was all she could do to stop herself from screaming the words. Polly could feel Jerome's puzzled gaze as she turned abruptly away from him and walked to her car. She was trembling violently as she opened the car door and slid behind the wheel, and when her passengers got in beside her, the little girl's high-pitched voice was like acid dripping into an open wound.

MICHAEL HAD JUST FINISHED with a patient and was writing details of the visit in the chart when Valerie knocked, then stuck her head in the door. "Dr. Gilbert's on line two for you."

Michael picked up the phone and greeted Luke warmly. He knew Luke Gilbert well. Luke and his wife, Morgan Jacobsen, were well-known and highly respected obstetricians in Vancouver, and their paths and Michael's had often crossed on the obstetrical ward at St. Joe's.

"Michael, I wonder if you'd do me a favor."

Luke's voice was tense, and Michael was surprised; Luke Gilbert was a self-contained Englishman, not given to revealing his feelings.

"Of course, Luke. What can I do for you?"

"It's my grandson, Duncan Hendricks, my daughter Sophie's boy."

Just the somber tone of Luke's voice told Michael the problem was serious. "He's five years old. He's been diagnosed with—"

Luke stopped and cleared his throat, obviously having a difficult time speaking.

"With astrocytoma of the main cerebral hemisphere, Grade Three."

The same diagnosis as Susannah's. A rush of conflicting emotion hit Michael like a fist in the gut. Uppermost was compassion for Luke and his family, the terrible understanding that only someone who'd lived this particular nightmare could feel for others trapped in the same situation. But there was also an immediate aversion, a certainty that he absolutely didn't want any involvement in this case. He knew, however, this was exactly what Luke was asking of him.

"I spoke to Rosof at the Center for Integrated Therapy," Luke went on. "He said that you're the one he'd recommend to supervise Duncan's treatment. You're experienced both in traditional and alternative therapies. I wondered, Michael, would you take him on as a patient? I realize it's asking a lot—I know it must bring back painful memories of your daughter.''

Michael struggled with the feelings roiling in him, and although he longed to refuse Luke, he knew he had no choice. This was a fellow doctor, a friend, asking a personal favor. There was no way to decline.

He forced a heartiness he was far from feeling into his voice. ''Of course I'll do the very best I can for Duncan, Luke. I'll have Valerie set up an immediate appointment. Is nine tomorrow morning a good time?''

Luke assured him it was, and for the next several minutes, Michael asked questions about Duncan, assimilating the answers Luke gave, assessing as objectively as he could the progress of the disease. The tumor, like Susannah's, was inoperable, situated too deep within the brain to make surgery possible. Duncan was undergoing a course of radiation.

''We all know what the track record is for this thing, Michael.'' Luke sounded tired and desperate. ''It's simply not curable through orthodox methods. I've searched the literature. Is there any alternative therapy that might work?''

Michael would have given anything to reassure Luke, but he couldn't do it. ''Nothing,'' he said heavily. ''Some alternative treatments can help support the body, but nothing I know will cure this particular type of tumor.''

"That's what I thought." Luke's sigh tore at Michael's soul. "Duncan's a bright kid. We've been as honest with him as we can be. We all feel it's important to explain exactly what's going on. The toughest thing for us is his optimism. He absolutely believes he's going to get well. I dread the moment he figures out he's not."

"I understand." Luke's words brought memories to the surface, hurtful memories. Susannah, at nine, had also been a bright child. Michael had always been delighted and amused at her interest in his job. He'd always answered her questions honestly, without shielding her from the harsher aspects of his medical practice.

When she became ill, she insisted Michael draw her pictures, show her the exact location of her tumor, tell her what to expect. And he'd done all that. He'd also insisted that her doctors inform her of exactly what they were doing every step of the way; after all, it was her body.

And so it came about that Susannah herself had ultimately been the one to decide not to continue with orthodox treatment. Her decision had been incredibly difficult for Michael to accept.

First, she'd asked her neurologist, Dr. Woodbine, point-blank whether the radiation would cure her. May Woodbine was a wonderful doctor, and she'd explained to Susannah that there were no guarantees; radiation was the best the medical profession had to offer. Susannah, being a doctor's child, had pressed her for statistics.

Both May Woodbine and Michael knew the treatment didn't offer any hope of cure. Its only purpose was to stave off the inevitable; the symptoms would improve temporarily, but the median survival rate for a glioma of the brainstem such as Susannah's…and Duncan's…was one year.

That was where total honesty became impossible for Michael; he didn't want his daughter to know that she had only a short time to live.

Susannah had guessed, however, and she decided not to go on with the radiation. Instead, she'd opted for a special diet and a number of other alternative treatments.

''We can always hope for spontaneous remission, Luke,'' Michael said.

''Yes, of course.'' Both doctors knew how rarely that occurred. ''Well, thank you, Michael, more than I can say. Sophie and her husband, Jason Hendricks, will be in your office in the morning with Duncan.''

THE FIRST THING that struck Michael at that meeting was how surprisingly young the Hendrickses were to have a five-year-old son. They looked like teenagers, and he learned later that Sophie was only twenty, Jason twenty-two. They were an exceptionally good-looking couple, and their child was beautiful. He had perfectly symmetrical features, a deep cleft in his chin, eyes so large and intensely blue and utterly clear that Michael felt he was looking at a slice of the sky.

They were already waiting in his office when he hurried in, parents seated side by side, holding hands, with the little boy perched on his father's knee.

Michael glanced at the clasped hands of Sophie and Jason and wondered how long it would be before the enormity of what was happening isolated them from each other, as it had Polly and him.

"Sorry I'm late," he apologized, shaking hands with them and explaining that he'd been held up on rounds at the hospital.

"I know how that happens," Sophie said with a strained smile. "Dad's always late. He barely even made it when my stepbrother Jacob was born." Banked terror showed in the huge gray eyes of the blond, plump young woman.

Her husband, Jason, could have modeled as a college football player. He was tall, broad-shouldered, muscular, with brown hair cropped in a crewcut. Although it wasn't hot in the office, he was sweating, and a nerve beside his eye jerked uncontrollably. Though young in years, these two were already experienced in anguish.

Tension filled the room.

Michael dragged a chair close to the little group and sat, wanting to ease the situation in any way he could. He smiled at Duncan, who gave him a searching look with those disconcertingly clear eyes, then put out his small hand trustingly when Michael offered his. Duncan had lost his hair as a result of the radiation, but his baldness didn't detract at all from his beauty. If anything, the stark skull emphasized the angelic face.

"Except for your blue eyes, I think you look exactly like your grandpa Luke, Duncan," Michael commented. The resemblance to handsome Luke Gilbert was striking, down to the deep cleft in Duncan's small strong chin.

"You know my grandpa Luke?" The boy's eyes lit up.

"I sure do. All us doctors know one another."

"My grandpa Luke's a baby doctor, and so's Morgan. She's my grandma, but she lets me call her 'Morgan' anyway. Her and Grandpa Luke help babies get born," Duncan said in a husky voice brimming with pride. "What kind of doctor are you?"

"I'm what's called a general practitioner. That means I get to do a little bit of all sorts of different medicine."

"You make people better, right?"

Michael's heart twisted. "Whenever I can, that's what I do." He braced himself for what he feared would be the next question, but it didn't come.

Instead, Duncan said, "When I grow up, I'm either gonna be a baby doctor or a carpenter. My other grandpa, Grandpa Andy, shows me how to make stuff outa wood.''

When I grow up…

At that moment Michael wished he were a carpenter himself instead of a doctor.

''Maybe you could do both, Duncan,'' he forced himself to say in a cheerful tone.

''Yeah. First I gotta get this tumor in my head better, though,'' the boy responded matter-of-factly, adding, ''Are you gonna have to stick me a lot? 'Cause I really don't like needles.''

''Nope. We may have to down the road, but certainly not today. All I'm gonna do this morning is talk to you and your mom and dad and have a look at you. Then I'll read this chart you brought me, and then you and I'll figure out how best we can make you feel better.'' *If only it were possible to heal you, child, I would.*

''Good.'' The boy nodded and grinned with relief. ''I sure don't like getting sticks all the time. I don't like my treatments, either. They make me feel *real* sick.''

''I know. Radiation can do that.''

''Morgan gave me a fish. His name's Oscar.'' Duncan had obviously had enough talk about illness.

''Is he a goldfish?'' It was impossible not to respond to this irresistible child.

''Yup. He's fat. He eats lots when I feed him

and then he poops in the water.'' Duncan's giggle was infectious.

Michael chatted about fish for a few moments, then turned his attention to Sophie and Jason, asking questions about the onset of the tumor, the symptoms Duncan had, the other doctors they'd seen, the medications he was taking, his appetite, his diet, his daily routine. Whenever possible, Michael asked Duncan questions directly, and he was impressed with how these parents encouraged their son to answer for himself.

During the physical examination, the boy was totally cooperative. The disease had affected his motor skills and his reflexes, just as Michael would have expected.

''What I'm going to do is suggest a number of alternative therapies that will make you feel better, Duncan,'' Michael explained when everything else was completed. ''I'll begin by recommending that the whole family change to a diet composed of natural foods.'' He wrote the titles of several cookbooks and the name of an experienced practitioner who would help with the transition.

He listed the other treatments that might prove helpful: Essiac, mixed respiratory virus vaccine, grape seed extract, green tea. He gave information on visualization and positive imagery and answered any questions they had.

As they were leaving the office, Sophie waited until Jerome and Duncan were out of earshot, then she blurted the question that Michael most dreaded.

"Is there a chance that all this stuff's going to make Duncan better, Doctor?"

Her gaze silently begged Michael for reassurance that he couldn't give.

CHAPTER SEVEN

IT TOOK ENORMOUS EFFORT for Michael to keep his voice steady, his words professional.

"No one can answer that, Sophie. There aren't any guarantees. The best thing we can do for Duncan is believe he will get better and help him believe it, as well." *Even though it's a lie,* an anguished part of his soul reminded him.

"But he does." Her face crumpled. "He absolutely believes he's going to get through this, and that's what breaks my heart. I know what his chances are. And sometimes…" She gulped and with her fingers rubbed at the tears coursing down her cheeks. "Sometimes I can hardly bear it, it hurts me so much."

"I understand." Michael knew he should put an arm around her, comfort her somehow, but he just couldn't do it. He felt as if something fragile in his chest would break if he touched her, that he'd do something humiliating, like start to cry. In self-defense he retreated behind his desk, where he fiddled with papers, waiting silently until she regained control.

"Thank you so much for seeing us," she said after a moment.

And Michael hated himself for being distant. He did his best to give her a facsimile of a smile, feeling like the worst of hypocrites.

"You can be certain we'll do absolutely everything you suggest, Dr. Forsythe."

"That's good. That's very important. Tell Valerie to make regular weekly appointments for Duncan. We'll all do the best we can for him, Sophie."

She nodded, and when the door closed behind her, Michael sank into his leather chair. His heart was hammering; he felt icy cold and nauseous. His hands knotted into fists and he longed to smash something.

He forced himself to study Duncan's chart, concentrate on the results of the numerous tests. It was all sickeningly familiar—the CAT scans, the blood tests.

He had no idea how long it was before Valerie tapped on the door to remind him his next patient was waiting.

With a supreme effort, he forced himself out of his chair, shoved the emotions into a dark place in his mind and somehow got on with being a doctor.

It was after seven that evening when Michael closed his own front door behind him. The long day had taken its toll, and it felt good to be home. Something smelled delicious and there was music playing, rock and roll. Polly hadn't played rock and roll for a very long time.

"Hi, Michael. I'm in the kitchen."

He hung his tweed jacket in the closet and made his way down the hall. Polly was stirring something on the stove, and she turned her head to smile at him.

"Long day, huh, Doc?"

She sounded cheerful. Although she looked disheveled, she was still terribly pretty in a narrow gray ankle-length skirt and a deep-green silky tunic that skimmed her slender hips. Her short, spiky hair was still a surprise to him.

"Very long day."

There was a smear of tomato paste on her cheek. Michael rubbed it off with his thumb and then kissed her quickly on the lips. "What're you making?"

She tasted sweet. Polly always tasted good, smelled good. That she managed to be fresh no matter what the occasion surprised him still. Coming home to such pleasant smells, such vibrant good health, after a day spent around illness was always such a pleasure.

"Vegetable stew and hot biscuits, and there's salad in the fridge." Her amber eyes shone with excitement. "Michael, you'll never guess what happened today."

"Tell me." Judging by her tone and her sparkling eyes, it was something good. A little of the weight lifted from his heart.

"Mom decided she wants Jerome to paint the outside of the house as well as clean up the rubbish. Can you believe that? She and I actually went out and bought the paint this afternoon—white, with green for the trim. She wanted turquoise, but I talked her out of it."

"Hey, that's wonderful, Pol." Michael leaned against the counter and smiled down at her. "I'm really glad she likes Jerome. Getting more work is good for him, too."

Polly nodded. "And guess what else? I'm going to help him. I'm going to paint with him. We're starting day after tomorrow, as long as it doesn't rain. Isn't that great? I called Norah and she can't believe this is happening—Mom changing her mind like this."

"You're going to paint the house with Jerome?" Michael frowned, not liking the idea at all. "Are you sure you want to do that, Polly? Painting a house is hard physical labor, you know. You'll have to be working up on ladders. I don't think that's such a good idea."

Polly shot him a disbelieving look and rolled her eyes heavenward. "For gosh sake, Michael." Her good humor evaporated. She threw down the spoon she'd been stirring the pot with and turned on him, eyes blazing. "This is something I *want* to do.

Can't you understand that? I *need* to do this. I need something to do that's creative.''

"What about your art? Why not get involved in that again?'' He gestured toward the closed door of the studio, and even as he did he knew it was the wrong thing to suggest. *Damn.* Almost everything he said to her these days was the wrong thing. Anger flared in him, mixed with frustration, at her, at himself.

Her voice was tense. "I can't draw anymore. I thought you knew that. Whatever talent I might have had is gone.'' She glared at him. "You don't get it, Michael. You just go off to work every single day. Your life has purpose and…and direction, and focus. Well, mine doesn't. Not anymore.''

He knew what was coming and he didn't want to listen, didn't want to hear it because of the pain it caused, because he couldn't do anything about it.

"Susannah was my job,'' Polly said slowly, her voice loud, as if by raising the volume she could make him hear, make him understand. "When we lost her, I no longer had anything to get out of bed for in the morning.'' Her huge, dramatic eyes glittered with anger and unshed tears, and although her voice trembled, she didn't stop.

He wished she would. God, how he wished she would.

"I lost my job as well as my daughter, Michael.

I'm not the same person anymore. I'm not an artist. I'm not a mother. I'm not really anything at all.''

"But you are, Pol.'' How could she not acknowledge it? It hurt him that he even had to point it out. "You're my wife.''

She nodded. "But that's not enough, Michael.''

The words were like nails hammered into his heart.

"I want another child. I've never pretended otherwise. But you won't agree to that.''

The look she gave him was filled with reproach, and he braced himself for still another confrontation.

But she didn't pursue the issue. "I have to find out what I can do to fill those empty places,'' she said. "However mundane it might seem to you, painting my mother's house might help. Who knows? It's something physical, and it doesn't take much brain power. Which is a good thing, because I still feel a lot of times as if my mind turned to mush somewhere along the way.''

Michael did his best to curb the torrent of emotions her words created—the guilt, the resentment, the denial and the awful recognition; so often, he still felt as if part of his mind had died, too, when Susannah had. At first he'd had trouble with procedures that should have been automatic, and if not for Valerie, he'd never have remembered the names of his patients in those first awful days and weeks. That was getting better, but it was a slow process.

He mustered his energy, trying to make her understand, knowing even as he did that the attempt was futile. Sometimes he thought they'd lost their understanding of each other along with everything else.

"It's your safety I'm concerned about, Polly. Working up on ladders is tricky. I don't want anything happening to you." The thought of her being injured or worse was unbearable, yet it was one that haunted him. There were so very many ways to lose her.

Unexpectedly, his concern softened her. She put a hand on his arm, and her voice was quiet.

"Nothing's gonna happen to me, Michael. I promise. I'll be careful. Just be glad for me, please. This is the first thing I've really wanted to try in a long time."

The pleading in her tone tore at his heart, and the old, familiar guilt gnawed at his gut. "Then do it, Pol. All I want is for you to be happy again." He reached out blindly and pulled her into his arms, holding her close against him, his nose buried in her spiky hair, every sensory nerve aware of her scent, the terrifying fragility of her bones, the softness of her beloved flesh, and before he could harness it, terror rode rampant through him, combined with shame and helplessness.

There was no sure way to keep her safe. There was nothing he could really do to protect her.

He was a strong man; he was a doctor; he was a person others relied on when they needed help, but he was a failure when it came to the first and most important task of all for a man—protecting those he most cherished, keeping his family safe from harm.

Her arms came up and looped around his neck. He kissed her hair, inhaling the fresh scent of her perfume, willing himself to think only of her. She tilted her head back and smiled at him, a lazy, inviting smile, and he bent and kissed her mouth.

The kiss deepened. It was evident immediately that she wanted him. Her lips opened beneath his, her tongue flicking. He pulled her closer, molding the thrilling, familiar body against his own. Firm breasts pressed against his chest; narrow hips strained against his groin.

He slid his hand down her back to cup the rounded swell of her bottom. He could feel the heat of her skin and the tiny bikini panties beneath the thin material of the skirt she wore. The thought of her lovely naked body shot a bolt of pure desire through him. She leaned into him, hips moving provocatively, and his lips devoured her, tongues dancing with need.

"Will dinner wait, love?" He murmured the words against her lips and groaned when she silently nodded, her mouth hungry.

Slipping an arm around her waist and another beneath her knees, he carried her into the living room to the overstuffed couch with its masses of goose down pillows. The blinds were drawn, the shadowy spaces of the large room lit only by the gentle spill of dusk from the skylight. With practiced ease, he pulled the skirt up past her hips, letting it bunch erotically around her narrow waist, then smoothly tugged her tunic up and over her shoulders and head. Her underwear was satin and lace, two tiny black scraps that he left so he could look at her, seductive and so nearly naked. His woman, his wife.

He removed his tie, tossed it aside. Then he slipped off his shirt.

"You're wondrously beautiful, my Polly." He dropped his trousers and underwear to the rug, slid his socks off, too, and lowered himself over her, covering her body with his, feeling the enticing softness and delicacy of her skin, concentrating on visual images, allowing them to enfold him in a cocoon of lust.

She skimmed her hands down his chest, tugging at the hair there; her arms encircling his back, and her legs parted and wound around him. Damp heat enveloped him.

"Now, Michael."

Her voice was throaty and she raised her hips, inviting him, nibbling kisses down his chin and under his jaw.

"I want you now. Don't wait, please, Michael."

His swollen penis pressed against her through the flimsy barrier of panty, and he pulled the garment aside, just enough so he could slide into her.

The heat... The tightness of her...

She lifted herself against him, and he slid farther inside.

A contraceptive. He needed a contraceptive. They were upstairs, in his bedside table.

Silently, he cursed his lack of foresight as his body throbbed with desire too long denied.

"I have to get a condom, sweetheart." He moved to stand up, but her arms locked him to her.

"No, Michael. Don't. My period's coming. Stay, please. Don't go. Love me now."

For one blind, ravenous instant, he almost gave in. But then the fear intercepted, cold and harsh. If she became pregnant...

"I'll be right back. Don't move."

By the time he came hurrying downstairs, though, the magic was gone. She was waiting, just as he'd asked, but it was a passionless waiting. Although he kissed her, fondled her, caressed every inch of her body, he could sense the distance that had crept between them like a cold dark shadow that, try as he might, he couldn't dispel.

He fought against it. His libido reacted to his wife's beauty as it always did, and when he became hard and pulsing again, he reached a hand around her backside and slid it up between them, touching every secret inch of her, willing her to soar with him. He slid the condom on and buried himself inside her, moving with the long, slow strokes he knew she liked, claiming mouth and nipples with lips and tongue in an echo of that other urgent movement.

"I can't, Michael. You come."

The whisper was defeat, another acknowledgment of his failure.

Passion drained from him, as if a plug had been opened.

"I love you, Polly." It was the truth, but it couldn't heal what was broken between them. He held her for several more long moments, then released her and headed for the bathroom.

For the rest of the evening, they were terribly polite to each other.

TWO DAYS LATER, with the morning sun beating down on her and the smell of lilacs from a neighbor's yard filling her nostrils, Polly remembered every detail of that miserable evening, and in spite of the blue sky and fresh air, she felt frustrated and angered by it all over again.

She was wearing denim shorts and a checked shirt, with a billed cap covering her hair, as she sat perched high on a scaffold that rested against the side of her mother's house and wielded a scraper, attacking the blistered, dried bubbles of ugly gray paint.

Far below her—it was shocking how high up she was—Jerome was talking to his daughter as he replaced the last pickets in the fence he'd repaired. He'd also fixed the railing to the back door, and emptied the front porch of its garbage.

Impatient to get on with the painting, Polly had offered to start scraping.

The good thing about being up that high and doing mindless physical work was the time it gave her to think about everything, Polly mused. She wrinkled her nose and admitted that the bad thing about it was exactly the same.

She thought about her and Michael and their diminishing sex life. With every fiber of her being, she'd wanted him to make love to her the other evening. She'd felt warm and loving and eager and sexy when he took her in his arms. But the damned business about the condom had acted like a dose of ice water.

Resentment added extra energy to her scraping. Why had Michael spoiled it for them? Why couldn't he just have let passion overwhelm them? *The way he used to.* Snippets of erotic scenes played in her head—the time they'd made love outside on the lawn three summers before, with the sprinkler's rhythmic arc soaking them every few moments, their laughter wild and desperate because they couldn't stop long enough to move out of the water. And the time at the Fieldings' party, when they'd looked at each other and terrible desire had sizzled between them, so that she'd pretended a headache and they'd hurried away. They hadn't even made it home; Michael had driven into a park and they'd made love like two teenagers, writhing in the back seat of the car, trying to stay sane enough to watch for the lights of a patrol car and in the end, blinded with pleasure, not caring.

"How's it going up there?"

Polly jumped, grabbed the side of the scaffold, and almost dropped the scraper.

"Steady, there. Sorry I scared you." Jerome looked up at her, eyes masked behind sunglasses. "I'm finished this fence now, so I'll be right up. I'm just gonna get a drink of water first. It's hot as blazes this morning."

"It is hot. And there's more to this scraping job than I expected." *Like X-rated love scenes from another life.*

"It won't take long with two of us," he assured her. "You want me to bring you up a drink?"

"Oh, please." She wiped a gloved hand across her forehead. "I brought a case of spring water. It's in the fridge. Have some yourself and bring me up a bottle."

Isabelle wasn't home. She'd announced when Polly arrived at nine that morning that she was going shopping and then out for lunch with friends, and she'd sailed off, wearing a blue seersucker suit and a smart straw hat.

Isabelle always looked elegant; it never failed to

amaze Polly that her mother could emerge from the chaos of her bedroom looking bandbox fresh.

A few moments later Jerome climbed the ladder and swung himself onto the scaffolding with athletic grace. He handed Polly the bottled water and then settled to the job of scraping.

"Daddy, see my bubbles?" Clover was sitting on a plastic lawn chair in the middle of the backyard with a basin of soapy water and a bubble wand Isabelle had given her that morning. Polly had heard Jerome telling her a moment ago that she was not allowed anywhere near the side of the house where the scaffolding was, that it was dangerous.

Now, however, the little girl slid off the lawn chair and made her way over until she stood directly beneath the ladder. "Daddy, I wanna come up with you," she whined.

Polly looked down at Clover, and it was all she could do not to snap at the child, to order her away from the ladder. Just as Jerome had said, it was dangerous.

"Move back, sweetheart." There wasn't even a trace of impatience in Jerome's tone, only concern. "Remember what Daddy told you—you're not to be near the ladder."

"But I want to come up where you are," she insisted, putting one foot on the first rung.

Again, Polly felt the urge to reprimand the little girl, but Jerome patiently coaxed her away, promising he'd come down and talk to her if she did what he asked.

She did, and he clambered down, then swung Clover up in his arms and reassured her in a low, calm voice, before planting kisses on her neck and making her giggle.

Polly watched, frowning. Why did Clover irritate her so? How could she dislike a small child?

She sipped at her water and reasoned with herself, observing the scene on the lawn below as Jerome settled Clover once again with her bubbles.

It was natural, after all, for a little girl to get bored and want her daddy's attention. But it would slow the job considerably if it happened all the time, Polly thought, feeling resentful.

"She gets bored. She really oughta be with other kids, instead of trailing around with me," Jerome said when he was once again on the scaffold. He started scraping, his muscular arms making easy work of the blistered paint.

"You got kids, Polly?"

Her steady scraping faltered. She should have expected the question, but she hadn't.

And how was Jerome to know it was the most difficult of questions for her?

CHAPTER EIGHT

"I HAD ONE DAUGHTER, named Susannah. She died a year ago last February when she was nine."

"That's a rough one."

Jerome was sympathetic, but he didn't seem to be ill at ease the way so many people were when Polly told them about Susannah.

"I had a brother who died when he was eight," he added after a moment. "Billy was just eleven months older than me. We were as close as twins. We always shared a bed, and we used to wear the same clothes. I still think about him, imagine what he'd look like as a man—how tall he'd be, what his voice would sound like. I suppose you do that with Susannah, too, huh? Sort of imagine her growing up?"

Polly was astounded. She gaped at him. "Yeah," she managed to say. "I do imagine that." His complete understanding had caught her off guard. She'd become so accustomed to people's awkwardness when she talked of Susannah, so aware of their relief when the subject changed and they could speak about something else. How absolutely unexpected to find in this young workman the acceptance so lacking in her friends.

Not just your friends, either, she corrected herself with bitter honesty. *Even Michael avoids conversations about Susannah. You know he does. He has from the moment of her death.*

The fact that her husband wouldn't verbally share with her their precious memories of their child was one of the things that hurt her the most deeply.

"What did she die of?"

Jerome's wide, sweeping strokes with the scraper formed a pattern for Polly to follow, as did his ease with this conversation.

"She had a brain tumor."

"Billy had leukemia."

"Were there other kids in your family, Jerome?"

"Oh, yeah. Seven of us—four boys and three girls—but we didn't grow up together," he confided. "Right after Billy died Social Services took the rest of us into care. We grew up in separate foster homes."

Polly tried to imagine what that would have been like for a little boy, and she wondered, as well, why it had happened. "It must have been really hard on you—losing your brother and then your whole family being separated like that."

He shrugged. "It wasn't so bad. I realize now that it was for the best. See, my mom and pop were

alcoholics. Living with them got really hairy sometimes. We never had enough food or anything in
the house. We couldn't count on them being there.
I used to think when I was a kid that Billy got sick
because we were hungry so much of the time. Of
course I know now that had nothing to do with it,
but you get funny ideas when you're little.'' He
glanced down at his daughter, playing with a wa-
tering can and the hose.

''Clover asked me the other day if her mom
went away because she was a bad girl.''

''What did you tell her?''

''It really threw me at first—I didn't know she
felt that way. I finally said that her mommy loved
her a lot, and she didn't want to leave her, but she
knew that Clover would be fine with me. And that
daddies never, ever, leave their little girls.'' The
hard, determined edge to his voice revealed more
than his words.

''That was a really good answer, Jerome.''

''Thanks.'' He gave Polly a grateful look and a
wide grin. ''Kids can really put you on the spot at
times, huh?''

''They really can.'' Polly smiled and shook her
head. ''I remember Susannah asking me about a
friend who was pregnant, why she had such a fat
tummy. I explained that she had a baby inside her,
and the next day Susannah went up to another
woman who was quite overweight and wanted to
know if she had babies in there.''

Jerome laughed, and a warm sense of companionship came over Polly. For the next hour, interrupted only by Clover's frequent demands, they scraped and talked, sharing stories of their childhoods. Polly found herself able to confide in Jerome, to relate with total honesty how Isabelle and Dylan had fought and separated and made up, how insecure she and Norah had been as a result of their parents' chaotic life-style.

He seemed to understand, and he told his own stories of being in a series of foster homes, never knowing how long he'd be staying with any single family. "It leaves you feeling that you're not as important as other people, that you're sort of a throwaway kid."

"That's exactly how Norah and I used to feel. Do you see your brothers and sisters at all, Jerome?"

He shook his head. "We lost touch with one another, getting shuffled around in different foster homes. I know where they are now. We exchange Christmas cards, but that's about the extent of it. Two of my sisters are up in northern B.C. The other one's living in Alaska. My brothers both joined the Canadian army. They're out in Ontario somewhere. They're all married, and I've got a pile of nieces and nephews I've never met. It's too bad none of them live here. It would be good for Clover to have relatives nearby—aunts and uncles and cousins."

"Susannah adored my sister, Norah. They were really good buddies. Norah was such a great aunt." Polly deliberately didn't mention Isabelle; her mother had been anything but a doting grandmother.

"What does your sister do?"

"She's a nurse on the obstetrical ward at St. Joe's hospital. She's not married. And Michael was an only child, so there weren't cousins for Susannah. You'll meet Norah. She's gonna drop by when she gets off shift this afternoon."

They climbed down the ladder at lunchtime, and sitting at the old picnic table in one corner of the yard, they ate the bagged lunches they'd brought. Polly made a real effort to befriend Clover, admiring a picture the little girl had drawn and offering her some of her trail mix, but the child was aloof, eyeing Polly suspiciously and huddling against Jerome on the wooden bench.

After lunch, Jerome put Clover down for a nap on the seat of his truck. He'd brought a pillow and a blanket, and he sat beside his daughter, stroking her hair, quietly singing her a country song until she was asleep.

Polly watched and listened from her perch high up on the side of the house, thinking what a familiar, intimate scene it was. It reminded Polly of how she used to rub Susannah's back at bedtime, while Michael would make up some farfetched story. The memory wasn't painful, although it made Polly nostalgic. It felt good to recall happy times with her daughter.

Jerome left his daughter sleeping and joined Polly. In another hour, with Clover still sleeping, they'd finished the scraping and began painting the trim at the top of the house. The intense bright green wasn't the color Polly would have chosen, but it was the only one Isabelle would agree to, and as the dingy brown began to disappear beneath the cheerful paint, Polly felt elated.

"Maybe I've got a whole new career happening here," she joked. "I could start my own business—painting houses."

"Better wait until we've done at least half this one before you hire yourself out. You might just change your mind." He grinned across at her. "So what brilliant career are you giving up for this painting gig?"

It was another question that always made Polly uncomfortable.

"I never had a real career," she confessed. "I went to art school instead of college, then I got married, and I never really worked at a regular job."

"What kind of art do you do?"

"Mostly I drew faces and bodies, life studies in charcoal, some watercolors. But I've stopped."

"Why's that?"

"I can't seem to do it anymore. I...I lost wherever it came from when Susannah died. I think I did my best work after I had her, and all during the years she was growing up. I'd take photos of her and draw from them when she was napping, and then when she started school I went to a life drawing class a couple times a week." Her eyes unexpectedly filled with tears. "I've tried, but whatever talent I had is just gone."

"It'll come back."

How could he be so certain?

"I hope you're right. But I doubt it." Polly dipped her brush and concentrated on the area she was painting. Her tears dried and she took a deep breath.

"That's probably why you're doing *this* painting," Jerome went on after a quiet few moments. "It'll get you back into your art—you wait and see."

Painting a house was so far removed from true art that Polly felt certain he was teasing her, but when she glanced at him she could tell he was totally sincere.

"Anybody ever tell you you're an optimist, Jerome?"

He grinned and nodded. "Yeah. Tiffany used to, when we were fighting." He adjusted his sunglasses. "With a life like mine, you've got to look on the bright side," he quipped. "It's either that or suicide."

Polly felt a surge of affection for him. He was

such a likable man, so good-natured and open and easy.

He was also able to give her pointers about the painting that made her more efficient, and as the afternoon progressed, they became a working unit, accomplishing much more than they expected. Isabelle came home at two and admired what they'd done, and when Clover woke up from her long nap, Isabelle brought out juice and an economy-size bag of cookies and let Clover devour as many as she wanted.

It was exactly what Isabelle used to do with Susannah, and it irked Polly the same way it had previously. Jerome didn't seem to pay any attention.

"Mom, all that sweet stuff isn't good for her teeth," she finally called down to Isabelle as cookie after cookie disappeared into Clover. "And she's going to be hyper with so much sugar in her system."

"You just mind your business up there and paint," her mother retorted. "As soon as she's full, we're going for a walk to the park, aren't we, Clover? Long as it's okay with your daddy."

Jerome enthusiastically agreed, and a few moments later, Isabelle and Clover meandered off down the back lane.

"That's nice of your mom to take Clover to the park," Jerome said, adding, "I'll be right back, I forgot to give them the sunscreen from the truck. Clover's skin's so fair she sunburns really easy.''

He hurried down the ladder, and Polly watched as he sprinted along the lane after his daughter and Isabelle. He was back a few moments later.

''Clover must take after her mother,'' Polly remarked. ''You don't look as if you've ever had a sunburn in your life.'' Although Jerome was blond-haired, his skin tone was a deep, rich walnut.

''You're right. I never burn. And Tiffany had black hair and sort of olive skin. She didn't have to worry, either. Clover isn't really like either one of us.''

Polly swiped on another line of green paint. ''Funny how that genetic thing happens, isn't it? Susannah wasn't like me at all, except for my eye color. She looked exactly like Michael.''

''Actually, I'm not exactly sure I am Clover's genetic father,'' Jerome confessed. ''Tiffany had an affair with some guy just before I met her. She told me she wasn't sure if she was pregnant already when we got together.''

Polly stared across at him, surprised and shocked. ''Doesn't that bother you? Not knowing if Clover is really your child?''

''Nope.'' The denial was absolute. ''Far as I'm concerned, she's my kid. I was there when she was born, and she and I both know I'm her daddy.'' That seemed to settle the matter for Jerome.

Polly thought about it, unable to understand how

he could fully accept the responsibility for a child who might not even be his. She couldn't do such a thing; she knew she couldn't. Once, when she and Michael were fighting about her becoming pregnant again, he'd suggested adoption, and Polly had known, instantly and conclusively, that she couldn't. She acknowledged it was selfish and horrible of her, but it was the truth.

She didn't comment on Jerome's remark, and after a few moments, he began to whistle. Apart from that it was quiet, up high where they were.

Polly considered how much she'd learned today about Jerome, and how much respect she had for him. Somehow, working together on a scaffold high up against this house had created a relaxed intimacy.

"Think we'll get the trim finished on this side of the house today, Jerome?"

"Sure. We make a good team. One artist, one jack-of-all-trades. Makes a fine combination, don't you think?" The grin he shot her way was entirely without sexual innuendo, and warmth filled Polly. This must be how it would feel to have a brother. She'd always wanted one when she was growing up.

"A couple of weeks after Susannah died, I checked myself into the psych ward for a few days," she surprised herself by saying. "I met a counselor named Frannie Sullivan, and I was able to talk with her. I don't think I could have survived without Frannie. Anyway, I was just thinking how honest we've been with each other today. Frannie always says that people normally walk around with armor on, never revealing how sad or frightened or insecure they really feel.'' She smiled at Jerome. ''It's true, because I do it myself all the time. 'How are you?' somebody asks, and you're dying inside, but you plaster this big grin on your face and say, 'Fine. I'm doing just fine.' But today's different, Jerome. With you I took all my armor off.''

He nodded, and she could see that he was both a little embarrassed and pleased. ''Same goes. I was kinda nervous about this—you being a doctor's wife and everything, and me barely finishing high school. But you're really easy to talk to, Polly.''

''Thanks.'' She dipped her brush in the tin again. ''It's a good thing we get along, because this is gonna take us more than a few days, by the looks of it. I didn't really understand how much work painting an entire house would be. We'll probably run out of things to talk about long before we run out of boards to paint.''

''I dunno about that. I haven't even started telling you about my wild years,'' he joked, and they both laughed.

''What's so funny, you two?'' Norah stood at the foot of the ladder, smiling and shading her eyes with her hand as she looked up at them. ''Is that all you've gotten painted in a whole day?''

"That shows you how much you know about painting houses," Polly retorted. "Jerome, this nasty critic is my sister, Norah Rafferty. Norah, Jerome Fox."

"Can you guys take a break? I brought some lemonade and a bag of fresh bagels."

"We'll be right down. This is hot, hungry work." Polly climbed down the ladder with Jerome right behind her, and they joined Norah at the picnic table.

"Where's Mom?" Norah poured chilled lemonade into plastic cups and handed out bagels.

"She's taken Jerome's girl, Clover, to the park." Polly had a long drink of the lemonade, sighing with pleasure.

"How old is your daughter, Jerome?"

"Clover's four. Polly says you work in maternity at St. Joe's. It must be exciting to watch babies get born every day. I saw Clover arrive, and it was tougher than any work I've ever done. Messier, too. I almost passed out."

Polly and Norah laughed.

"That happens to dads a lot," Norah told Jerome. "Far as I'm concerned, working on obstetrics is the greatest job in the world. I love my work. Each shift just flies past. How about you, Jerome? What do you do besides paint houses? Do you enjoy your work?"

Polly listened and observed as Jerome and Norah got to know each other. As usual, Norah wasn't wearing makeup. She had on nondescript beige trousers and a checked gingham shirt that, in Polly's opinion, did nothing for her; yet when she spoke about her work and deftly encouraged Jerome to talk about his, she had an incandescent beauty about her.

Polly glanced at Jerome, and it was obvious that he, too, thought Norah was attractive at this moment. He was watching her, nodding and paying attention to everything she said.

"I'd do my job whether I got paid or not," Norah commented. "I can't see ever quitting obstetrical nursing."

"I don't feel that way about construction, but I'm gonna save my money and someday start my own minibrew store," Jerome replied. "I've been making beer from old traditional recipes for a couple of years now, and I find it really interesting. I'd love to have a place where people could experiment, try out different methods of brewing."

"I've made wine a few times. It's such a thrill when it turns out," Norah replied.

And they launched into a lively discussion of natural methods versus chemical that Polly didn't understand.

She let their conversation flow over and around her: ate her bagel and thought about people's jobs, about Norah and her babies and, inevitably, about the baby she herself longed to have.

After Susannah's death, when nothing would

help the agony of her loss, she'd cut a picture of a baby out of a magazine, a sober, round-faced, blue-eyed child, placid, totally unlike volatile Susannah, with her dark curls and dramatic temperament.

Polly had matted the picture, and in the endless long nights when sleep wouldn't come despite medications, she'd hold that photo and dream, visualizing having this baby, loving her, sitting at night in a room filled with gentle shadows and feeding her from breasts overflowing with milk, just as she had Susannah. The soft, sweet-smelling child would fill the emptiness that threatened to swallow her up. The baby would be a part of Michael and Polly the way Susannah had been. She would be a link to the part of herself Polly felt she was losing, the nurturing, mothering part of her that had been the epicenter of her life since the moment her daughter was born, the part that had been stolen from her.

Anger and frustration filled Polly whenever she acknowledged that it was Michael who wouldn't let her have this baby she longed for, no matter how she reasoned or begged or harangued him about it—

"Polly?"

The insistent, puzzled note in Norah's voice told her that she'd entirely missed part of the conversation.

"Sorry." She forced a smile. "I was daydreaming. I didn't hear what you said."

"I said I'm off tomorrow, and I'd be happy to come and help paint. That okay with you?"

"Absolutely. I think it's a great idea. We'll get done that much faster if you help." Polly forced enthusiasm into her voice, even though her immediate reaction was, of all things, a bleak sense of disappointment. She didn't want her sister helping with the painting. The disturbing truth was, she didn't want Norah there. She wanted Jerome all to herself.

CHAPTER NINE

NORAH LEFT, and Polly and Jerome scrambled back up the ladder to the scaffold.

As they worked, Polly acknowledged to herself that she'd been looking forward to the easy flow of conversation with Jerome, the chance to talk freely in a way she hadn't done lately—the way she and Michael used to talk.

Suddenly, she felt afraid. The ability to talk to Michael about anything and everything had always been such a powerful bond between them. But it wasn't there anymore, and here she was, sharing her innermost thoughts and feelings with a man she'd known only a few days. It pointed out to her as nothing else could have how deep and wide the chasm between her and the man she loved had become.

''I'll be back shortly.'' Polly hurried down the ladder and went into her mother's house, retrieved her cell phone from her purse and dialed Michael's office number.

Valerie answered, and a moment later Michael came on the line. Polly forced all traces of the agitation she felt out of her voice and instead purred in a low, sexy tone, "Dr. Forsythe, I'm an admirer of yours and I'm calling to ask you for a date."

"I'm certain that could be arranged."

She could tell by his guarded response that he was with a patient.

"Tonight, for dinner. Eight o'clock, at Le Veggie."

"Sounds good. How's the painting going?"

"It's obscenely green. My mother is delighted."

He laughed, as she'd hoped he would.

"Be careful on that ladder."

"I am."

She hung up, thinking that many things were far more dangerous than a ladder.

LATER THAT EVENING, Polly sat across from her husband in the quiet restaurant on Denman Street that she'd chosen because it was intimate and restful. The waiter had taken their orders, and they were sipping wine. Soft music played unobtrusively in the background, and Polly felt relaxed and attractive; she'd hurried home from her mother's and spent two hours scrubbing off specks of green paint, soaking in a tub of fragrant bubbles, repairing her manicure and trying on one outfit after another until she settled on the simple ivory knit dress she was wearing.

Michael had been late, as usual. He'd raced in

the door at seven-thirty full of apologies, and hurriedly showered and shaved.

He looked handsome, sitting opposite her now, but then, he always did.

He also looked weary. There were lines around his dark eyes that hadn't been there a short time ago.

"Michael, we have to talk."

"Yeah, we do, Pol." He sighed and set down his glass on the gleaming white cloth. He didn't look at her. Instead, he gazed out the window, although she could tell he wasn't really seeing the pedestrians on the busy street.

"I've been avoiding it, but we've got to discuss this money thing."

"'Money thing'?" Polly had been wondering how best to bring up the issues that were bothering her, that had become evident today when she'd talked with Jerome.

"What money thing, Michael?" She frowned at him, then belatedly remembered. "You mean, Raymond Stokes?"

Michael nodded. "I spoke with the R.C.M.P. again today. They reiterated that there's very little chance of recovering any of the money, even if, by some miracle, they locate Raymond."

"But you said we were okay. You said our situation wasn't desperate."

"It's not. Not yet. But we'll have to be careful, Polly. We'll have to reduce our expenditures every way we can for the next while. I'm going to extend my office hours and take on extra work in order to make up the loss.''

Polly gave him an incredulous look. ''But you're already working long hours, Michael. You're hardly ever home as it is.'' She knew she sounded accusatory, but it was the simple truth. How could he extend what was already overextended?

The waiter brought their food just then, and Polly waited with barely controlled impatience until he was gone. ''Look, maybe we ought to just borrow enough to get us through so there won't be so much pressure on you.''

''Borrow?'' Michael made a noise intended as a laugh. ''I already have borrowed—to cover our bills for the month. We're at the limit on our line of credit, and we're mortgaged on the house as high as the bank will allow.''

Polly put down her fork. She was barely able to swallow the mouthful of food she'd taken. ''Are…are you saying we're…we're going bankrupt, Michael?''

''No, I'm not saying that. Of course not.'' But he sounded impatient instead of reassuring. ''What I am saying is that we have to cut our expenses drastically for the foreseeable future, until I can get caught up. Until I can provide a financial cushion again, like the one we had before Raymond stole it away. You'll have to watch your spending for a while.''

Controlled anger and sharp bitterness laced his voice; Polly had rarely heard such a voice from her husband. She recognized that he was under enormous pressure, and with a sinking sensation in her stomach, she knew this was not the time to bring up the intimate problems in their marriage that were causing her such heartache. No matter how serious they were, Michael was already on overload. Confronting him with emotional issues right now could be disastrous.

Impossible as it seemed to her, they'd simply have to bungle along the way they had been, until the money issue was less urgent, until Michael could listen to what she had to say without the issue of finances tightening like a noose around his neck.

''Of course I'll do everything I can to help.'' Guilt over how much she'd already charged on their accounts this month rose up in her. There'd been clothing, and the set of dishes, and Norah's watch, and…the truth was she couldn't even remember precisely how much she'd charged, but it was a lot. She'd grown accustomed to buying anything and everything that took her fancy. Michael had never once restrained her in any way.

Shame overwhelmed her. What was wrong with her? Where money was concerned, she'd acted totally irresponsibly, like a spoiled child instead of a reliable adult and partner. And Michael had treated her that way, as well, she realized with a start.

That made her angry. ''Why didn't you tell me right away how serious this Raymond thing was, Michael? I'm your wife—I had a right to know. We're supposed to be partners. We're supposed to share the bad stuff as well as the good, aren't we?''

''There hasn't been a whole lot of good for a while now, Polly. I guess I thought you didn't need this on top of everything else. You've seemed…better…lately. I didn't want to upset you all over again.''

''Better? Damn it all, Michael, I'm not an invalid. Losing Susannah wasn't some disease I'll recover from. How dare you treat me like a patient, or like…like a child you have to humor?'' Her voice had risen, and other diners were staring at them. Polly didn't care. His words, what she perceived as his condescension, infuriated her.

Suddenly she wanted to pour out all the other grievances, all the ways he was hurting her and their marriage.

Michael must have sensed it, because he said in a quiet, controlled tone, ''This isn't the place to discuss it, Polly. If you're finished with your food, we'll leave.''

''I'm done.'' She'd barely touched her food, but she couldn't eat another bite.

He got up, signaled the waiter and went to the cashier to pay the bill, and by the time they were out on the sidewalk, she'd calmed down enough to reaffirm that this wasn't the time to bring up all the other issues. But she couldn't separate them; if she brought up one thing, she'd have to bring up the rest, and for the first time in their marriage, she was afraid of confronting him.

She walked stiffly beside Michael to where they'd parked the car. He didn't say anything about what had occurred in the restaurant, and neither did she.

They rode home in strained silence, and when they reached the house he disappeared into his study, muttering about bringing his files up-to-date.

Polly swallowed the medications she'd been trying to give up, and in a short time fell into a deep, drugged sleep. She didn't hear Michael come to bed, and when she awoke the next morning, groggy and sluggish, he'd already left for the hospital.

She quickly showered and hurried over to her mother's house, grateful beyond belief to have a job to go to, a place where she was needed, people to talk with who'd make it easier to forget for a few hours that her marriage was collapsing around her.

Norah was already there, and so was Jerome.

The three of them joked and laughed and worked. If Polly's laughter was a little too loud, her jokes a little forced, the other two didn't seem to notice.

The following day Norah had to return to work, and Polly was alone with Jerome. For the next week, from early morning until late at night, she worked as hard as she'd ever done physically. She concentrated on the job, not allowing herself to think of the problems between her and Michael. She was too exhausted each evening to do more than prepare a quick meal for herself and then fall into bed.

She found she didn't need the medications these nights. Sleep was instantaneous, long and deep. She saw very little of Michael. He was working even longer hours than before, and he didn't even object when she and Jerome decided to paint on Sunday afternoon.

THE SILENT HOUSE settled in around Michael, weighing down on him like a heavy dark cloak. Half an hour earlier, Polly had stuck her head into the study to tell him she was going to her mother's to paint. He'd been working for hours on the endless stack of forms the government required, but when the sound of Polly's car accelerating down the drive faded, he shoved the untidy mass of paper aside and got to his feet to wander restlessly from one room to the next. Every now and then he'd pause in front of the wide front window in the living room.

Sunday. It had always been the best day of the week for him. He used to get up early and make his one culinary specialty—buckwheat pancakes. He and Susannah would take a cup of coffee up to Polly to entice her out of bed, and they'd all have breakfast together before church.

The old order changeth, yielding place to new…

But, contrary to the Tennyson poem, there was no new order, he reminded himself with bitter irony, just this constant sense of desperation in his gut, and the growing certainty that he was losing the only woman he'd ever loved and he seemed unable to do a damned thing to prevent it.

It was suddenly all he could do to stop himself from driving his fist through the plate-glass window.

He hurried to the hall, grabbed a jacket and his car keys. St. Joe's Emergency would be teeming with people needing assistance, and the staff there were growing accustomed to having him volunteer his services.

POLLY'S FRIENDSHIP with Jerome deepened as the days progressed. They laughed over silly things— the way Polly's hair became speckled with white paint, the time Jerome accidentally dropped his brush directly onto the neighbor's black cat. The comfortable intimacy between them was undeniable.

To Polly's surprise, Isabelle had grown fond of Clover. She told the girl to call her ''Auntie,'' and she began taking Clover to the park every day, either in the morning or late in the afternoon, freeing Jerome to concentrate on the painting. Isabelle's generosity puzzled Polly. Selfless service had never been a part of her mother's nature, and Clover was anything but an appealing child.

It was Norah who discovered the truth. She'd fallen into the habit of dropping by on her way to or from work, and one afternoon she and Polly were in Isabelle's kitchen, mixing up a pitcher of frozen juice. The unusually warm weather had lasted through the end of April, and Isabelle, as usual, had taken Clover to the park.

"A group of older men play horseshoes over there, and there's one of those big checkerboards painted on the concrete. I guess these guys meet every day, and Clover gives Mom an excuse for hanging out where the action is." Norah shook her head and laughed. "Trust Mom to figure out where the boys are, huh?"

Polly wasn't amused. "Honestly, she's the limit." She gave the juice a vigorous stir. "The way she fought with Dad you'd have thought she hated men. But the minute he was dead, she started acting like a teenager again, and she's still at it. I wish she'd just grow up."

Norah picked up the plastic glasses and headed for the door. "Mom is what she is, Pol. She's never gonna change, so we might as well get used to it. Besides, she's helping Jerome out, so at least he benefits."

It was easy for Norah to excuse Isabelle, Polly fumed as she followed her sister out the door. Norah had never had a kid; she didn't know how it had felt to have Isabelle parade one man after the other in front of Susannah.

"Are they really all my uncles?" Susannah had asked once, and Polly had dreaded the time when Susannah would realize her grandmother was promiscuous. In so many ways, Isabelle had deliberately undermined how Polly was raising her daughter.

Outside, the late afternoon was hot. Jerome was sweating, and he'd stripped off his shirt. He was wearing only a pair of tattered blue jean cutoffs. His hair had bleached to a silvery blond, and his brown, muscular body gleamed in the sunlight. He drank the entire glass of juice in one long, thirsty draft, then tilted back his head to gaze up at the wall they were working on.

"We're gonna be finished here in the morning, Polly. All we've got left is that one back wall to second-coat. Then I'm going up to retouch the trim—for some reason the paint on the eaves went on really uneven on this side—but that won't take long. How about we go out for lunch tomorrow and I buy us all a burger and a beer as a celebration."

Norah shook her head. "I'd love to, but I can't, I'm on days tomorrow."

"I accept," Polly said. "I think that's a great

idea. We need a celebration after all this hard work.''

''I'll ask Isabelle if she wants to come along,'' Jerome added.

A little of Polly's anticipation faded.

''The house looks absolutely beautiful. You've both done such a great job,'' Norah said. ''What are you going to do after this, Jerome? Do you have another job lined up?'' Norah continued quickly, ''The only reason I'm asking is that there's a job posting at the hospital for a maintenance person and the pay is quite good.''

''I really appreciate you telling me.'' Jerome's white teeth flashed in a wide smile. ''I've been trying to scout out a job on construction, but things are slow right now. Think I'd have any chance of getting on at St. Joe's, Norah?''

''I don't see why not. I'm sure Michael would give you a good reference.'' Norah hesitated, then acknowledged shyly, ''I would, too, if you wanted to apply. In fact, I could give you a ride over there right now and show you around. You could pick up the job posting and talk to the maintenance supervisor.''

Polly felt a stab of resentment mixed with…it couldn't be jealousy, could it? She immediately shoved the idea out of her mind. ''Why don't you do that, Jerome. I can finish this last bit of siding. And Clover's fine with Mom. They likely won't be back for another hour or so.''

Isabelle would stay until dark as long as there were men at the park fawning over her, Polly thought scathingly.

"Okay, I'd really like to get my name in right away if there's a chance of a steady job." Jerome hurried inside to wash up, and in another few moments, he and Norah drove off.

Polly watched them go, feeling unreasonably lonely and bereft. With much less than her usual enthusiasm, she painted for a while, then set down her brush. She tugged off her gloves and dug her cell phone out of her bag, then sat down cross-legged on the grass and dialed Michael's office, thinking how often she used to call him like this and how he'd always take a few moments to talk to her and Susannah, no matter how busy he was.

When had she stopped doing that? She'd hardly called him at all since she'd begun painting here, and even before that, the calls had been few and far between.

"Valerie, hi. It's me. Is he busy?" The greeting was a rite.

"I'll get him."

"Polly? Is anything wrong?" Michael sounded harassed.

"Nothing my favorite doctor couldn't fix," Polly replied, deliberately injecting a sexy, teasing note into her voice. "This job is nearly done. I wanted to see if you could come by and take a look at our handiwork."

"I'm sorry, Pol. I just can't. I'm really backed up here. Bob Larue is on holiday and I'm seeing his patients as well as my own. Don't worry about dinner. I'll grab something later." There was a short pause, and when she didn't say anything, he added, "I'd better go. I was with a patient when you called."

"Okay." Her stomach ached all of a sudden. "I guess I'll see you when I see you, then."

"Don't wait up, love. I've got house calls to make when I'm done here."

Polly pressed the button that disconnected the call and slowly tucked the phone back in her bag. She stared at her mother's house, resplendent in its new paint.

As of tomorrow she'd be out of a job. Because of their finances, there was no way she could return to the pattern of spending her days driving around the city, visiting boutiques and shopping malls. Neither could she stay at home. The very thought of being there alone, hour after hour, day after day, with nothing to attend to, made her tremble.

What on earth was she going to do with the rest of her life?

IN SPITE of being physically exhausted, Polly slept badly that night. At three in the morning she awoke from a panicked dream in which she was locked in a windowless room, terrified because some nameless, dreaded danger was almost upon her.

Realizing that Michael wasn't in bed beside her, and feeling lost and desolate, she got up and pulled on a cotton robe and then made her way downstairs.

A light was on in the den. Polly pushed the half-opened door wide. Michael was slumped on the leather sofa, wearing a gray T-shirt and sweatpants, staring at the television, where an old black-and-white movie flickered soundlessly across the screen. He wasn't paying any attention to it. He seemed lost in thought, his expression unbearably sad.

CHAPTER TEN

"MICHAEL?" Polly stepped into the room. "What's wrong?"

Startled out of his reverie, he mustered a smile and reached out a hand to his wife, then pulled her down beside him on the sofa and looped an arm around her shoulders. "Oh, I was just thinking about a patient. Can't sleep, love?"

"Nope. Bad dreams. You, too?"

"I haven't been to bed yet."

She frowned at him. "It's three in the morning and you get up at six. That's crazy, Michael. You can't work as hard as you're doing and not sleep."

"Yeah, I know."

"Are you worrying about money?"

"No, Pol, I'm not." He'd been thinking about Duncan Hendricks. The boy had been in his office that afternoon. Something about Duncan made it impossible for Michael to maintain any objectivity. The boy was totally open, trusting, absolutely confident he'd soon get better, and that perfect faith was Michael's undoing, just as it was Sophie's. The course of radiation was done, and although at the moment Duncan was still experiencing mild seizures and acute nausea, he should soon improve.

Temporarily. Duncan would die—it was only a matter of time. And each minute of his dying would bring memories of Susannah, making Michael feel as though he were trapped in some bizarre time warp, fated to live the worst moments of his life over and over.

"What are you watching?"

Polly's question brought him out of his reverie. He peered at the screen. "I don't know. Isn't that Bette Davis?" He hadn't consciously realized the television was on.

Polly reached for the remote and clicked it off, then turned so she was looking straight at him. "I want to talk about us, Michael. I've been putting if off, waiting for the right moment, but it never comes. Something's wrong between us and it's getting worse all the time."

He began to protest, but she put a finger on his lips, silencing him. "We don't communicate anymore. I hardly ever see you. You come to bed after I'm asleep and you're gone when I get up. We don't make love. I...I actually feel at times as if you're avoiding me. *Are* you avoiding me, Michael?"

"Don't be ridiculous, Polly." He could feel tension flood through his body. He was irritated with her, and his voice reflected it. He didn't need this right now. "I told you I'd have to work longer and harder to get us out of this financial mess. And you've been busy, as well, painting over at Isabelle's. We're both dead tired by nighttime.''

''You've always been busy, yet we would talk three or four times during the day, no matter how rushed you were. You always had a second for me. You don't anymore. And every time I want to talk about Susannah, you change the subject. If we can't even talk about our daughter, what can we talk about, Michael?''

She paused, and he thought of Duncan. He couldn't tell her, couldn't explain that it was his own inadequacy he couldn't speak of.

When he didn't say anything, she gave a weary sigh. ''I know you've always refused, but now I'm asking you again. Won't you come with me and talk to Frannie? I really feel we need some counseling, and I trust her.''

Exasperation and exhaustion made him short-tempered. ''I'm not going to Frannie Sullivan. I know she's been wonderful for you, and I'm grateful, but just because something's right for you doesn't make it right for me. People deal with grief in different ways. I'm sure she's told you that.'' He was really angry now, and he moved his arm from around her shoulders and shifted his body back from hers so they weren't touching. An almost overwhelming urge to get away came over him, but at three in the morning, there was nowhere to go, no way to avoid these things he didn't want to hear or think about. And she was persisting, even when he'd made it plain he wanted the conversation to end.

"I know from Frannie that sometimes people don't deal with grief at all, Michael," she went on. "They lock it away somewhere inside and it ruins their lives. I feel as if that's what you're doing, and in the process you're separating yourself from me and refusing to see what's happening to our marriage."

He swore under his breath. "Stop psychoanalyzing me. You keep on and on about our marriage, Polly. As far as I'm concerned, we're doing okay." He knew it wasn't true, but he couldn't bring himself to admit it to Polly. "You're being more than a little dramatic here, aren't you?" He was aware the sarcastic accusation would inflame her, and it did.

She bolted to her feet and turned on him, hands on her hips, eyes flashing fire. "Don't you dare speak to me in that condescending tone. I'm not being dramatic. I'm being honest, which seems to be something you're incapable of these days." Tears glittered in her eyes. "I can't reason with you anymore. You won't agree to counseling. You…you make me so mad I don't even want to talk to you."

She scrambled to her feet and ran out the door, and he knew she was crying.

He slumped back on the sofa and told himself

How to validate your
Editor's FREE GIFT "Thank You"

1. Peel off gift seal from front cover. Place it in space provided at right. This automatically entitles you to receive two free books and a fabulous mystery gift.

2. Send back this card and you'll get brand-new Harlequin Superromance® novels. These books have a cover price of $4.25 each in the U.S. and $4.75 each in Canada, but they are yours to keep absolutely free.

3. There's no catch. You're under no obligation to buy anything. We charge nothing—ZERO—for your first shipment. And you don't have to make any minimum number of purchases—not even one!

4. The fact is thousands of readers enjoy receiving books by mail from the Harlequin Reader Service®. They like the convenience of home delivery...they like getting the best new novels BEFORE they're available in stores... and they love our discount prices!

5. We hope that after receiving your free books you'll want to remain a subscriber. But the choice is yours— to continue or cancel, any time at all! So why not take us up on our invitation, with no risk of any kind. You'll be glad you did!

6. Don't forget to detach your FREE BOOKMARK. And remember...just for validating your Editor's Free Gift Offer, we'll send you THREE gifts, *ABSOLUTELY FREE!*

GET A **FREE** MYSTERY GIFT...

YOURS FREE!

SURPRISE MYSTERY GIFT COULD BE YOURS _FREE_ AS A SPECIAL "THANK YOU" FROM THE EDITORS OF HARLEQUIN

The Harlequin Reader Service® — Here's how it works:

Accepting your 2 free books and mystery gift places you under no obligation to buy anything. You may keep the books and gift and return the shipping statement marked "cancel." If you do not cancel, about a month later we'll send you 6 additional novels and bill you just $3.57 each in the U.S., or $3.96 each in Canada, plus 25¢ delivery per book and applicable taxes if any.* That's the complete price and — compared to the cover price of $4.25 in the U.S. and $4.75 in Canada — it's quite a bargain! You may cancel at any time, but if you choose to continue, every month we'll send you 6 more books, which you may either purchase at the discount price or return to us and cancel your subscription.

*Terms and prices subject to change without notice. Sales tax applicable in N.Y. Canadian residents will be charged applicable provincial taxes and GST.

he didn't care. He wanted her only to leave him in peace, he assured himself. If her anger was the price, he'd pay it. But he couldn't sit there any longer, and going to bed was out of the question now.

He got up and rummaged around until he found his track shoes in the back of the hall closet. He pulled them on and slipped quietly out the front door.

It was raining, not a true Vancouver downpour but a gray drizzle. The street lamps made an eerie, hissing sound; the other houses on the street were dark and silent. He hadn't run in months, and his muscles and lungs protested before he'd gone two blocks, but he kept on, long after he was gasping for breath and soaked to the skin.

Common sense told him this was how men had heart attacks. At the very least, he'd be miserably sore for days, exhausted when he had to leave for work in the morning, now only a few hours away.

But he went doggedly on, and the physical pain brought a mental oblivion he welcomed.

BY THE TIME Polly managed to drag herself from a drugged sleep the following morning, Michael was already gone. He hadn't slept beside her; she assumed he'd used the spare bedroom. A sense of utter desolation overcame her when she reviewed in her mind what had happened between them. It was painfully obvious Michael wasn't willing to do any of the things she felt were necessary to improve their relationship. And she couldn't go on much longer with things the way they were. Did that mean their marriage was over? It was the first time Polly had allowed herself even to consider separation.

She stood under a hot shower until the pain in her head eased. She didn't want to go to her mother's house; she didn't feel like celebrating with Jerome. But the hours loomed empty and aimless at home. Going to her mother's would at least fill part of the day. A glance out the window confirmed that although it had rained in the night, the sun was out again. The last of the painting could go ahead.

When Polly arrived at Isabelle's, the extension ladder was up and Jerome was already at work, balanced on the scaffold.

Clover pedaled a battered tricycle back and forth across the backyard. Polly smiled at her and said hi, but as usual, the girl didn't respond.

"'Morning," Jerome called in a cheery tone. "Thought I'd get this out of the way before we got going on that final wall."

"I'll start the second coat there." Polly pulled on her gloves and found her paint can and brush, then made her way around the corner to the side of the house where the final bit of painting would complete the job.

She dipped her brush in the paint and began the

long, even strokes that were automatic now. She could hear the radio in her mother's kitchen blasting out a Western tune, and a dog down the block barked monotonously. She hoped Jerome would finish soon so he'd come and work beside her and they could talk. She desperately needed conversation this morning, something that would occupy her mind so she didn't think every moment about her husband and her marriage.

Cold fear filled her stomach each time she remembered Michael's reaction the previous night. He hadn't acknowledged a single thing she'd said; it was as if he no longer cared enough even to try to find a solution to their problems.

Her heart ached in an entirely new way when she considered his indifference. What was wrong with them? Had Susannah's death signaled the death of their love for each other?

Sick at heart, she paid little attention at first to the sound of Jerome talking to his daughter in the kind, reasonable way he always did.

"Clover, please don't ride into the alley on your bike. Trucks drive there and they might not see you, okay, honey?"

Polly went on painting, trying to stop worrying about her and Michael, thinking vaguely how much she'd love a cup of coffee. She hadn't had any appetite for breakfast. She'd just finish this portion, she decided, then go in and have a cup of Isabelle's strong brew.

"Clover, get back in the yard." Jerome's tone was uncharacteristically sharp. "Clover, get back here. There's a truck coming…"

Real alarm was in his voice. Knowing he was up on the scaffold, Polly hastily put down her brush.

"I'll get her," she called, but as she moved around the corner to the backyard, she heard the awful sound of the ladder sliding across the wall. She heard Jerome cry out, and just as she rounded the corner, the ladder hit the ground with an ear-splitting clang.

"Jerome," Polly hollered, watching him fall, feeling as if she were trapped in a nightmare.

He hit the ground hard, landing on his side, and he screamed, a shrill animal sound that sent shivers of horror through Polly.

"Jerome. Jerome, oh, my God." Polly knelt beside him.

His face was contorted with pain and he was struggling for breath, his leg twisted at an unnatural angle beneath him. He writhed, and Polly gasped. It was obvious his right thighbone was broken. Blood stained his pantleg.

"Oh, my Lord, I heard the ladder go. Is he hurt bad?" Isabelle came hurrying down the back stairs.

"Go call 9-1-1. Hurry, he's broken his leg. And then bring out a blanket." Polly whipped off her sweatshirt and tucked it around Jerome's shoulders and upper body, trying desperately to remember what else she ought to do for shock.

She was a doctor's wife. How could she know so little first aid? The only thing she was sure of was that Jerome needed to be kept warm and shouldn't be moved.

Isabelle ran into the house, and Jerome somehow drew in a breath, but the sound that came from him when he released it was one of pure agony. He gritted his teeth.

"Clover?" he managed to groan.

"Stay absolutely still. I'll get her." Polly, trembling hard, staggered to her feet, then immediately saw the child, just coming through the back gate on her tricycle. Clover pedaled over to where Jerome lay, going slower and slower the closer she came, eyes riveted on her father.

"Daddy? Get up, Daddy." Her face contorted. "Daddy? Get up, okay?" She burst into noisy tears.

Jerome's face showed his torture. He tried to respond to Clover, but the effort was clearly beyond him. Polly could see him making an effort not to moan so as not to frighten his daughter, but the pain must have been overwhelming, because the sounds that escaped him were anguished.

"Clover, honey, don't be scared," Polly said, trying to put her arms around the little girl. Clover struck out at her, and Polly had to let her go. "Don't cry. Your daddy's hurt his leg. The ambulance is coming right away and the men on it will help him,'' she babbled.

Isabelle came hurrying back outside, a plaid blanket over her arm. ''They'll be here in a couple of minutes. They said don't move him and keep him warm.''

Together, she and Polly cautiously tucked the blanket around Jerome. His face was ashen and his lips had a bluish tinge, and he had black bags under his eyes, like bruises. Although his face was covered in sweat, he was shivering. Again, he struggled to speak, making several attempts before he could get the words out.

''Take...care...of...Clover?''

''Of course I'll take care of her. Don't worry about her. I'll keep her with me, I promise.'' Once more, Polly tried to put her arm around Clover, but once more the little girl pulled away. She collapsed on the grass beside her father and sobbed so hard her entire small body shook.

''Da...ddy, da...ddy,'' she wailed.

Jerome was drifting in and out of consciousness, and it seemed an eternity to Polly before a siren heralded the ambulance's arrival. Isabelle ran to the front of the house to tell the driver he should go down the alley.

At last, the paramedics came running, a man and a woman. ''B.C. Ambulance Service. Can you tell us what happened to you, sir?'' They knelt beside Jerome. When it was obvious he couldn't respond, they asked Polly questions about how the accident had happened.

They gave Jerome oxygen, and when they slit his pantleg Polly felt her stomach heave. The large bone of his thigh protruded from the skin.

"His right wrist's fractured, as well, and some ribs," the female attendant said. "I've got them stabilized. Okay, Ed, let's scoop and run. We'll have you in Emergency real quick, Jerome. Just bear with us here while we get this spine board on...now onto the stretcher."

Jerome was quickly loaded into the ambulance.

"Tell him we'll bring Clover. We'll follow in my car," Polly told the attendants. Isabelle had lifted Clover into her arms and the girl wasn't struggling now. She clung to Isabelle, sobbing hysterically and calling for her father.

The route to St. Joe's was familiar, but Polly was trembling so much, driving was a challenge.

By the time she pulled her car into the parking lot, Jerome had already been whisked into the hospital.

CHAPTER ELEVEN

POLLY, with Isabelle and Clover trailing close behind, hurried through the wide sliding doors and into the controlled bustle of St. Joe's Emergency.

Leslie Yates was the nurse on triage, and Polly raced over to her, grateful to see someone she recognized. As quickly and clearly as she could, Polly explained what had happened and asked if Leslie knew Jerome's condition and whether Michael had been notified.

"Mr. Fox told the paramedics that Dr. Forsythe is his family physician, so we called his office immediately and he's on his way. Dr. Brulotte and the trauma team are with Mr. Fox in room two. Sit down over there—" she indicated a waiting area "—I'll have someone come and tell you how he's doing."

Polly and Isabelle sat. Clover had stopped crying, and Isabelle set her on a chair between them. Polly could see by the stain on the child's overalls that she'd peed herself, and her small face was a study in misery. Wanting to comfort her, Polly tried to take her hand, but Clover yanked it away.

Polly felt immense relief when she saw Michael

come striding in. She got up and half ran to him, all their differences forgotten in the face of this calamity. He caught her in his strong, capable arms and held her close for a moment. Held tight against his solid, familiar body, she realized she was still trembling.

"He fell, Michael." The words came tumbling out. "Jerome…he fell off the ladder and his leg, his thigh—the bone's broken really bad. There was blood coming out. And his wrist—it's broken, too. It was awful. He looked…he sounded…" Her voice broke and she fought the tears that threatened.

"Easy, love. Calm down. He's in good hands here. Hello, Isabelle. Hi, Clover. I'll go right now and find out exactly how he is." Michael eased Polly into a chair. "I'll be back in a short while."

He hurried off, and it seemed to Polly they waited interminably. It was a nurse, not Michael, who finally came out of the treatment room and over to them.

"Jerome's stable now. He'll be going up to surgery in a moment. Dr. Forsythe is talking with the ER doctors. He said to tell you he'll be here right away. Jerome has a compound fracture of the femur, a fractured right wrist and several broken ribs."

Michael walked over just then. "They've taken him up to surgery. He'll be there for at least a couple of hours." He crouched so that he was at

Clover's eye level. "Your daddy's getting all fixed up, but it's going to be a while before you can see him. Right now, how about a treat? You've been a very brave girl, and I'll bet you'd like some ice cream."

Clover nodded, slid off the chair and took Michael's hand. They headed off toward the cafeteria.

"It sounds like Jerome'll be in hospital for a while," Isabelle commented. "Who's gonna take care of Clover?"

"I promised Jerome we would." Polly turned to face her mother. "Will it be okay if she stays with you, Mom? You get along with her, and she knows you better than she does me." It was the best and most logical solution. After all, Isabelle had spent time with Clover during the painting of the house, and Clover knew Isabelle and responded to her.

"Well, this is a fine kettle of fish," Isabelle exclaimed in an irritated tone. "Of course I feel sorry for Jerome and for Clover—goodness knows I do—but I certainly can't have her staying with me."

"Whyever not?" Polly could feel her temper rising, and she made an effort—futile though it was—to control herself. "Mom, that kid calls you 'Auntie.' She likes you. She certainly makes it plain she has no use for me. And I know Jerome doesn't have anybody else who'd take her—his relatives are far away and he hasn't lived in B.C. long enough to make friends. Would it be such a sacrifice to keep her for a few days?"

Isabelle's chin went up and she cast a defiant look at her daughter. "I shouldn't have to explain anything, but if you must know, I have a new friend who sleeps over most nights. Of course Eric is a perfect gentleman, but I certainly can't have Clover around. You can understand that."

Being directly confronted with her mother's sex life was disconcerting and embarrassing. "Eric?" Polly sputtered. "Who's this Eric?"

"His name is Eric Sanderson. He's a retired businessman."

"Where'd you meet him?" Polly realized she was beginning to sound like a suspicious parent, but she couldn't seem to help herself.

"At the park two weeks ago, when I took Clover over to play. He goes there to play checkers."

"Two weeks ago?" Polly blurted. "You met this guy two weeks ago and you're going to bed with him already?"

"Oh, phooey. Don't be so old-fashioned," Isabelle snapped. "It's not as if I'm going to get pregnant. And even if it wasn't for Eric, I'm not up to caring for a child full-time at my age. I raised you and Norah. I would say I've earned my freedom. I'm sorry, but she'll have to go home with you, Polly. I could maybe still take her to the park some afternoons, but she absolutely can't stay with me. It's out of the question."

"Sometimes I can't believe how selfish you are, Mother." The words were out before Polly could stop them. "That kid hates me. You're the one who's made a fuss over her every single day." Polly took a shuddering breath and said what she'd always held back. "But then, you didn't make time in your life for Susannah, either, so why the heck should I think you'd do it for a stranger?"

Isabelle flinched, but she straightened her shoulders and gave Polly a scathing look. "Don't you speak to me in that tone, miss. Why, it's...it's partly because Clover reminds me so much of Susie that I'm fond of her. You seem to think you're the only one who misses that dear girl. She was my granddaughter, Polly, and I loved her, regardless of how much time I spent with her."

"*Clover* reminds you of Susannah?" Polly was aghast. Comparing the two girls was preposterous. How *could* her mother even think a thing like that, much less say it? It...it was a sacrilege.

All of a sudden, Polly was furious with Isabelle. She knew if she tried to say anything more to her she'd end up screaming accusations, making a terrible scene, and this wasn't the place. Michael worked here at St. Joe's, she reminded herself. She couldn't embarrass him in front of the staff by yelling at her mother.

Where *was* Michael, anyway? Where had he disappeared to with that child, just when Polly needed him? She couldn't bear to sit beside her mother one more instant.

Finally she saw him, making his way slowly back along the hospital corridor, Clover clinging to him with one hand and holding an ice-cream cone with the other.

On legs that felt shaky Polly jumped up and hurried toward them, struggling for control. She was on the verge of tears again, but this time they were angry tears at her mother's insensitivity.

"Well, Clover," she managed to say in what she hoped could be mistaken for a cheerful tone. "You're going to come and stay with Michael and me for a while, at our house, until your daddy's better. Isn't that nice?"

Michael shot her a surprised look, but the murderous expression on Polly's face must have warned him not to question her further.

"Don't want to."

Clover scowled and her mouth bunched up, but she didn't cry. It was obvious she wasn't any more in favor of this plan than Polly was.

"I think we'll go home right now, have a bath and get some fresh clothes on, okay?" The child reeked of urine, and her face was streaked with tears and ice cream. Her nose was running; her pale eyes watered; her thin muddy-blond hair straggled out of cheap plastic hair clips and into her eyes. She looked like a ragamuffin, Polly concluded.

A mental image of Susannah imposed itself between Polly and this unattractive child. Beautiful, exotic Susannah, with her thick dark curls, her cat's eyes and amazingly long lashes, her tawny skin, her long graceful child's body... A new wave of fury spilled through Polly as she regarded Clover. How could Isabelle think for an instant that this homely little girl was anything like Susannah?

Michael once again crouched so he was at Clover's eye level. "Clover, the doctors are taking good care of your daddy here. What you can do for him is go home with Polly now so Daddy doesn't worry about you, okay?"

Clover eyed him and at last nodded reluctantly.

"Good girl." Michael stood and put an arm around Polly's shoulders. "Jerome'll be in surgery another couple of hours, and I have to get back to the office—patients were lined up three deep when I left. The staff here will call me and report on Jerome's condition as soon as he's done, and I'll phone you and Clover." He bent his head and brushed her mouth with his, then affectionately rubbed a hand across Clover's head.

"This little girl needs a nap—she's been yawning. It was a pretty upsetting morning for her."

And what about me? Polly squelched the thought, embarrassed at being so immature.

"I'll try to get home early, Pol, and give you a hand."

"*Please, please* do, Michael." The rest of the day stretched ahead of Polly like an eternity. She'd be trapped at home with this contrary child, subject to her needs, her demands, her sullenness.

Isabelle joined them, and Polly studiously avoided even looking at her mother. ''Could you drop Mom off, Michael? It's on your way to the office.'' It was also on her way home, but the thought of spending even another twenty minutes in Isabelle's company was abhorrent. ''I have to stop at a mall and get some things—milk and juice and soup and something for Clover to wear.'' It was the truth. She didn't have much in her cupboards suitable for a child to eat. A box of clothing Susannah had outgrown stood in an upstairs closet, but Polly wasn't sure anything would fit. Or was it only that she couldn't bear the thought of her daughter's clothing on another child? On *this* child.

''Sure, I'll take Isabelle with me. 'Bye, you two. Clover, thank you for being such a brave girl.''

Polly waited until Michael and her mother were gone before heading for the exit herself. She reached down to take Clover's hand, but again the child yanked hers away and Polly didn't try any more. She was aware of the little girl marching stoically along at her side as she made her way outside and over to the parking lot where she'd left her car, but she didn't touch her except to secure the seat belt once she was in the vehicle.

It was hot in the car, and Polly wrinkled her nose at the odor of urine. She opened all the windows.

Ice cream dribbled down, and Polly was grateful the seats were leather and could be wiped clean.

Clover said nothing during the drive to the supermarket, and inside, when Polly tried to determine what she might like to eat, Clover was stubbornly mute.

Polly found herself cringing when other shoppers glanced at the grubby, sullen child, then at her.

My Lord, they think she's mine. I don't want them to think she's mine.

A wave of shame at her own pettiness washed over her, but it didn't change how she felt. There was a section in the store with inexpensive children's clothing. Polly quickly selected a packet of panties, another of socks and several pairs of shorts with matching T-shirts. She found a cotton knit nightgown and tossed it into the basket, as well, along with a pair of jeans and a sweater. Clover watched, but even when Polly asked her what colors she wanted or if she liked a certain garment, the little girl refused to comment.

Polly paid for her purchases and hurried out. Twenty minutes later she stopped the car in her driveway and made her way around to get Clover. The child slid off the seat, staring around her.

"You gots a *big* house," she blurted in an awed voice.

It was the first remark she'd volunteered since they'd left the hospital, and Polly had to smile in spite of herself. ''Yeah, I guess it is pretty big. Come on, let's get these groceries inside.''

Clover was eager to help when Polly opened the trunk of the car. She struggled with a huge mesh bag of apples, and Polly wrestled the heavier grocery sacks to the front door. She set them down to unlock the door and ushered Clover in ahead of her, then led the way down the hallway to the kitchen. The child followed, staring around with big eyes.

Polly dumped the grocery bags on the counter and grabbed the bag of clothing. ''Okay, Clover, c'mon upstairs. Lets get you cleaned up a bit before lunch.''

In the bathroom, she filled the tub with warm water, spilling in a generous amount of sweet-smelling bubble bath.

''My mommy have some of that.'' Clover pointed at the elegant bottle and doffed her clothing. For a moment Polly's heart caught at the sight of the fragile little body. The girl climbed into the tub with Polly's help and sank into the bubbles with a sigh of pure feminine bliss.

Polly handed her a sponge and a long-handled brush and let her play for a few moments before shampooing her hair. Clover was stoic about the shampoo and rinse water; without a word of complaint, she let Polly pour pitchers of water over her head.

When she was out of the tub, however, she refused Polly's offer to help with the new clothing.

"I can by my own self," she insisted, pulling panties and shorts on, struggling into a T-shirt. With a ferocity that made Polly flinch, she attacked her hair with the brush.

Downstairs again, Polly heated a tin of soup and opened the jar of peanut butter. It was the first time she'd had peanut butter in the house since Susannah had died, and the familiar smell brought back a cascade of memories.

Clover ate two spoonfuls of soup and a quarter of one sandwich between yawns. It was evident she was too exhausted to eat. Polly led the way upstairs once more and opened the door to the spare bedroom.

"This is where you can sleep, Clover. This can be your room while you're here."

No response. Accustomed to Clover's silence, Polly glanced around the sunny room. It was certainly evident Michael had been sleeping here more than he had with her. A pair of his trousers and a shirt were tossed over the chair; an undershirt and a pair of socks lay on the deep window seat; several medical journals sat on the floor beside the bed.

Having Clover here meant that he'd just have to grit his teeth and sleep in their bed, Polly thought spitefully as she gathered up his things.

She turned back the bedcovers, wondering if she

ought to put a protective plastic sheet over the mattress. To heck with it, she decided; all of a sudden, like Clover, she was exhausted.

"Time for a nap."

The child readily climbed into the bed, wriggled her head into the pillow and popped her thumb in her mouth. Before Polly even had her tucked in properly, she'd fallen sound asleep.

Polly closed the door and headed for her bedroom. In the shower she tried to let the stream of hot water wash away the stress of the day. After she'd dried off, she lay down on the bed, thinking she'd rest for just a few moments.

The dream was vivid and alarming. Polly was sixteen. She knew she had a fatal disease and she was dying. The only person who could save her was an old woman, but Polly couldn't find her. Frantically, she searched. The search led her through department stores, where instead of the old woman, Polly kept collecting children like a pied piper. All the children were little girls, and all of them clung to her, slowing her down in her frantic search. She studied them, searching for Susannah, knowing that if her daughter was among them everything would somehow be all right. But Susannah was nowhere to be found, and Polly grew increasingly anxious—

The ringing of the telephone woke her, and she fumbled her way out of the dream and reached for the receiver.

"Pol? It's me."

"Umm. Michael, hi. I was asleep—give me a minute here." Polly cleared her throat and tried to orient herself. "What time is it?"

"Five-thirty. Sorry I woke you. Look, Pol, I know I promised I'd get home early. I've been trying to get out of here, but I got behind on appointments and I won't be there for at least another hour. I heard from the hospital. Jerome came through the surgery very well, and he's doing fine. He'll be in recovery for a short while, then they'll move him down to orthopedics."

"Oh, that's good. I'm so glad he came through okay." Polly was having trouble waking up. She felt groggy and thick-headed, unable to believe she'd slept so long. How could it be five-thirty already? She'd lain down at two. Apparently, she'd slept the entire afternoon away. She couldn't remember when she'd last done that.

"How are you making out with Clover, Pol?"

Clover. Oh, Lordie. Michael's question sent guilt and anxiety shooting through her. She'd totally forgotten about the child. Clover must have awakened long ago. What if...

"Michael, I've gotta go and check on her. She was having a nap, and...we'll talk when you get home, okay?" she babbled.

Without waiting for a response, Polly dropped the telephone and lunged off the bed.

She was responsible for Jerome's daughter, and

she'd left her unsupervised for hours in a strange house. Clover was only four. The calamities that could befall an unsupervised four-year-old in a strange house were endless and terrifying.

Nervously, muttering a prayer, Polly snatched the first dressing gown her hand touched—a luxurious rose silk robe Michael had bought her for Christmas. She shoved her arms into the sleeves and tied the belt as she ran out of the bedroom.

CHAPTER TWELVE

JUST AS POLLY FEARED, the bed in the spare room was empty.

"Clover? Clover, where are you?" Heart hammering, she hurried along the corridor, checking the bathroom, the studio, the sewing room...all empty.

But the door to the room at the top of the stairs, the door to Susannah's room, was ajar. Polly hesitated and then pushed it wide. There was always an instant when she first entered this room that Polly imagined Susannah was still here, asleep on the bed, smiling from the window seat, twirling in a beam of sunlight to some unheard music. This was where her daughter's spirit still lived, Polly fancied. It was the reason she'd kept this room exactly the way it had been the morning they'd taken Susannah to St. Joe's.

Today, there was only Clover, sitting in Susannah's rocking chair, holding a doll from one of the low shelves that lined one wall. She was taking off its clothes, peeling the small garments roughly from the doll's body, mumbling as she did so.

"Clover. What are you doing in here?" Polly's

tone was sharp. She felt violated, furious with this ignorant child. "You're not supposed to be here." She advanced into the room. "This room is off limits. You are not allowed in here—ever. Do you understand?"

Startled, Clover dropped the doll and shrank back in the chair. She gave Polly a fearful look, and her face contorted. Then she opened her mouth wide and began to cry.

Polly was immediately ashamed. "Clover, I'm sorry. I'm sorry for scaring you. Please don't cry." She picked up the doll, replaced its clothing and put it back exactly where it belonged, then took the girl by the hand, led her out of the room and closed the door firmly behind them.

Clover was still howling, and Polly was at a loss about what to do to make the situation better.

"Let's go downstairs. Do you want some juice and cookies, maybe?" Polly had to raise her voice to be heard over the clamor.

Clover, still howling, nodded, and Polly led the way down the stairs to the kitchen. She poured apple juice and set out oatmeal cookies.

The little girl quieted, although sobs still escaped. Polly handed her a tissue, and she blew her nose and mopped at her eyes, than climbed up on the high stool and reached for the apple juice. Too late, Polly realized she'd filled the tall glass too full. It tumbled to the floor and shattered dramatically. Juice and glass sprayed all over Polly, down the walls, across the floor.

"Oh, *damn, damn.*" Polly brushed at the silk gown.

Clover flinched, her eyes on Polly's face, and immediately began to cry all over again.

"Clover, it's okay. Don't worry about it. It's only juice," Polly jabbered, cursing herself for scaring the kid all over again. "It was an accident. I spill stuff myself all the time." Ignoring the mess and carefully avoiding the splinters of glass, Polly filled another glass—a plastic one this time—and gave it to the child, then pushed the cookies over so they were within reach. "Here, you have this, and I'll clean up the mess." She pulled the sticky dressing gown around her and used handfuls of paper towels to gather up the shards of glass. When the worst was in the garbage can, she glanced at Clover. The girl hadn't touched the juice or the cookies. She was watching Polly with a forlorn expression, her eyes red-rimmed, her mouth downcast.

"Aren't you thirsty?"

Clover shook her head. "I want my daddy. Is my daddy all better now?" The question was plaintive. "Is he coming to get me? Does he know where you lives?"

Feeling infinitely weary, Polly slumped onto a stool. "Your daddy's in the hospital, Clover. Michael called and said his operation went fine, and he's sleeping now. He's gonna get all better, but it won't happen today. You'll stay here with us until your daddy gets out of the hospital. He knows you're here. Your daddy knows we'll take very good care of you for him.''

We'll take care of you? She was hallucinating, believing for even a single moment that Michael would be around enough to be any help.

It's you and me, kid, so we'd better get used to it. She sighed. Michael didn't spend enough time at home even to water the plants, never mind care for a kid. It was a bleak thought in a sea of bleak thoughts.

Clover shot Polly a rebellious look, her lower lip jutting out. ''Tomorrow my daddy will come for me.''

A vision of the days ahead, with this conversation repeated again and again and again, flashed through Polly's head. Children Clover's age didn't understand time; the little girl couldn't realize how long it was going to be before Jerome was well once more.

Polly took a deep breath and prayed for patience. ''Not tomorrow, either, Clover. Nor the day after that. It's gonna take quite a few sleeps before your daddy's okay.'' How long? Polly wondered desperately. How long would she and Clover be trapped here with each other?

Clover's expression was mutinous. ''I don't

wanna stay at your house. I gots my own house. I want my daddy.''

''I know you do, Clover.'' Polly struggled to find a way to explain. ''Sometimes we can't have what we want most. When that happens, we have to do what's best for everyone, and it's best that you stay here. Drink your juice, now, and have a cookie.''

''No. Don't want juice. Don't want cookie. I...want...my...daddy. I don't like it here.''

Polly stared at the defiant little face. Her patience was wearing thin, and she didn't know how to handle this child at all. And it could only get worse. Silently she cursed her mother, her mother's house, the new paint job, the ladder. Yet a part of her couldn't help but feel sorry for this lost little girl who obviously didn't like Polly any more than Polly liked her.

There had to be a way to survive this, and she had to find it for both their sakes, Polly decided. Maybe she could put Clover in a day care for at least a few hours a day, to give them both a break. But reason told her such a move would only make the girl even more insecure.

''Look, Clover.'' Polly searched for a solution. ''How about this? Michael will take you to see your daddy this evening at the hospital, I promise.'' If this happened to be the one night Michael didn't have to visit St. Joe's, then too damned bad. He was taking this kid there anyway.

"And until then, I'll find you some toys and...and maybe you'd like some stuff to draw pictures with. We can put your drawings up on the walls in your bedroom."

Clover obstinately shook her head, but Polly went in search of paper and felt pens anyhow, not knowing what else to do.

"Why not make a picture for your daddy? You can take it to him when you go see him tonight." She spread a large sheet of drawing paper in front of the girl and gave her the set of multicolored pens.

For a while, Clover ignored them. But then she sighed dramatically, took out a red pen and began to scribble on the paper. Within a few moments she was engrossed, and Polly breathed a sigh of relief. She hurried upstairs, shucked off the stained and sticky robe, quickly washed the juice off her legs and pulled on underwear and a denim dress. She was still fumbling with the buttons as she raced back downstairs, wondering what new trouble the kid could get into in the few moments she'd been gone.

But Clover was still drawing, and she played quietly with the pens and paper while Polly threw together a stir-fry and put a pot of rice on to steam.

Polly was setting the table when Michael arrived. She glanced at the clock, amazed that the time had gone so quickly.

"Well, ladies." Michael sounded deliberately

cheerful. "How's everything going? That's a great drawing, Clover."

"It's for my daddy."

Clover gazed up at Michael, her face wreathed in smiles. Polly felt a stab of annoyance, knowing it was petty but still feeling irritated. The kid hadn't come close to smiling at her once, despite the fact that she'd done her level best to amuse her.

Michael grinned back at Clover and kissed Polly on the cheek, obviously eager to forget the quarrel they'd had the night before, the accusations she'd hurled at him.

Was she willing to forget, as well? Polly wondered. She certainly didn't have the desire or energy to pursue any of the issues again right now; she and Michael had more pressing things to discuss at the moment.

"Michael, could you come into the studio for a moment, please? Clover, you make another picture, okay? We'll be right back." Polly turned off the heat under the pots and led the way out to the spacious, bright room that adjoined the kitchen.

She closed the door behind them and faced her husband. She could see by his wary expression that he thought she was going to bring up the quarrel they'd had.

Instead she said, "Michael, exactly how long will Jerome be in hospital?"

He visibly relaxed. "I can't say for certain. It

depends on how soon he can get around. I'd estimate a month, maybe even six weeks, seeing there's no one at home to help him.''

"Six weeks?" Aghast, Polly gaped at her husband. "Six weeks? My Lord, I thought people were up and out of the hospital faster than that these days.''

''Usually they are, but a compound fracture of the femur's pretty serious.'' He turned and looked at Clover through the glass door. ''Are you planning to take care of Clover the whole time?''

''I promised him I would.'' Polly was trying to get her mind around the idea of six entire weeks baby-sitting Clover. The prospect was daunting. ''I don't know how I'll manage, because we don't get along very well, she and I.''

''I'll help out as much as I can.''

His words suddenly infuriated Polly. She snapped, ''Let's not pretend here, okay? Just like I said last night, you're never home anymore, so don't make promises you won't keep.''

His mouth tightened, but he didn't respond, and that made Polly even angrier. It also frightened her.

Before, they used to have real, honest fights, the kind two passionate people had who knew the foundation of their relationship was strong enough to withstand the occasional violent storm. There was such safety then, because Polly had never doubted they'd ride it out together.

Not now. Either he clammed up like this or

walked away, leaving her with a hopeless, helpless sense of frustration and failure and loss. And nothing ever really got resolved between them.

Polly felt fear, as well, a terrible, bone-deep fear that they'd never recover whatever it was they were losing. It was as if the lifeblood of their marriage was leaking away. Surely there had to be a way to make Michael see that, to make him understand.

But before she could begin to put any of her feelings into words, the door opened and Clover appeared, holding out a sheet of paper covered with messy coloring.

"I made a picture for my daddy, see, Doctor?"

Polly could feel Michael's relief at the interruption.

"That's a beautiful picture, Clover."

"I promised her you'd take her to St. Joe's to see Jerome after dinner, Michael. I hope that fits into your busy schedule." Polly was being deliberately sarcastic, still hoping that something would break through the wall he'd built around himself. "And please tell Jerome I need some of her clothes and toys."

All he said was, "I will. Let's go eat right now, and then we'll go to the hospital, Clover. I have a few patients to check on, and you can visit your daddy." He took the girl's hand and led the way to the dining room.

Polly followed, wondering if a person could literally explode from frustration.

CHAPTER THIRTEEN

DURING DINNER, Michael chatted politely with Polly, relating anecdotes from the office as if her outburst in the sunroom and the fight they'd had the night before had never happened.

He also talked to Clover. To Polly's chagrin, the little girl prattled away to him, telling him about the clothes Polly had bought her, a bird she'd seen outside on the lawn, even the apple juice she'd spilled and the bath she'd had. She held out her hand coquettishly so Michael could smell the perfumed bubble bath. She was an altogether different child with Michael around.

When the meal was over, he helped Clover carry her dishes into the kitchen and showed her how to load them into the dishwasher. Polly could tell the little girl was impressed and fascinated by the appliance, as if she hadn't seen one before.

Once the dishes were all cleared away, Polly said, "Now, Clover, maybe you'd like to wash your face and hands and brush your hair before you go see your daddy."

For the first time, Clover was agreeable to what Polly suggested. She ran off to the bathroom, and a few moments later, clutching the picture she'd drawn for Jerome to her chest, she waited at the door for Michael.

Polly waited, too, half hoping he'd suggest she accompany them to the hospital, but he didn't. He kissed her goodbye without the slightest trace of passion, and she watched through the window as he helped Clover into his car and adjusted the seat belt around her.

As they drove away, Polly turned slowly from the window. It was a relief to have Clover gone, but suddenly the house felt emptier than ever.

MICHAEL GLANCED over at his small passenger. "We need to get a child's seat for you, Clover, so you can see out the front window."

"My daddy gots one in his truck."

"Maybe we'll ask him if we can borrow it, just while you're staying with Polly and me."

She didn't respond, but he saw her forehead crease in an anxious frown. Poor little kid, she must be really confused by all that had happened to her.

"Your daddy's going to be better soon, Clover, but for now he needs to be in the hospital. You won't mind staying with us until he's better, will you?"

"Where's your own little girl? When's she coming back?"

The abrupt question caught Michael off guard,

and for a moment he didn't know how to reply. *How did she know about Susannah?* If he'd learned anything about children over the years, it was that the only way to really communicate with them was to be totally forthright and honest.

"Our little girl got very sick and died, Clover." He was aware that children even as young as Clover often had a concept of death and euphemisms only confused them. But above all, he didn't want to frighten her. "That hardly ever happens to little girls, though. You're not to worry it might happen to you, because it won't."

Clover nodded, seemingly undisturbed. "My kitten died. Daddy buried him behind the 'partment. Daddy said he went to stay in heaven, where the angels live."

Michael couldn't, even for Clover's sake, reinforce a belief in heaven or in angels.

"What's her name? Your girl."

"Susannah." Saying her name was difficult. He'd avoided it for so long now.

"Susannah. Susannah. That's a nice name, Susannah."

They drove in silence for several minutes.

Clover finally turned and shot him a look from under her eyelashes. "Your mommy gots mad at me for touching the doll," she said accusingly. "I went in your girl's room and your mommy said I have to stay out of there."

Susannah's room, which Polly refused to change

in any way. They'd quarreled about it, only once but fiercely. Michael had wanted everything gone from that room immediately after the funeral, and Polly had screamed at him and pounded his chest with her fists for suggesting it.

She'd be angry, all right, if this child or any other disrupted her shrine. He suspected Polly went and sat there often. His heart contracted. He hadn't set foot in there himself since...

"I gots my own dolls at my house." Clover was defensive. "My rabbit's there, too, on my bed." A tiny pause, then, in a rush, "I wanna go home to my own house, okay? I want my daddy and my own dolly, and my rabbit. Okay, Doctor?"

The vehement plea touched his heart. What she wanted was perfectly natural.

"You will go home, when your daddy's better. But right now let's see how he's feeling." He was relieved when they turned into the hospital parking lot.

Inside, he took her hand and shortened his stride, and on the elevator encouraged her to push the button for the orthopedics floor, where Jerome had been taken after a short stay in Recovery. At the nursing station, Michael learned that Jerome was still groggy from the anesthetic. Michael introduced Clover to the nurses, then led the girl down the hall to Jerome's room.

"Daddy?" She wasn't at all sure those first few seconds that the figure in the hospital bed with casts and an IV pole was her father. Jerome was sleeping, but at the sound of her voice he opened his eyes and turned his head.

"Clover? Hey, my sweetheart, come over here and say hi."

His voice was weak, but there was no mistaking the delight in his tone, and she ran to him. Grasping the hand he extended to her, she pressed her face into his palm and sniffed at him like a puppy.

Michael saw tears spring to Jerome's eyes when she passionately declared, "Daddy, I *luff* you, I miss you. I made you a picture, see?" She thrust it at him. "Can we go home now, Daddy? *Please?*"

The entreaty burst from the child, and the tears that had gathered in Jerome's eyes now slid down his cheeks. "Not for a while, sweetheart," he managed to say. In the gentlest way, he showed her his casts and told her he had to stay where he was, that he couldn't walk, couldn't take care of her just now.

"Then can I stay here with you, Daddy?"

Jerome reluctantly said she couldn't do that, either, and Clover burst into stormy tears. Jerome stroked her head and Michael lifted her up on the bed. She sat in the crook of Jerome's left arm, and after a few moments she quieted, although huge sobs still shook her now and again.

At last she touched the dressing on Jerome's

chest with a gentle hand, before reaching up to press her lips to it.

"I kiss it better."

"Thank you, sweetheart. That helps."

She settled against him, and her thumb stole into her mouth. Soon her eyelids drooped and she fell asleep.

Quietly, so as not to wake her, Michael said, "Are there any questions you have that I could help with, Jerome? Is there anything you need?"

Jerome shook his head. "Dr. Bellamy was real good about explaining everything. The only thing I'm worried about is her." His voice trembled with weakness and concern. "They think it'll be at least six or eight weeks before I'll be able to take care of her myself." His eyes were troubled. "I've been racking my brain to figure out who else might take her, but I can't come up with anybody. If you and Polly can't keep her, Doctor, she'll have to go into foster care. I don't know how she'd do with that. She's still real upset over Tiffany leaving. She cries for her mother nearly every night, and now she's gonna think I've deserted her, as well."

"She's fine with us, Jerome. I'll bring her up often to see you, and I know Polly will take good care of her. We'll need some of her clothes, though, and she should have her toys, to make her feel at home."

"The keys to the apartment are in the drawer of that table. There's a toy rabbit she sleeps with every night—she calls him 'Wilbur.'" He hesitated. "Are you really sure it's okay with you, Doctor?"

"Absolutely." It was fine with him; Michael was fond of Clover. He wasn't as certain about Polly, but she was the one who'd promised, and Polly was always good to her word. At any rate, there seemed no reasonable alternative except a temporary foster home, and Michael knew all too well how difficult it was for social workers to find suitable placements for any child. He hated to think of Clover, lost and lonely, in some group home where the workers did their best but couldn't hope to address the needs of every child.

She was best off with them. And Michael vowed he'd do his damnedest to make good on his promise to Polly to share in caring for Clover.

"I have some other patients to see, Jerome. Shall I move Clover to that empty bed?"

Jerome shook his head. "I want her here with me for a little while."

"If you get uncomfortable, ring for the nurse. I'll tell them Clover's in here with you. I shouldn't be much more than half an hour."

But it was an hour and a half before Michael came back. He'd had a minor emergency to deal with; Everett Simms, one his patients scheduled for gallbladder surgery the next morning, had suddenly decided to sign himself out. It had taken time and all of Michael's persuasive powers to convince Everett that surgery was necessary.

When he finally got back to Jerome's room, Clover was still snuggled in, and father and daughter were both fast asleep. Michael gently scooped Clover into his arms, and a nurse wrapped a blanket around her. She didn't wake, and neither did Jerome.

At home, Polly must have been watching for his car; she opened the door for him and without a word led the way upstairs to the spare bedroom. She turned the covers back on the bed and together, still in silence, they undressed Clover and got her into a cotton nightie. She struggled and whined a little and her mouth puckered into a grimace, but the moment the covers were tucked snugly around her, she slept again.

Polly had put a night-light in a low wall socket, and it glowed as she pulled the door shut behind them.

"It's really something how kids can sleep like that," she remarked. "Remember the times we got home late and put Susannah down just this way?"

"Yeah, I do." Why did she constantly have to remind him? Michael wondered wearily. It was like having someone pick at a scab.

"You want a glass of juice or maybe some wine?"

"Wine sounds great."

Her earlier anger seemed entirely gone now, and

he felt enormously relieved. They made their way back downstairs, and he poured them each a glass of white wine from a bottle in the fridge.

Polly perched on a high stool in the kitchen and Michael took the seat across from her. He lifted his glass in an old and automatic toast. "To us, my love."

A shadow flitted across her face, but she held her own stemmed glass aloft and repeated, "To us."

Michael reached in his trouser pocket for Jerome's keys. "I can go over there first thing in the morning, if that would help, and get Clover's stuff."

Polly shook her head. "I'll go. It's probably better if I take her with me. That way she can bring whatever things she wants." She dragged a hand through her hair, and Michael noticed the dark circles under her eyes, the fatigue there.

"Polly, remember there's always Community Services for Clover." Whatever the other considerations, he wouldn't have her worn down by this. "I know you feel a responsibility because Jerome is your friend, but if this is too much for you, I'll make other arrangements for her."

"No." Polly shook her head. "I promised him, and a promise is a promise. I talked to Nora. She's gonna take Clover on her days off." Polly scowled. "My mother should have volunteered to have her at least part of the time. I'm really furious with her over this, Michael. She made friends with Clover. She's the logical person to care for her. But no. She's got some man on the string who's staying with her overnight—can you believe that?''

Michael grinned, equally amused by Isabelle's antics and Polly's reaction to them. ''It doesn't really surprise me that she's sexually active. Isabelle's an attractive woman. I just hope she's practicing safe sex.''

Polly shot him a look, but she had to smile. ''You might not think it was so funny if she were your mother.''

''Oh, I don't know. My mother turned herself into a self-pitying martyr after my father died. She might have lived longer and been a lot more pleasant to be around if she'd decided to have an affair or two.''

Michael was an only child, and his mother had made his life difficult before her death ten years earlier. She'd quarreled with everyone in the seniors home, demanded that Michael visit her every single day, then complained nonstop about everything. She'd been a thoroughly miserable, self-centered woman, and it had almost been a relief when she'd contracted pneumonia and died suddenly.

Michael had always privately thought Isabelle was by far the easier of the two women, even though she, too, was monumentally self-centered.

What Michael liked about Isabelle was her indomitable spirit. He'd never told Polly she'd inherited that same fiery spirit from her mother. He knew his wife wouldn't consider it a compliment.

"Do you really think Mom's promiscuous, Michael?" There was consternation in Polly's voice. "I've joked about it, but I'm not sure I really believed it."

"She could be." Michael thought it more than probable. "But what difference does it really make, Pol? You're not responsible for her actions."

"Maybe not, but we'd have to take care of her if she got some disease. What if she got AIDS?"

"I think Isabelle's wise enough to protect herself, but if that happened, we'd just have to do the best we could. Anyhow, the things we worry about aren't usually the things that happen, Pol."

That wasn't entirely true, of course. Although he'd never once considered the possibility of losing Susannah, he'd always worried about losing Polly, and that fear had come all too close to reality; she'd almost died when Susannah was born. She'd bled out and had to be transfused, and her heart had stopped during the procedure.

Having Susannah had nearly lost him Polly; now, ironically, losing Susannah seemed to be doing the same thing. Tranquil moments such as this were increasingly rare between them. More often than not, Polly was angry with him, or he with her.

Cold and terrible fear clutched at his bowels and he set down his wineglass and suddenly took her in his arms, kissing her lips, running his hands down her lovely body, reassuring himself that for this moment in time, she was still here, still his.

CHAPTER FOURTEEN

"LET'S GO TO BED, Polly."

Michael's words were an invitation, and she acknowledged it with her lips, kissing him with deepening passion, winding her arms around his neck and pressing her body against his.

Holding her close to his side, he led the way upstairs. In their bedroom, he again took her in his arms and kissed her, long, sensuous, endless kisses that brought her body alive in his arms until she moved restlessly against him, wordlessly pleading for more.

Still kissing her, he undid the buttons on the front of her denim dress and slid it off her shoulders, letting it drop to the floor. Beneath it, she wore a white lacy bra and silk panties, and he bent and closed his lips around lace and taut nipple, teasing first one breast and then the other before he reached behind her and undid the clasp to free them to lips and teeth and tongue.

Polly moaned, and Michael lifted her and placed her on the wide bed, then stripped off his own clothing and propped himself up beside her, his heart lurching at the softness of her velvety skin, the incredible delicacy and perfection of her slender body. He pulled her to him, trying to fit every inch of her diminutive frame against his own long length.

Softness, heat, sensuality.

"Sweetheart, I love you, I love you so," he breathed, his mouth traveling from lips to neck to breasts and back again. He knew her body intimately, but familiarity brought only increased excitement.

He sensed the exact moment when desire became need, when need turned to urgency, when urgency became desperation. Only then did he enter her, slowly, tantalizingly, controlling his violent urge to plunge again and again, choreographing every long slide, pausing with exquisite delight to encourage her climb and inadvertently his own.

She trembled, hovering, and with one final long, desperate stroke he brought them to the summit, and together they tumbled into ecstasy...and immediately became aware of a child wailing just outside their closed bedroom door.

"Damn. Damn it to hell." Polly scrabbled under her pillow for a nightgown, and Michael yanked the bedcovers up an instant before the door swung open.

Polly tugged on her gown and made her way to the door, her voice husky and still trembling slightly from the force of their loving. "What's wrong, Clover?"

"I...want...my...da-a-addy. I...want...Wilbur."

"Daddy's not here. Go back to bed, now."

"I...want...my...rabbit."

"Come on, it's time for sleeping."

Clover's wails grew fainter as Polly led her down the hallway, but they didn't stop. Michael got up and fumbled in his drawer. He found a pair of pajama bottoms and a T-shirt, pulled them on and made his way toward Clover's bedroom.

Polly was tucking her firmly in, and although Clover didn't resist, she was sobbing into the pillow, deep, heartbroken sobs that shook her body.

"Go back to bed, love. I'll get her settled." Michael pressed a quick kiss on Polly's neck and sat on the edge of Clover's bed, rubbing his hand up and down her small back. He could feel every vertebra, as well as the child's agitation.

"We'll get your rabbit tomorrow, sweetheart," he soothed. "How would it be if I told you a story now?"

Through her sobs, Clover nodded.

"Once upon a time..."

He hesitated, at a loss for a beginning. It had been a very long time since he'd made up tales for a small child. He tried without success to remember stories he'd told in the past.

"Once upon a time there was a fish named Oscar," he began, thinking suddenly of Duncan.

"Oscar lived in a glass fishbowl and he belonged to a little girl called—"

The sobbing had stopped and Clover rolled over on her back, eyes on Michael's face.

"Susannah. The girl's name is Susannah," she prompted, sniffing hard.

Could he do this? He swallowed the lump in his throat and made himself go on. "Oscar was a very special goldfish because he knew how to talk, but only to—" He forced himself to say it. "Only to Susannah. No one else could understand him, because no one listened the way she did."

The ideas and words were beginning to come easier; his daughter's name not so difficult to say.

"Oscar had a small round glass fishbowl filled with water, because fishes need water to breathe. But he wasn't happy there. He'd put his face against the glass and look out at the big world where Susannah lived, and wonder what it would be like to get out. Gradually, it was all he thought about. It was what he wanted more than anything. Now, one day a terrible thing happened. Susannah's daddy hurt his leg and had to go to the hospital to get better."

"Just like my da-daddy."

The hitch in Clover's voice touched his heart. "Just like your daddy, yes." Michael nodded and stroked the damp hair back from her forehead. "Susannah's daddy made sure there were good people to take care of her while he was away, but she was very frightened and terribly lonely. She cried all the time. She wrapped her arms around Oscar's fishbowl and she cried and cried and cried. Oscar tried to tell her that everything would be okay, but she wasn't listening properly and so she couldn't hear him, and that made her even sadder. Her tears fell into Oscar's water, more and more and more of them, and they were salty, because tears are like that, very wet and very salty. Soon Oscar began to feel a little sick because he was breathing in all the tears Susannah was crying.

"'Stop, stop,' he pleaded. But she couldn't hear him. She wasn't listening. Slowly, the fishbowl filled up more and more with her tears, until at last it was filled to the very brim. All the salt made Oscar float to the top and suddenly, he floated right out and into Susannah's lap, all wet and fishy and gasping for water, because fishes can't breathe air.

"Now, the shock of that made Susannah stop crying. She stared down at her lap and said, 'My goodness, Oscar, what are you doing out of your fishbowl?' And she waited for him to answer, but of course Oscar couldn't. He'd gotten what he wanted, which was to be out of his fishbowl, but now he didn't like it at all. He flipped and flopped because he was a fish out of water, and at last Susannah realized that her tears had filled up the bowl and floated poor Oscar right out. Quick as a wink, she put nice fresh water into the bowl, and cupping her hand carefully around him, she put

Oscar back. 'Thank you, oh, thank you,' he gasped, and now she could hear him again, because she was listening. And he told her what he knew to be true—that very soon her daddy would be coming back to her—and Susannah knew that what Oscar said was right, because he always told the truth. And from that day on, Oscar never wanted anything except what he had—which was a lovely round fishbowl, lots of water—and a good friend he could talk to.''

Clover sighed; her eyes drifted shut, opened again.

Michael made his voice softer and softer.

''And Susannah stopped crying, and very soon her daddy was all better and he came home to her.''

She was asleep.

''And they all lived happily ever after,'' Michael whispered, pulling the warm quilt up and gently tucking it around her.

He closed Clover's door and made his way back to the bedroom. The bed lamp was on and Polly was propped up on pillows, a magazine against her bent legs.

''Is she asleep?''

Michael nodded, slipping under the covers, reaching out to take her in his arms.

But she resisted. She tossed the magazine to the floor and flopped back on her pillows, arms crossed on her chest. "We're going to go through this every single night, Michael. I just know it."

"Probably not. She'll get used to being here. Right now she's in a strange place and she feels very alone. She misses Jerome. He's all she's got."

"I know that, and I do feel sorry for her. I just wish I could like her a little more." Her ambivalence toward Clover troubled her still. "It's awful not to like a child. You don't seem to have that problem with her."

It sounded almost like an accusation.

"She's not an easy kid," he acknowledged. "When Jerome first brought her in to see me, she fought like a little tiger."

"She's sullen, which makes me crazy. Susannah was cheerful almost all the time."

Michael didn't answer. He reached over and turned out the bedside lamp. Why did Polly have to bring their daughter into every single conversation? Even Clover had named the girl in his story after her.

"Would you believe my mother actually said that Clover reminds her of Susannah?" Polly's voice mirrored her outrage. "As far as I can see, there's not one single thing about Clover that could possibly remind anyone of Susannah."

A long-forgotten bit of poetry flashed unbidden into Michael's head.

"She is a little lonely child, lost in hell.
Persophone, take her head upon your knee,
Smile and say, my dear, my dear, it is not so
lonely here..."

The words were painful. He pulled up the blanket. "Polly, can we just go to sleep? It's been a long day, and I'm wiped out."

"Sure." Her anger was evident in her tone. "Sure, we can go to sleep. Anything at all to avoid talking to me, right, Michael? You can spend an hour telling a story to a kid, but when it comes to having a serious discussion with your wife, you're too tired."

He didn't answer. He forced his breathing to mimic sleep. After a long, interminable time, when he could tell by her rhythmic breathing and the slight trembling of her limbs that she was asleep, he crept out of bed and made his way downstairs to his office.

He always had patient files to update, government forms to fill out, paperwork that both numbed his brain and demanded his attention. Through the small hours he worked, and just before dawn, he stretched out on the leather couch and fell instantly into exhausted sleep.

POLLY AWOKE SLOWLY. Gray morning light filtered through the draperies. It was raining outside; she could hear the steady patter of water hitting the glass panes of the window. Michael was gone, but she suddenly had the definite feeling that she wasn't alone. She turned over quickly and propped herself on an elbow.

Clover stood at the side of the bed, staring at her. How long had she been there? Polly stared back for a moment, feeling as if her privacy had been invaded. Then she tried for a smile and cleared her throat.

"Good morning, Clover."

"It's time to get up."

The words were accusatory, and for some reason they made Polly feel guilty. "Yeah, I guess it is." She squinted at the clock and yawned. "It's only ten past eight. That's not exactly the middle of the afternoon, you know."

Clover didn't respond. She was already dressed, in the same shorts and top she'd worn the day before. She looked tousled and unwashed.

"I'm hungry. Where's Doctor gone?"

Good question. "He's probably at work. He has to go and make all the sick people better." *And get away from his wife.*

"Sick people like my daddy?"

"Yup." She swung her legs out of bed, and Clover followed as she headed for the bathroom.

"I'll be out in a minute." Polly shut the door firmly behind her. When she emerged a few moments later, Clover was sitting on the floor, by the door, waiting.

"We should have a shower before breakfast," Polly said determinedly.

"Both together?" Clover immediately took off her shorts and top. She'd forgotten to put on panties, Polly noticed, and she'd pulled on her shorts backward. She was still a baby in so many ways.

"I guess so—we're both girls." It was the most efficient way to do things. Polly turned on the shower and soaped them both down, then shampooed her head and Clover's. Afterward, she used dusting powder and cologne liberally on Clover as well as herself. The little girl was fascinated with Polly's cosmetics, and Polly let her dab on moisturizer and lip gloss. She used conditioner and volumnizer on both their heads, deciding on impulse to take Clover to Louie and see what he could do with her hair. It desperately needed cutting. The sparse bangs hung in her eyes; the rest was too short to braid or pull into a ponytail. She also had to drop by Jerome's apartment to pick up Clover's things, Polly remembered.

Those errands might take up the morning. Clover napped so they'd have to be home by noon. Somehow, someway, she'd have to make it through the day, Polly thought. There were weeks of this ahead, she reminded herself—and her heart sank. She felt trapped.

During the past months she'd never thought of herself as free. She'd viewed her days as stretches of time to put in, hours to fill with shopping, lunches, hairdressers, masseurs. Now that she had to build her days around this child, Polly understood for the first time how independent she'd been. She'd had freedom, and never once appreciated it.

"Okay, kid, let's go down and have breakfast."

Clover looked clean, if not pretty, in fresh pink shorts and T-shirt, and she trotted along at Polly's side cheerfully enough. At least the day had started off fairly well. That was a hopeful sign.

In the kitchen, Polly made coffee, poured two glasses of orange juice, set out cold cereal and milk.

"I don't like orange juice," Clover announced, pushing away the glass and scowling. "I don't like this cereal. I only like Sugar Pops."

"Want some toast, instead?"

Clover shook her head. "Don't like toast. I want bacon'n'eggs."

"We don't eat bacon and eggs. How about oatmeal?"

"Don't like oatmeal." Clover thrust out her bottom lip ominously.

"Then what the heck are you going to eat for breakfast?" All the fragile camaraderie of bathing and doing makeup disappeared in an instant, and Polly was right back where she'd been the day before, feeling resentment and animosity toward this four-year-old child and disliking herself for it.

Clover sullenly agreed to peanut butter on plain untoasted bread, and much against her better judgment, Polly marked Sugar Pops on a grocery list.

She knew it was silly, but Clover's fussy eating habits got under her skin. Susannah had been the easiest child in the world when it came to food, Polly recalled. After her illness was diagnosed, a macrobiotic practitioner had suggested a strict diet of grains, steamed vegetables and rice. Susannah had adopted it wholeheartedly, never complaining.

Sipping her coffee, Polly called and managed to wheedle an appointment with Louie, who told her that he usually didn't ''do'' children but would bend his rule just this once to accommodate her; it just so happened he'd had a ten o'clock cancellation.

It was already nine-thirty. Polly rushed them out and over to the salon, only to find that Clover was terrified of scissors. She took one look at Louie holding the tools of his trade and began screaming. No amount of reasoning or even bribery worked. When Polly tried to lift her into the chair, Clover stiffened and kicked. Everyone stopped and stared. Louie moved well out of range, rolled his eyes and looked disgusted.

Polly finally slunk out of the salon with Clover clutching her pantleg. Every eye in the place was on them. Polly had an irresistible urge to turn and scream, ''She's not mine—I'm only baby-sitting.''

She didn't. She hurried them into the car, took deep, calming breaths and drove to Jerome's apartment, a two-bedroom walk up in a run-down building in Richmond.

"There's my house," Clover crowed as they drove up. Polly unlocked the outside door and Clover raced in ahead of her, the trauma of the aborted haircut forgotten. She danced up the stairs and waited impatiently as Polly opened the apartment door.

Clearly, Jerome did his best to keep the place clean, but clearly, too, money was in short supply. The furniture was old, well worn and mismatched. An antiquated television stood in one corner. The stove and battered fridge looked ancient. A toaster sat on the kitchen counter, but there was no microwave, blender, food processor or juicer, and certainly no dishwasher.

Two bikes leaned against a wall—an adult's and a child's with training wheels.

"That's my bike. I ride with my daddy. This is my bedroom," Clover announced with great pride, ushering Polly in and climbing up on the narrow bed. The pink quilt was thin from many washings, but plenty of toys lay scattered around, many of them homemade. Clover had several dolls, a set of building blocks and a unique dollhouse that Polly admired.

"My daddy made it for me." Clover snatched a grubby toy rabbit off the bed and held it lovingly to her chest.

"It's beautiful. And that's Wilbur, huh? Let's gather up your clothes and whatever toys you want, and take them to our house, okay?" Polly had brought a roomy sports bag and several boxes, but the few garments in the closet and the sparse collection of underwear, pajamas and socks left plenty of room. "Shall we take your dolls?"

Clover didn't answer, so Polly added the dolls to the bag anyway.

"How about your dollhouse, Clover?"

Clover was now sitting on her bed, clutching Wilbur. She shook her head.

"Okay, then what else would you like to bring?"

No answer. Polly added toys at random and zipped the bag, then carried it to the doorway. Clover didn't move.

"Come on, Clover, we have to go now. If there's anything else you want we'll take it. Your bike, maybe?"

Clover shook her head again, scuttling back on the bed so that her back was against the wall.

Polly went to the door and waited. "Clover, c'mon, now." A foreboding came over her. "We have to go."

No answer. Polly blew a breath out from between her teeth, dropped the sports bag and went back into the bedroom.

Clover sat exactly where she'd left her, back against the wall, rabbit clutched to her chest.

"Clover, you can't stay here. There's no one to take care of you." Polly reached out to pick her up, and Clover bit her on the thumb. Her sharp teeth pierced the skin. Polly shrieked with pain and jerked back, rubbing her hand. Blood popped out of the bite marks.

"Ow-ww, damn it all, biting is not allowed." Polly realized she was shrieking. Her thumb hurt like fury. What she wanted to do was smack Clover, but she made a huge effort to control herself.

She lowered her voice. "You really hurt me, Clover Fox. And hurting people is not allowed. Now, get off that bed and come with me. You can't stay here—you know that."

But that was exactly what Clover intended to do. She didn't move. Chin set, eyes slitted, she glared up at Polly.

Polly glared right back. What on earth, she wondered, was she going to do with this impossible child?

CHAPTER FIFTEEN

POLLY FINALLY REACHED OUT and lifted Clover, holding her tight against her and being careful to face the child away from her to make sure that biting wasn't easy.

Clover kicked and thrashed and began screaming. The back of her head caught Polly on the cheekbone, and for a moment she saw stars. She fumbled for the doorknob, got the door open and began to struggle her way down the steps.

Clover went right on screaming and squirming, and an elderly woman coming up the stairs needed to back against the wall to avoid being kicked. She looked up at the open door of Jerome's apartment and stared at Polly suspiciously.

"That's Clover Fox, isn't it?" She had to holler to be heard over Clover's screams. "Who are you? Where are you taking her? Where's Jerome?"

Polly, red-faced, mortified, out of breath and out of patience, had no desire or energy to hold a conversation.

She jockeyed past the woman, stumbled down the final steps and out to the car, wrestled kicking

child and keys and car door and finally dumped
Clover inside on the front passenger seat.

As soon as Clover was in the car, she stopped
fighting. She bent forward and rested her forehead
on her skinny knees, sobbing as if her heart would
break.

Sweating, trembling, feeling as if she'd just been
wrestling a lion cub, Polly leaned against the side
of the car and tried to figure out how to get the
sports bag she'd dropped in the apartment. Could
she leave Clover alone in the car for the scant four
minutes it would take to retrieve it and lock the
apartment door?

She stood undecided, wishing with all her heart
she'd never laid eyes on Clover Fox. Her thumb
still stung, her cheekbone throbbed and felt as if it
was swelling and Clover's shoes had put dirt marks
all over her clean khaki pants. She undoubtedly
had bruises on her thighs, as well.

Slowly Polly became aware of a siren approach-
ing, and she jumped back when a police car
squealed to a stop a scant four feet from her car.

The R.C.M.P. officer was out of the car and
standing beside Polly almost before the wheels had
stopped turning. Simultaneously, the door of the
apartment building opened and the woman Polly
had passed on the stairs stood there, hands on her
hips.

"Officer, she's kidnapping that little girl," she
screeched. "I know Jerome—I'm his landlady.

That's his little girl. His wife ain't been around awhile but this woman sure ain't her.''

The confusion took forty long, humiliating minutes to sort out.

The officer made calls to the hospital to confirm that Jerome was a patient and calls to Michael's office to confirm that Polly was who her driver's license said she was. Apparently Michael was at the hospital delivering a baby, but Valerie must have been convincing, because finally the policeman apologized and drove off.

While she was under suspicion of kidnapping, Polly decided categorically that as soon as she was out of sight of the law, she was dropping Clover off at Social Services. The idea lost appeal, however, when she thought about the explanations she'd have to make, the upset it would cause Jerome.

Instead, she drove straight home, exchanging murderous looks with Clover at every stoplight.

At home, Clover meekly followed Polly inside, ate without protest the soup and sandwich set in front of her and, clutching her rabbit, marched off to take a nap without being told.

Polly sank into a chair and held a bag of frozen peas to her aching cheekbone. The phone rang, but she let the machine take it. She listened to Michael's voice apologizing for not being available when the police phoned and urging her to call him as soon as she got home.

She went upstairs and checked on Clover, who was sound asleep and looking almost angelic. Polly went into the bathroom, stripped off her filthy clothes, then filled the tub with hot water and lavender bath oil. She soaked her aching body and her bitten finger and contemplated her life, her marriage, the vast well of anger that never seemed to empty.

Making love with Michael the night before had been wonderful, but she'd felt alone and bereft afterward, furious with him and resentful of Clover. She thought about the intensity of her feelings toward the child. *Against* her, she corrected. It wasn't natural to dislike a little kid this way. She needed help.

After a while she climbed out of the water and got dressed. Then she called Frannie Sullivan's number at St. Joe's, only to be told that Frannie was on holiday and wouldn't be available for ten days.

"Ten days?" It seemed an eternity. Polly's dismay must have been evident in her tone, because the receptionist said, "If it's urgent, Mr. Canning can see you, Mrs. Forsythe. He's relieving for Mrs. Sullivan. He has an opening—"

"No, no, it's all right. I'll wait for Frannie. Make an appointment for me as soon as she's back."

Feeling totally abandoned, Polly wrote down the date and time the woman gave her.

The rest of the day passed uneventfully, which Polly considered a blessing. When Clover woke up, she asked to have the television on.

"I like cartoons. I wanna watch. My daddy always lets me," she whined.

Polly, who deplored whining and had always been critical of allowing children to stare at a television when they could be doing something imaginative, silently led the way to the family room and switched on the machine.

Clover was still sitting in front of it when Michael arrived. Polly had been flicking restlessly through art magazines and feeling guilty about using the television as a baby-sitter. Now she gaped at Michael and then looked at the clock in amazement.

It was only five-thirty.

"What are you doing home so early? Is anything wrong?"

"Nothing at all." He came over to her, gave her a chaste kiss and examined her cheek with gentle fingers. "What happened to you?"

"Clover bonked me with her head."

"Was this before or after you had a run-in with the law?"

"Before. Just after she bit me." Polly held up her thumb.

Michael looked at it. "You probably should have a tetanus shot. Kid's got a mean strike," he commented.

But Polly could tell he was more amused than disturbed.

Clover heard his voice just then and came running.

"Hiya, Doctor." She gave him a radiant smile and put her hand in his.

"Hi, Clover." Michael smiled at her. "So is this Wilbur, the famous rabbit?"

She'd clutched the stuffed toy to her chest all afternoon, cringing and scowling at Polly if she came near, as if Polly were about to steal the bedraggled thing. Now Clover offered Wilbur to Michael, who looked over the toy and admired it extravagantly before giving it back to her. "I had Valerie reschedule some appointments so I could take you girls out for a pizza."

He hadn't been home this early in months. Polly tried not to resent the fact that his appearance now was solely due to Clover's presence.

"Pizza sounds good," she managed to mumble with a semblance of grace.

It drove Polly nuts to acknowledge yet again that with Michael around, Clover was a different child. At the pizza parlor, Polly watched and listened as she chattered to Michael, telling him about something she'd seen on television, gesticulating with both hands to earnestly illustrate a point. She ate two large slices of vegetarian pizza and without a single complaint drank the orange juice Michael ordered for her.

Afterward, Michael drove to a nearby park that had slides and swings and climbing apparatuses, and Polly sat on a bench and again watched as Michael played with Clover. The little girl's shrieks of laughter were a reproach as well as a source of irritation. Seeing Michael push the swing high, hearing him laugh with Clover, bothered Polly deeply, and she couldn't dispel her negative feelings no matter how much she tried.

Back at the house, it was Michael who put Clover to bed. From the bottom of the stairs, Polly could hear the muted sound of his voice as he told the little girl a story, probably one of the same unlikely tales he'd made up for Susannah when she was small. For some reason it hurt Polly so much she felt like storming up the stairs and screaming at him to stop, but of course she didn't.

When at last he came down, she pretended to be absorbed in a television documentary on the homeless.

"I have to do house calls, Pol, then check on a patient at St. Joe's."

He picked up his keys from the hall table, adding the phrase she'd come to expect and hate.

"Don't wait up for me. I'll be late."

It was a relief to have him gone, she told herself.

And then she burst into tears.

AFTER THAT FIRST DAY, Polly did her best to avoid confrontations with Clover. She let the girl eat what she wanted, choose her own clothes, brush her own hair. She invented errands they could do each morning, to pass the time until Clover napped. In the afternoon, steeling herself, she'd dig out a bag of toys and the box of clothing. Clover accepted both without enthusiasm.

The only serious problem was Susannah's room. Polly caught Clover in there repeatedly, and each time she barely held her temper. "You know you're not supposed to be in here," she reprimanded.

Clover would nod vigorously. "Off limits," she'd parrot in a stern voice.

But the moment Polly's back was turned, she'd sneak in again. Polly gritted her teeth and counted the days until her appointment with Frannie.

Just as he'd promised, Michael managed to come home early most evenings, and Polly was relieved to turn Clover over to him. He took the child with him to St. Joe's to see her father, and he bought her a small tape player and a handful of children's tapes when he found she liked music.

As a result, Clover adored him. She'd watch for his car from the front window, then run to greet him, shrieking, "Doctor's home. Doctor's home."

It grated on Polly's nerves.

The fourth day of Clover's stay, Polly realized she still hadn't gone to see Jerome herself, so when Clover woke up from her nap, they headed for St. Joe's.

Polly bought an enormous bouquet of spring flowers and a funny card before she made her way up to orthopedics. The moment the elevator doors opened, Clover went running down the hallway and disappeared into Jerome's room.

Polly followed, surprised and a little disappointed to find Norah sitting beside Jerome's bed. Polly greeted them both, then impulsively leaned down and kissed Jerome's cheek, laughing at the lipstick imprint that remained there.

"It's great to see you, Polly," Jerome said with a warm smile. "I've wanted to thank you for taking care of Clover for me."

Polly was shocked at how much older he looked. It was obvious his injuries had taken a severe toll. His skin now had a grayish cast, and lines of strain edged his mouth and eyes.

"We brought you flowers, Daddy." Clover had climbed up on the bed, careful of the IV and his casts. She put her hand on his face and patted him tenderly. "I *luff* you, Daddy," she said.

Polly was touched. "We all *luff* your daddy, Clover. We want him to get well really quick. Now, what can I put these flowers in?"

"There should be something here." Norah opened a cupboard and found a container, and Polly followed her sister into the hallway when she went to fill the vase.

"You seen Mom lately?" Norah's voice was low and tense.

Polly was leaning over the sink, carefully arranging the flowers in the water. "Nope. Not since the day Jerome got hurt." Was that only four days ago? It seemed like half a lifetime. "She hasn't called. She probably thinks I'll ask her to baby-sit. You been over there?"

Norah nodded. "Yesterday afternoon. Nobody home. I called her this morning, really early. Still nobody home. I used the key she keeps hidden under the steps and went in—I was afraid maybe she'd fallen down the basement stairs or slipped in the bath or something. But she wasn't there." Norah sounded anxious. "I'm gonna drop by again sometime today."

Polly snorted. "She's probably in bed with that guy she's having the big affair with."

"But I thought you said they stay at her place."

"She said that to get out of keeping Clover."

"Mom doesn't lie, Polly."

A definite warning note sounded in Norah's voice, and Polly glanced at her in surprise.

"If they weren't staying at her house she'd have said so."

"What's the matter, Norah? How come you're so touchy all of a sudden?"

"I told you. I'm worried about Mom."

Polly snorted. "I wouldn't waste my time or energy. She sure doesn't return the favor."

"Don't always be so hard on her." This time there was outright hostility in Norah's voice.

Polly decided not to pursue the issue. She had enough to think about without arguing with her sister. She carried the flowers over to Jerome's bed and set them on the bedside table. "This is a heck of a way to get out of taking me to lunch, Jerome," she teased, deliberately flirting a little to cheer him up. "We were supposed to go to the pub as soon as we finished the painting, not meet this way in the hospital."

"I'll give you a rain check, Polly. The moment I'm out of here we'll go."

"It's a date," Polly agreed.

Clover was sitting contentedly beside her father, looking at a magazine she'd taken from the side table.

"Thanks for the flowers and the card, Polly," he said. "Is this girl of mine behaving herself with you?"

Clover jerked up her head and looked at Polly with wary eyes.

Surreptitiously, Polly rubbed at the bandage on her thumb. "I'm sure she's doing her best," she managed.

"I hope so. I'm sorry about the misunderstanding with the landlady the other day. She's a busybody—always got her nose stuck into everybody's business. I couldn't believe she called the cops on you."

"What happened, exactly?" Norah asked. "Jerome mentioned you had some problem."

Polly told her an abridged version of the story, editing out the massive fight she'd had with Clover and making the incident sound funny instead of awful.

Jerome laughed, but Norah didn't.

Polly was aware the whole time that Clover was watching her anxiously. It was obvious the girl didn't want her father to know she'd misbehaved. Norah, on the other hand, was giving her disapproving glances. All in all, the atmosphere in the room was strained.

Polly chatted on, deliberately trying to amuse Jerome but more and more aware of Norah's silence. "Is there anything you need?" she finally asked him. "I'm going shopping later. I could drop it off here."

"Nothing at all, thanks." He turned his head and smiled at Norah. "Norah's been wonderful. She brought extra juice and some shaving stuff, and that fruit over there. She's been stopping by every couple of hours and bringing me whatever I need."

Polly glanced at Norah. Her sister's face was turning bright red and she avoided Polly's gaze.

"I'm working right on the next floor. It's easy to pop down whenever we're not in the middle of a delivery," she said, trying for nonchalance and failing.

Every couple of hours? It suddenly dawned on Polly that Norah was in love.

CHAPTER SIXTEEN

POLLY STUDIED her sister, seeing changes in her she'd been too preoccupied to notice until now.

Norah was actually wearing eye makeup and lipstick, which she hardly ever did. She had on a blue dress that Polly had never seen before, a dress that revealed her slender figure in a flattering way. Her silky hair was still in its customary shoulder-length bob, but a portion on the crown was drawn back into a silver clip, and the style softened her features.

All of a sudden Norah was pretty. Her hazel eyes were shining; the high color on her cheeks accentuated her clear, pale skin.

Also for the first time, Polly noticed how Jerome's blue eyes softened when he looked at Norah. She suddenly felt like an idiot for not realizing that the two were attracted to each other and wanted to be alone.

She got to her feet, but she could see by Clover's rebellious expression that the girl was going to throw a full-scale tantrum if Polly suggested they leave so soon.

Inspiration struck. ''I don't suppose you could

keep an eye on Clover for a while, Norah. I've got to go—I have a ton of errands to run and it's boring for her to tag along. I think she'd much rather be here with her daddy. Right, Clover?''

Clover nodded vigorously.

''I could come back and get her in an hour or two.''

''I'd love to have her.'' Norah smiled at Clover. ''I just got off shift, so I'm free for the evening. I'll bring her home later. We'll stay here until Jerome gets tired and then maybe go check out the kiddie train in Stanley Park and grab some dinner. Would you like that, Clover?''

Again, Clover nodded with enthusiasm.

Polly cheerfully said goodbye and hurried out. The elevator was empty; she leaned against the wall and closed her eyes, letting the false smile fade at last.

She was stupid, stupid, not to have realized sooner that Norah wanted Jerome all to herself. And there was absolutely no reason to feel this lonely and left out. After all, she didn't have to even think about Clover for a few hours.

She'd lied about the errands. What should she do for the rest of the afternoon? She had to go to the bank—she had hardly any money in her wallet. Was there any money in the bank? She should have asked Michael more about their finances in the past few days, but they'd reached some sort of polite truce that Polly was loath to disturb.

Certainly she couldn't go shopping. She'd given her word that she would cut back and she meant to keep it. Where could she go, what could she do, that didn't cost money?

Art galleries, she decided. She'd tour the art galleries, big established ones as well as the little ones that exhibited work from unknown artists. She and Michael used to do that sometimes on Saturday afternoons when Susannah was at a movie with her friends.

Michael had always insisted that Polly's work would someday be displayed in a gallery, she remembered wistfully. He'd been her biggest fan.

Twice, with Michael's encouragement, Polly had taken a portfolio of her sketches to one of the galleries. Both times the owner had commented that although her work showed promise, it wasn't what he was looking for. In other words, it wasn't good enough.

After the second disappointment, she'd never tried again, although she'd gone on drawing. She'd stopped when Susannah got sick, and had never drawn again.

So she wasn't an artist any longer. Michael never mentioned the dozens of sketches of Susannah that she'd turned to face the wall in her studio. He never went in there anymore. She hardly did herself. It was another portion of her life that had ended abruptly.

But she could still look at other people's work

and appreciate it. She could still dream, she assured herself now. Dreams were free, and fortunately visiting galleries was, as well.

If only she had someone to go with her, someone with whom to share her impressions the way she used to with Michael. A terrible aloneness came over her, and she longed for him, for the intimacy of intellect and heart and imagination they used to share. She felt almost as if he'd gone on a trip to a far country, a place where she couldn't follow.

Most of the afternoon was unremarkable. The art she viewed was technically good, but it didn't resonate viscerally. It started to rain as she was heading for Concepts, a new, small gallery on Fourth Avenue, and finding a parking spot on the busy street was difficult. When at last she left the car in a lot blocks from the gallery, she hesitated before she stepped out into the downpour. Maybe she should just go home.

But the thought of the empty house and the hours to fill before night made her grab an umbrella from the back seat.

The narrow window at Concepts had a single painting displayed, a surrealistic tulip. Even before she stepped inside the gallery, Polly felt her spirits lift at the artistic explosion of color and raw energy the large canvas conveyed.

"'Afternoon."

The cheerful greeting came from an attractive

woman seated at a desk at the rear of the narrow
gallery. She looked to be in her fifties, and she had
coal-black hair with a startling white stripe down
the middle.

"I'm Jade Crampton. If you need any information, let me know."

Polly nodded, overwhelmed by the effect of the
floral paintings that surrounded her.

The small gallery obviously featured only a single artist at a time. All the paintings were of flowers—huge, outrageous, otherworldly flowers, each
of which held in its center something hazy waiting
to be born, an embryo, a half-glimpsed vision from
another reality that the viewer couldn't quite iden-
tify.

The paintings stirred Polly's imagination and her
emotions. The colors were so vibrant that Polly
could feel them on her skin, and the contrast between their intensity and the fragile center was
mesmerizing.

She felt as if she'd stumbled into a dream that
promised depth and peace and joy if only she could
understand the artist's symbolism.

A small dais held a picture of the artist, an or-
dinary-looking elderly woman from Saskatchewan.
Polly read her bio, and a shudder went down her
spine. This woman, too, had known loss.

The bio said she had done only watercolor land-
scapes until the death of her beloved husband three
years ago. After his death these dramatic flowers

with their secret, hazy hearts exposed came to her in dreams and obsessed her. She felt they were a gift from him, from his spirit to hers.

One last time, Polly moved slowly from one painting to the next. Could a spirit communicate in a dream? So often she dreamed of Susannah, but the dreams were always troubled. What was her daughter trying to tell her?

She left the gallery and drove home through the heavy traffic and the rain, but neither affected her the way they might have. She felt excited, as if she'd almost discovered a truth she'd been searching for for a long time.

Unfortunately, the excitement didn't last long. When she walked in, the house felt chilly and damp, and Polly's spirits flagged. She turned on the gas fireplace and lit the lamps against the sudden stormy darkness.

Then she ventured into her studio. In spite of the rain, light still poured from the enormous skylights she'd had installed. The cleaning-service people had been the only ones in here during the past months. Her easel was empty, her charcoals, pencils, jars of watercolor and tubes of paint lined up in neat, unnatural order.

On a three-tiered workbench dozens of her drawings lay neatly stacked, and against two walls, the works she'd had framed stood like shy sentinels, their wired backs facing her.

Resolutely, Polly turned some of them around.

Although she knew what to expect, the sight of Susannah, smiling, laughing, posturing, dancing, tore at her heart and made her breath catch. For a very long time she stared at them, breathing hard, willing herself to get beyond the subject and assess their worth in an objective, artistic sense.

Of course she couldn't. They were her children almost as much as Susannah had been, and it was impossible to be impartial about them.

They were also the past, she thought sadly. What would the future hold, if ever she dared to begin again?

I sure as hell don't feel any flowers coming on. But it's past time to try again.

Determinedly, she pinned a sheet of paper to her easel and chose a pencil. She'd always drawn Susannah, and her daughter's face and form were clear in her mind's eye.

Two hours later, she'd just crumpled up the fifth attempt and tossed it into the overflowing wastebasket, when the doorbell sounded.

Relieved beyond measure at the interruption, she hastily turned out the lights in the studio and went to open the front door.

"Hi, Clover. Come on in, Norah."

"Hi." Norah collapsed a red umbrella and shook the raindrops free before she stepped inside. "It was too wet for Stanley Park, so we're home a bit early. I stopped and got Clover a video."

"How about dinner? I was just about to make something." She was hungry, Polly realized.

"No, thanks. We had a burger and ice cream, and I should really get home."

"Oh, c'mon, stay for a cup of tea at least," Polly pleaded. "Michael's late, as usual, and I'd enjoy the company."

Norah hesitated but then slipped off her raincoat.

Polly took it from her, adding, "Clover, please take those shoes off before you walk on the rug. They're all muddy."

Clover plopped down and did as she was told, then asked, "Can I watch my movie?"

"Sure, go ahead. Do you know how to program the television?"

"Doctor showed me." She ran to turn on the television, and Polly led the way into the kitchen.

"I drove past Mom's house again and there's still nobody there." Norah stood by a stool at the island, but she didn't sit. "It's been twenty-four hours now, and I'm really concerned, Polly. I think we should call the police."

Polly was exasperated. "Oh, for heaven's sake, Norah. We'll just end up looking really stupid when they find out she's been on some marathon senior-sex binge at her boyfriend's place."

"Why does it bother you so much to think that someone finds Mom attractive?" Norah's usually moderate voice was shrill and accusatory. "You act as if you're the only one who deserves a sex life, the only one who should have a man who cares about you.''

Polly set down the teapot with a thump and stared at her sister, astonished. ''What's that supposed to mean? What are you mad at me about all of a sudden? I didn't murder Mom and hide her body in the cellar, for gosh sakes.''

''Sometimes I think that if you could get away with it you would, you hate her so much.'' There wasn't a trace of humor in Norah's tone. ''You don't seem to realize that I'm really worried about her. You never consider anybody's feelings but your own, Polly. You're so much like Mom I can't believe it.''

Polly's mouth dropped open. ''Me, like Mom? You've got to be kidding.'' She was angry now, her voice as loud as Norah's. ''That's a rotten, unfair thing to say. Why would you accuse *me* of being like *her?*''

Norah's voice was out of control. ''Because it's the truth, Polly. You always talk about how she flirts. Well, take a look at yourself. You do the same. You go on about her having to be the center of attention. Well, you can't bear it if everyone isn't dancing attendance on you. Today, at the hospital, for instance—'' Norah stopped abruptly. Her face turned magenta. It was obvious she'd said more than she'd intended.

Suddenly, Polly understood. ''You're jealous, Norah. That's what this is all about, isn't it?

You…you're in love with Jerome, and you actually think there's something between me and him.''

Norah couldn't meet Polly's eyes. ''I don't think you're having an affair, if that's what you mean. I know Jerome, and I respect him. I don't believe he'd do something like that.''

''And you think I would?'' Polly was incredulous and deeply hurt.

Norah's shoulders slumped and she plopped onto a stool. ''No, I don't really think that. I know you love Michael. But you don't always act like it, Polly. You flirted with Jerome the whole time you were painting Mom's house—you know you did. In fact, you've flirted with every man I've ever been interested in. And you force them to compare us. Naturally, I come off second best. I always have. I've always been your homely little sister. Well, the fact is, you've never grown up, Polly. You don't act like a responsible adult. You were Daddy's little girl, and then Michael took over spoiling you. He's given you everything he has to give, and sometimes I don't think you even appreciate it.''

Norah's voice was quiet now, and icy cold. ''You're spoiled, Polly, and you're self-centered. You always have been. You have no idea what it's like to be really alone, to be responsible for yourself, to have to pay your own bills and be alone in the night. I know you lost Susannah. I know that's the worst loss anyone could have. But we all lost her, and you even shut us out when we tried to share that grief.''

"Share?" Polly's voice, too, was out of control. "You didn't try to share. You disappeared after Susannah's funeral, just when I needed you most.''

Norah looked stricken. "I'm sorry, Polly." She stumbled to her feet. "I'm going home. I've already said too much.''

Speechless and numb with shock and hurt, Polly couldn't move. She heard the front door open and close behind her sister.

Long, silent moments crept by until at last, with trembling hands, Polly poured a cup of tea and sank onto a stool. Norah's accusations rang in her ears, even though she assured herself that none was true. They were affecting her so much simply because Norah had never done this before—never lost her temper, never said things she couldn't possibly mean. She'd probably phone any minute now and apologize.

But an hour passed and the phone was silent. Michael came home, and like an automaton, Polly made supper while he put Clover to bed. It was a routine they'd fallen into. As usual, Clover had obviously been waiting for him. The moment she heard him open the front door, she came running to greet him, full of stories about her afternoon with Norah and the video she was watching. The sense of aloneness that had plagued Polly all day grew deeper and more painful.

When he came downstairs again, he seemed distracted, and barely responded to her remarks about the weather. Polly, too, fell silent, the memory of the quarrel with Norah haunting her.

They ate a simple meal of soup and sandwiches at the kitchen counter, and she longed to tell Michael what had occurred, but each time she opened her mouth to begin, fear stopped her.

What if Michael thought she was all the things Norah had claimed? He'd never say so—she knew he'd never hurt her like that—but she knew him so well she'd be able to tell by his expression whether or not he agreed. And if he did, she didn't think she could stand it.

Norah's words were going 'round and 'round in her head as she stowed the dishes in the dishwasher, and she was barely paying attention when Michael suddenly said, "Polly, we have to sell this house right away. I spoke to a real estate agent this afternoon. He'll be coming by tomorrow to evaluate and suggest a selling price."

CHAPTER SEVENTEEN

POLLY, bent over the dishwasher, straightened and turned to him, certain she'd misunderstood. But the somber expression on Michael's face filled her with anxiety. A plate slipped from her hand and shattered on the tile floor. She ignored it and so did he.

"I'm sorry, Polly."

He didn't sound sorry. He sounded formal, distant, as though he wasn't talking about their home, their life.

"The bank won't loan us any more money, and I can't meet the mortgage payments much longer. I've been juggling, paying only what's absolutely essential, doing my level best to get us out of this mess, but I can't." His voice remained even. "I've known for the past week this was coming. Berina called me this afternoon. He convinced me the only answer is to sell this house, pay off our debts and find somewhere much less expensive to live. Upkeep and taxes here are way more than we can afford now."

Polly couldn't speak. She looked around her kitchen, at the gleaming pots and pans dangling from their hooks above the island, at the framed selections of Susannah's art that hung near the ceiling in a frieze around the room. Into her mind came images of the pool, where she loved to swim; the birdhouse she and Susannah had built; the swing Michael had hung from the maple tree. And, oh, God, her daughter's room, filled with the only essence of Susannah she had left.

His words slowly penetrated. "You…you've known about this for a week? And you…you didn't say anything to me?" That showed as nothing else could have how far apart they'd grown.

"I should have, I know." Wearily, he rubbed a hand over his face. "I've been trying to think of a way out of this, a way to protect you."

"Protect me?" The words spilled out. "I don't want to be protected, I want to know what's going on. Husbands and wives talk to each other. We used to talk. It was you who stopped, not me. You…you have no right to, to…shield me as if I were unfit, to keep such important things from me."

You've never grown up, Polly. You don't act like a responsible adult. Michael took over spoiling you.

Norah's words rushed to her mind, burning like acid, and with them the awful suspicion that maybe Norah was right. Maybe Michael felt he had to protect her because she hadn't matured. That thought scared her, and with fear came unreasonable anger and blame.

"How can you calmly tell me that we have to sell this house? This was Susannah's home. How can I move away from here, from all that's left of her?" Even as the words poured out, Polly knew they were unfair, but she was past the point of caring. All she could do now was feel, and what she felt was anguish. Her already precarious world was collapsing all around her.

"She's gone." Michael's voice was suddenly hard and cold. "Susannah's dead, Polly. Nothing either of us can do will bring her back. When are you going to get that through your head? Keeping her room the same, having her pictures up on the wall, talking about her all the goddamn time—none of it, nothing, will bring our daughter back. Why the hell can't you just accept that and let go?"

She gasped. His heartless words were like arrows in her chest. "How can you say such things, Michael? How can you talk in that tone of voice about our daughter? I thought you loved me. I thought you loved Susannah."

With that, at last his control snapped. He brought both fists down on the counter with such a crash that Polly jumped, dropping the plate she was about to put in the dishwasher. It shattered on the floor. His dark eyes blazed.

"Love you? Goddamn it, I'd die for you if I had

to. I'd have died for Susannah if it would have saved her. But I couldn't do it, Polly. I'm a doctor, but I couldn't save my own daughter.'' His voice reverberated through the room; his face was contorted. "I can't save this house for you, either. The money's gone, Polly, and there's not a damn thing I can do about that.''

She should have recognized the anguish beneath his words, but her own hurt was too deep. "Money? This isn't about money, Michael.''

"Then what the *hell* is it about?''

His anger was terrible because it was so unfamiliar to her. "It's...it's about us. It's about our marriage,'' she stammered. "Our marriage is falling apart, but you don't notice. You go off to work every time I try to talk to you. You won't discuss Susannah. You won't remember her with me. And I need you to do that. You're the only one who knew her the way I did.'' She sucked in a sobbing breath. "You've deserted me, Michael, in every sense.''

He stared at her, his eyes hard. "I'm a doctor, Polly. I have an office, patients to see.'' His voice was quieter, but it held a hard, warning note. "My job is to provide care to them, and that doesn't stop because eight hours have gone by. You know that. You knew when you married me that I didn't have a regular nine-to-five job.''

"Sure I knew. And I never complained when Susannah was alive, because I knew you wanted to be home with us even when you couldn't be.'' She realized she should stop, but she no longer cared what she said. ''Then after she died it dawned on me that you were using your job as an excuse to avoid coming home, to avoid being with me. It wasn't until Clover came here that it got really clear.'' Her tone was nasty. ''It's amazing— isn't it?—how you can find time to get home early now that *she's* here?'' She heard herself and was appalled, but she still went on. ''I'm the only one you're trying to avoid, Michael. Why don't you just admit it?''

He was glaring at her. ''If we're being honest, Polly, then you should take a hard look at the way you feel about that little girl. The reason I've been racing home every afternoon is that it's patently obvious you don't like her, and Clover knows it. That resentment doesn't exactly make the best environment for a child.''

''I'm as kind to her as I can be.'' His words filled her with guilt. ''I told Jerome I'd take care of her, and I'm doing it as best I can. She's not an easy kid—you said so yourself.''

''She's a child, Polly.''

''Doctor?''

Clover stood in the kitchen doorway, her rabbit stuffed under her arm. Her eyes were wide and frightened, and Polly felt sick, wondering how much she'd heard, how much she understood.

''My tummy hurts,'' she said in a quavery voice.

"Does it?" Michael picked her up and she burrowed her head into his shoulder. "Let's get you back in bed and see if a story helps." His voice was infinitely gentle now, and he headed for the stairs, murmuring comfort to Clover.

Polly felt as if she couldn't breathe. In a daze, she got the broom and swept up the broken crockery, then loaded the rest of the dishes. Michael didn't come back downstairs.

Outside, the rain had stopped. Distraught, Polly pulled on a jacket and went into the backyard.

The pool was still empty; she'd decided not to fill it until after Clover left. It was hard enough to keep an eye on her without worrying about the danger of the swimming pool.

Polly walked around it and made her way to the iron table and chairs on the cement patio. She and her family had had such fun here. Vancouver had enjoyed unprecedented good weather the summer the pool was installed, and she and Susannah had spent most of every day out here, joined by Michael in the evenings. Her family had seemed so secure back then.

She looked up at the gracious lines of the house, and her entire body hurt at the thought of leaving it.

Where would she be living six months from now?

Her family, her husband, her home.

She'd lost her daughter. She was losing her

home. That left only Michael. She thought of the devastating quarrel they'd just had, the terrible things they'd both said that were hurtful and that would be difficult to forget.

Six months from now, would she still be Michael's wife?

THE HORRENDOUS QUARREL sapped Michael's energy. It took a long time to settle Clover down, and when at last she was sleeping, he couldn't face another confrontation. He made his way to his study and fell into an exhausted sleep on the sofa there, only to awaken abruptly at four-thirty in the morning with a sense of overwhelming urgency.

He had to make things right with Polly. Somehow, he had to make her understand it wasn't her he was angry with. It was his own inadequacy.

He made his way up to their bedroom with some hazy thought of taking her in his arms and making love to her until the remnants of the quarrel were burned away in the fire of physical passion. In the dim light of dawn, he climbed into bed beside her and gathered her in his arms, but she was deeply asleep.

The vials of medication that she'd stopped using in the past weeks were once again open on her bedside table, and he knew he was the reason she'd had to resort to them again. If he awakened her, what could he say that would make everything better?

He released her gently and lay beside her, watching her sleep. Her face was flushed and relaxed, innocent and intensely beautiful to him. He stroked a finger across her cheek and then got up. After showering, he looked in on Clover, who was curled up like a kitten, then he drove through the gray dawn and the deserted streets to his office. He was immersed in paperwork when Valerie arrived at eight, bringing him a coffee and muffin.

Michael's heart sank when he learned his first patient was Duncan Hendricks. The boy came in with his mother, Sophie, and Michael had to struggle hard to summon up his professional mask of cheerfulness and assurance.

Fortunately, Duncan didn't notice anything amiss. With his usual wide smile and a cheery, "Hi, Doctor," he walked over and stuck out his hand for the special secret handshake Michael had taught him on one of his early visits. It had become a ritual between them, and it allowed Michael to gauge reflexes, strength and coordination without the boy suspecting he was being tested.

All three showed no improvement.

"How are you feeling, Duncan? How are the headaches?"

"They hurt. But I'm gettin' better soon."

Duncan's attitude was amazing. Michael had never heard the little boy complain, and his response was always the same when he was asked how he felt—a stalwart assurance that he was getting better, even though his symptoms hadn't improved in the slightest. In fact, they had worsened somewhat.

Michael smiled at the child, and in some unexplainable way his own heartache eased a bit, just looking into Duncan's sweet, open face.

"How's Oscar?" Duncan didn't realize it, but the goldfish had become a focal figure in the stories he told Clover each night. As had Susannah. Clover insisted every story had to include her.

"Oscar's good. How long do goldfish live, Dr. Mike?"

"I'm not sure, Duncan, but I think they live quite a long time."

"I hope so. I wanna keep Oscar till I grow up."

If only this child could grow up. At one time Michael had believed that anything was possible, but he didn't anymore. Now he knew the unthinkable happened, that the deepest and most terrible of fears were often the ones that were realized. He suspected the goldfish would outlive Duncan.

He chatted with the boy about his fish and his favorite television shows for a moment before turning to Sophie and quizzing her closely about Duncan's appetite, his sleep patterns, his bowel movements.

Keeping up a running dialogue, Michael did a further neurological workup, checking motor skills, looking at Duncan's eyes. The tests revealed what Michael already knew: the radiation to the head had had no influence on the symptoms, and it should have by now.

"I'm gonna go to kindergarten after summertime, Doctor," Duncan announced. "Mommy and I went to the school to register, and we met the teacher, Mrs. Poke…Mrs. Poka…"

"Mrs. Pokara," Sophie supplied.

"Yeah. And there's this really neat turtle named Alphonse that gets to come home with you sometimes, right, Mommy?"

"Right, Duncan." Sophie smiled at her son, but when she turned to Michael, her eyes were shining with unshed tears. The chances of Duncan being around to start kindergarten in September were extremely slim.

Sophie and Duncan left, and as usual, it took Michael several moments to compose himself enough to carry on with the rest of the day's appointments.

Valerie tapped on his door and stuck her head in. She eyed the untouched muffin and the cold coffee. "Polly's on line two. You better start eating something, Doctor. You're losing weight. And whenever you're ready, Mr. Benedict's waiting in examining room three."

Michael almost groaned aloud. The morning couldn't get much worse. Malcolm Benedict was a new patient with severe headaches. He'd had a very minor motorcycle accident six months before, and extensive tests at the time had ruled out any organic damage. Several doctors had arrived at the diagnosis of severe personality disorder, and Michael heartily concurred. Benedict was brilliant and totally obnoxious, and he'd challenged Michael on every aspect of his treatment for the headaches—which of course were stress related. Benedict had been so vehemently certain of an organic cause that he had finally worn Michael down and Michael had ordered a CAT scan.

"Mr. Benedict's lab reports are here—the delivery service just dropped them off." Valerie handed over a manila envelope and closed the door.

Michael tossed the envelope on his desk, on top of Duncan's file. He picked up the phone.

"'Morning, Polly." Like a black cloud, the aftermath of their fight hung between them, and much as he wanted to dispel it, he couldn't think how to begin. More than anything, he wanted to tell her about Duncan, to share the tumultuous feelings the boy and his illness aroused, but of course he couldn't do that. It would only upset her, the way it was upsetting him.

"The real estate agent's here."

Polly's abrupt and distant tone told him how angry she was.

"He's suggested a price and wants to know if it's agreeable with you. I told him whatever you two decide is fine with me. I'll put him on."

She was gone before Michael could respond.

He talked with the agent for several moments, thinking of Polly instead of the house.

"Could I speak with my wife again, please?"

He'd get Valerie to shuffle the appointments; they'd go out to lunch together; he'd apologize for last night.

"She's out with your little girl. She gave me a set of keys. I'll lock up when I leave."

With a heavy heart, Michael hung up. He dialed Polly's cell phone number but got no response. That left him with a cold, hard knot in his stomach, but there wasn't time for despair, not here, not now.

Benedict was waiting, Michael reminded himself, and he'd need all the patience and fortitude he could muster to deal with the angry, disagreeable man. At least the CAT scan would provide undeniable proof that Benedict was creating his own stress, Michael thought wearily. He opened the lab report and skimmed the results. Astounded, he read them a second time, then a third.

Chronic subdural hematoma.

Malcolm Benedict had a mass of blood under his skull that certainly would account for persistent headaches, and would require immediate surgery. Benedict had been right all along: there *was* an organic reason for his problem. Michael and the other doctors had been wrong. The first test results had been misinterpreted, and no one except Benedict had considered redoing them.

Michael stared at the lab report. He looked from it to the file underneath—Duncan's file.

Why hadn't Duncan's tumor responded the way it should have to the radiation? He hurried out to find Valerie.

"Schedule a CAT scan for Duncan Hendricks, A.S.A.P."

He'd reexamine the original slides and compare them with the new. It hardly seemed possible that a mistake could have been made, but there was no harm in checking.

CHAPTER EIGHTEEN

SITTING IN HER CAR in front of her mother's house, Polly waited for her sister. Norah had phoned just before the real estate agent arrived that morning, and without any greeting said in a tense voice, "Mom's still not home. I've been calling since six this morning and there's no answer. I've called her friends and checked with her neighbors. Nobody's seen her for three days. She's disappeared, Polly, and we've got to do something. Meet me at her place. We'll see if maybe there's a note or something I missed the other day."

Polly had agreed, and Norah hung up without saying goodbye.

"Why can't we go in and see Auntie?" Clover was whining. "I need a drink. I have to pee."

Clover's petulant voice grated on Polly's nerves.

"Auntie's not at home. We'll go in when Norah comes. You can get a drink then and use the bathroom."

"Where did Auntie go? Why didn't she take me?"

Good question. Polly was caring for a child she couldn't like, her marriage was a shambles, her sister hated her, and her house was about to be sold. Frannie was on holiday just when she needed her most, and now Isabelle had disappeared. For a mad moment, Polly almost gave in to hysterical laughter. Her life was turning into a soap opera.

Norah drove up and parked, and Polly got out.

"Hiya, Norah." The moment Polly let her out of the car, Clover ran over and grabbed Norah's hand as if it were a life preserver.

They stood for a tense moment, looking at each other, and Polly struggled for something to say that might break the charged atmosphere.

"This is like the showdown at the OK Corral," she joked. "I left my gun at home, so you're safe."

Her sister gave a strained smile. "So did I. Let's go in and see what we can find."

Polly's heart sank. Gun or not, it was all too obvious that Norah was still angry.

They found the key and opened the door. The old, familiar odor of cigarette smoke mingled with a stronger smell of rotting garbage.

"Yuck." Polly checked the can under the sink and found it overflowing. "I'm taking this out."

She dumped the garbage into the tin in the alley and paused on the way back to admire the paint job, the pristine backyard, the steps Jerome had repaired. The place looked better than it had since her father was alive, which was ironic, considering that everything else was falling apart at a rapid rate.

"There's no note down here that I can see," Norah announced when Polly came in. "Let's go up and look in Mom's bedroom."

Polly followed Norah and Clover up the stairs. Clover was still clinging to Norah like a piece of Velcro, Polly noted.

The bed in Isabelle's room was unmade and the room was in its customary state of chaos. Two dresses, several pairs of panties and a slip had been tossed on the trunk Isabelle used as a night table. More discarded clothing fell from the chair, and a black bra peeped out from under the dresser, the top of which was littered with costume jewelry, empty coffee cups, overflowing ashtrays and a thick layer of dust.

The usual collection of cardboard boxes holding god only knows what were stacked against one wall, and dozens of the paperback Westerns Isabelle adored cluttered the board-and-brick bookshelf under the window.

Norah stared at the open doors of the bulging closet. "Could you tell if any of her clothes were missing, Polly?"

Polly shook her head. "Not a chance. She's got so many, nobody could tell. Any sign of her purse? If she's gone somewhere, she'll have taken her purse with her."

"Which one d'you think she was using?" Norah gestured at the closet, where a welter of handbags was piled on the shelf.

Polly tried to remember and couldn't. "Maybe a straw one? I'm not sure."

"It's white," Clover said with conviction. "Auntie's purse is white. It gots a little green one inside it where she keeps all her money."

"You're right—I remember now!" Norah exclaimed. "Good for you, Clover." She did a quick survey. "It's not up here, and I didn't see it downstairs, either."

They checked the other two bedrooms.

"This is where Polly and I slept when we were little girls like you," Norah told Clover.

"Where did Susannah sleep?" Clover looked up at Norah.

"Susannah didn't live here," Polly said shortly.

"She lived at your house, right?" Clover asked Polly. "'Cause you're her mommy, right?"

"Right." Why was this kid so obsessed with Susannah?

"And Isabelle is our mommy," Norah explained. "Now, let's go look a bit more downstairs."

They searched, but the purse wasn't around. And there wasn't any note. Nothing indicated where Isabelle might be or when she might be back.

"I give up. I need a cup of coffee." Polly felt exhausted.

"I could use a cup, too," Norah agreed.

In the kitchen Polly emptied the half-filled coffeepot and washed it before starting a fresh pot to drip.

Norah gave Clover a stack of old *National Geographics*. Isabelle had at least twelve boxes filled with them. They found a pair of scissors, and Clover sat at the kitchen table, happily snipping away at a photo spread of elephants.

Polly filled two mugs and silently handed one to Norah. The air was once again thick with all the things unsaid between them.

"Let's go sit in the living room." Norah led the way, and when they were seated, Polly on the old sagging sofa and Norah on one of the rump-sprung chairs, Norah gave a huge sigh. "Polly, I apologize for the things I said last night. I got myself into a state over…" She gulped and went pink. "Over Jerome," she finally said. "I hardly slept all night I felt so bad about taking it out on you."

Polly thought back over the previous evening and shuddered. "Maybe you weren't all wrong," she said in a gloomy tone. "Maybe I am like Mom."

After all, Michael had pretty much said the same things, hadn't he?

"Oh, you're not. I mean, you're like her in that you're both beautiful and charismatic in a way I never have been. I've always been a little jealous of that. See, I…I care about Jerome, and I very much want him to feel the same way about me, so much that it scares me silly," Norah confessed.

"Oh, Pol, it's easier to get mad at you than to take a hard look at myself." She swallowed the coffee as if it were medicine and stared down at the dusty carpet. "More than anything I want what you've got, Pol." Her voice was wistful. "You have a rock-solid marriage, a husband who adores you. Losing Susannah was awful for all of us, but you've got such courage. You went for help. You worked hard at getting through it, while I..." Tears welled up and rolled down Norah's cheeks. She wiped at them with her fingers and choked back sobs.

"I ran away. I went to Seattle and locked myself in a hotel room for four days and bawled. I was so shattered I couldn't be around anybody, and I feel so guilty about that—about not being there for you when you needed me."

A hard core of resentment began to melt inside Polly. She *had* blamed Norah; she'd thought her actions insensitive and outright cruel. Hearing what had really happened made her heart go out to her sister, because she understood.

"Losing Susannah was so enormous. I loved her so. I *do* love her so." Norah wept.

"I know you do. *She* knew you did. You were the best auntie a kid could have."

"I want children so much, Polly," Norah acknowledged. "Sometimes it's like a physical pain inside me. I hold the babies in the nursery and I ache for my own."

Polly knew all about that ache. "I didn't know you felt this way. I thought you wanted a career instead of a marriage."

"I'd convinced myself I did because every time I met someone I cared for, something went wrong. I've always blamed the men," Norah admitted. "I finally figured out when I couldn't sleep last night that I go into relationships believing they won't work, that I'm not good enough, so I look for ways to end them. That way it's me doing the dumping instead of the other way around." She dug in her jeans pocket and came up with a tattered tissue, which she used to mop her eyes and blow her nose. "Pretty dumb, huh? I'm thirty-four. It's taken me all these years to figure this out and now it sounds so simple."

But it didn't sound simple at all to Polly. She'd spent enough time with Frannie to know that insights into one's psyche were hard-won and painful. She told Norah so, and something Norah had said echoed inside her brain.

You have a rock-solid marriage, a husband who adores you...

If Norah only knew the truth. And why shouldn't she? Polly wondered suddenly. Norah was her sister, and she'd just been bone honest.

Polly sucked in a deep breath and told Norah some of what was really happening in her life. She began with Stokes and the financial crisis, and how she'd contributed to it by spending money recklessly after Susannah's death. The only thing Polly couldn't bring herself to admit was how bad things were between her and Michael. That hurt was too painful, her fear too deep.

Instead, she talked about the loss of the house, her inability to draw, the sense of inadequacy she'd always had because, unlike Norah, she had no formal career. "That's what I've always envied about you, Norah. I'd give anything to have a job I cared about, somewhere I had to go every day, a purpose to my life." She'd been holding the tears back, but now she let them come. "I lost all that when Susannah died."

"Oh, Pol." Norah moved over to the sofa. She hugged Polly, holding her and stroking her hair as if Polly were her little sister instead of the other way around. Both were crying now, healing tears that rolled down their cheeks and made wet splotches on their T-shirts.

They became aware of Clover standing a few steps away, her forehead wrinkled in a frown.

"Are you crying 'cause your mommy went away?" she asked, adding in an understanding tone, "I cried when my mommy went away."

"Oh, sweetheart, c'mere."

Norah sniffled and she and Polly enfolded Clover in their arms. At that moment, Polly felt closer to the little girl than she ever had before.

"Sometimes crying helps, doesn't it, honey?" Norah's voice was tear-choked.

Clover endured the embrace for a few seconds, then announced, "You're squeezing me too tight and I *still* gots to pee."

Tears gave way to laughter as Clover scampered down the hall to the bathroom.

"She's such a funny, sweet little thing, and I want to get to know her better, Polly. I'm starting my long break tomorrow. Would you mind if I had her for a couple days?"

Rubbing the thumb that still ached from Clover's teeth, Polly decided to let Norah find out for herself that the kid wasn't always sweet. "You free tomorrow morning, by any chance? I've got an appointment, and I was wondering what to do with Clover." Their newfound intimacy prompted her to add, "It's with Frannie, at the hospital. I need to talk to her again. I could drop Clover off at your place."

"I'd be delighted."

Having a sister who was also a friend was so comforting. Polly could tell by the warmth in Norah's eyes that she felt the same.

But there was still the matter of Isabelle. "What the heck are we gonna do about Mom, Norah?"

"Go to the police, I guess. What else can we do?"

"I'd better call Michael first. I haven't told him yet that Mom's even gone missing." Norah looked surprised, and Polly added, "We...haven't been talking a whole lot lately. We're having some problems.'' It was as near as she could come to sharing the open wound that was her marriage.

Norah nodded, her gaze compassionate and warm. ''You'll work it out, Pol. You two are meant for each other.''

Not long ago Polly had believed that to be so. Now she wasn't certain at all. She dialed the office number, and when Michael finally came on the line, her heart grew heavy at the weariness in his voice.

She quickly told him about Isabelle, the search they'd made of the house. ''Norah thinks we ought to call the police.''

''I think she's right. Polly, about last night... I'm sorry. I didn't mean to hurt you.''

''I know that.'' Did she? She swallowed hard. ''I'm sorry, too.''

''We'll talk later. Let me know what happens with the police. And, Polly? I do love you.''

Feeling lighter, Polly hung up and dialed the Vancouver City Police nonemergency number. The constable she spoke with asked if she and Norah could come to the nearest station and file a missing person complaint. It would help if they could provide a recent photo of Isabelle.

They dug through cardboard boxes of Isabelle's photographs. There were dozens of Susannah but not a lot of Isabelle; she was always the one taking the pictures. Polly tucked several into her handbag;

she'd make copies and give them back to Isabelle—not that her mother would even miss them.

They finally located one of Isabelle and Susannah, taken at Christmastime.

It was Susannah's last Christmas. She sat curled beside her grandmother in the love seat in Polly's living room, fragile, incandescent, smiling.

Polly stared at it, struck by the resemblance between her daughter and her mother. "I never realized before how much Susannah looked like Mom. I always thought she was the image of Michael."

"She was, but she had lots of Mom in her, too. I always said they looked alike."

"I never believed it." Because of the way she felt about her mother, it wasn't something Polly wanted to know, even now.

"I wanna see." Clover reached for the photo.

"Is that your girl with Auntie?" Clover studied the picture.

"Yup," Polly said. "That's Susannah."

Clover nodded. "She gots a fish called Oscar, and he can talk."

"Who told you that?"

"Doctor. He tells me stories 'bout Susannah and Oscar."

Polly stared at Clover. Michael, who'd barely mention his daughter's name, made up stories about her to tell Clover? All of a sudden Polly felt betrayed in a whole new way.

"Clover, get your sandals on." Norah shot an anxious glance at Polly, sensing something was wrong. "We're gonna go down to the police station now."

At the station, the young female constable was businesslike and sympathetic. She gave Clover apple juice while Polly and Norah answered dozens of questions and filled in forms. They were told that Isabelle's picture and description would be circulated among all the Lower Mainland detachments immediately.

By the time they were done, Norah had to hurry to St. Joe's to begin her shift and Clover was cranky and sleepy.

Polly drove home. She was just tucking Clover into bed, when the phone rang.

"Polly?" Isabelle's voice came lilting over the line. "Hello, dear."

"Mom, where the heck are you? Are you okay? Norah and I are half out of our minds worrying about you."

"Of course I'm okay—why wouldn't I be? And there's no need to holler at me, Polly."

Polly's temper was slipping. She forced herself to lower her voice so as not to disturb Clover, but the urge to scream at her mother was almost overwhelming. "You've been gone for three days— none of us had any idea where. Norah and I just spent all morning at your house looking for a note, trying to figure out what to do. Where exactly are you, and what in *hell* is going on?"

"I'm in Oregon. In a campground, outside of Eugene. It's lovely here, lots nicer than Canada." Isabelle sounded jubilant. "They have a little café and a pub, there's live music and dancing every night, the beer is good."

"And what *exactly* are you doing in Oregon?" Polly would cheerfully have throttled her mother at this moment.

"Surprise, surprise," Isabelle crowed. "Eric and I got married—Eric Sanderson. You haven't met him yet, but you'll love him when you do. We eloped. I just thought it would be easier on you and Norah that way. No fuss about a wedding or reception—you're both so busy. Besides, it was a spur-of-the-moment decision. He has a travel trailer. We're staying in that. We've decided to be snowbirds."

Giddy laughter that made Polly want to scream followed.

"Eric's very tidy and so romantic. He waits on me hand and foot." Isabelle's giggle was girlish, and Polly's sense of outrage grew.

"You'll have to call and tell Norah the good news for me," Isabelle went on. "I tried to phone her a while ago, but she wasn't home."

"That's because we were at the police station. We gave them a picture of you. They've sent out a bulletin. You're officially listed as a missing person. You're on their Wanted list.'' That gave Polly some small satisfaction. Her mind was reeling. "In fact, the first thing you'd better do after this is call the constable we talked with—her name is..." Polly fished in the pocket of her jeans for the card the officer had given her and read off the name and number.

"Oh, you do that for me, dear, won't you?" Isabelle was unconcerned. "Tell them I'm on my honeymoon."

Polly was furious. "You call them yourself, Mom. They'll just think I'm trying to cover something up."

Like matricide.

"Oh, all right. But there is something you must do for me, you and Norah. I want you to sell the house."

"Sell...the...house?" Polly was no longer angry. Instead, she was utterly dumbfounded. It was the last thing she expected from Isabelle.

"We plan to travel. No point in paying taxes on a house we're not going to live in. I'm mailing a list of things I need. You girls can send them. Other stuff has to be put in storage. I'll sign whatever legal papers you need. Here's my address."

In a daze, Polly found a pencil and scribbled it down.

"And of course you girls are to divide the family heirlooms between you," Isabelle said magnanimously. "Now, I must go, but first Eric wants to say hi. Here's Polly, lover," Isabelle cooed.

Polly stood frozen into place as a hearty male voice with a pronounced English accent came on the line.

"Hello, Polly. I just want you to know that I plan to take good care of your mother. Don't you girls worry about her for a moment. We'll be traveling a fair bit, but when we get back to Vancouver I look forward to meeting you and your sister." Gruffly he added, "Always wanted daughters— never had any. Give your sister my love."

Polly mumbled something polite and hung up. She stared blindly at the wall for a while, then dialed the obstetrical floor of St. Joe's and asked for Norah.

"She's with a patient at the moment."

Childbirth would simply have to wait, Polly decided.

"Tell her it's an emergency."

CHAPTER NINETEEN

THERE WAS A PAUSE, and at last Norah came on the line.

"Polly?" Her voice was filled with concern. "What is it? Is something wrong?"

"Depends how you look at it. Mom just called. She's alive and well and living in a travel trailer in Oregon. And...she's gotten married. Eric Sanderson is our new stepdaddy. Such a trusting soul—he sends us his love, sight unseen. Mom wants us to sell the house, but first we get to sort through all her stuff, pack up what she wants, then send it to her. We're to store the rest. Oh, yeah, we also get to divide the family heirlooms between us."

After a moment of stunned silence, Norah used an expletive Polly would have sworn could never cross her sister's lips. Then Norah started to giggle, and in a moment, Polly, too, was chuckling.

"I suppose you want the *Geographics*," Norah gasped. "Which means I get the paperback Westerns." That set them off again. The laughter was like strong medicine, lifting Polly's spirits.

That evening, Michael laughed, too, when she

told him about her call from Isabelle. He brought her a clay pot filled with purple hyacinths, and he kissed her and held her close until Clover insinuated herself between them.

More than anything, Polly wanted to accept his apology, forget the angry words they'd exchanged. The trouble was, she kept remembering what Clover had revealed—that Michael had named a character in one of his stories after Susannah.

How could he do such a thing, yet coldly tell Polly she had to let Susannah go? She wanted to ask him, but the memory of last night's devastating row was still too fresh and too painful to risk another. It felt as though she were walking gingerly across a minefield; there were so many places she didn't dare step for fear of an explosion.

Michael asked if she'd go along to St. Joe's to see Jerome, but Polly refused. Then, as he and Clover drove off, she couldn't help the feelings of abandonment that swept over her.

She tried again to draw, using the photos of Susannah she'd found at her mother's house, but that didn't work. Her efforts had no life, no originality, and she tore the sketches to shreds, feeling a hopelessness that reached to the depths of her soul.

Michael came home and put Clover to bed. Feeling like a spy, Polly hovered in the hallway, waiting to hear the story he'd tell, but tonight Clover asked that he read a book about dinosaurs.

When Michael came downstairs, he opened a

bottle of wine. Polly drank more of it than usual, and later, when he made love to her, she felt anesthetized enough to lose herself in the mindless pleasure of sex.

Don't think, she told herself as his mouth brought her sweetly to orgasm. *Don't think,* she warned as he touched her belly, kissed her breast, claimed the familiar space between her thighs.

Don't think—don't think—it's far too dangerous.

Thank God Frannie was back. She was seeing her the next day.

When the alarm sounded in the morning, Polly awakened with a sense of dread mingled with relief, and when she reached Frannie's office at nine-thirty, she sank into the familiar armchair, remembering how many times she'd sat there before, how frantic she'd felt most of those times.

"'Morning, Polly. You've cut your hair. I like it.''

Frannie, tall and slender, looked striking in a simple peach linen dress. She sat beside the small desk, just a few feet from Polly. When she'd first started seeing Frannie, that easy physical proximity had been disturbing, but now it was reassuring.

"Is this a recent photo of the kids?" Polly reached for a framed snapshot on the desk. "Zoe is really getting big." Zoe was Frannie's step-daughter. She was holding baby Harry.

"She's seven. She's so mature for her age I

worry about her sometimes. She's like a little mother to Harry.''

"He's almost sixteen months now, isn't he? Next Tuesday.'' Polly always knew exactly how old Harry was because Frannie had gone into labor with him during one of Polly's counseling sessions, back when she was still trying to decide whether or not she wanted to go on living.

"He looks absolutely huge, Frannie. And so handsome.''

Frannie smiled, and pride in her son made her deep blue eyes glow. "Thanks, although I can't take any credit for either his size or his looks. He's the absolute image of Kaleb.''

Polly had met handsome Kaleb Sullivan at the St. Joe's Christmas party. He was a fireman. His sister, Lily, was an ER nurse, married to ER physician Greg Brulotte.

The phone rang, and Frannie apologized as she lifted the receiver. "I have to take this one call. There's an urgent situation with a child.''

Frannie talked and Polly glanced around the small room, noting the homey touches and thinking about how much of her agony this room had witnessed, how much of her rage.

Today, her feelings were less extreme. She tried to sort through the hodgepodge of confused emotions so that she could be concise when she and Frannie talked.

There was the extreme antipathy she felt toward

Clover; the sense of shame and self-recrimination this roused in her; the deep, gut-wrenching ache in her heart at the prospect of leaving the home she loved; and, underneath all of it, the terrible anxiety about her marriage.

Poor Frannie, Polly reflected with dark humor. What could anyone do in a single hour to solve such a mess?

Frannie hung up and programmed the machine so it would take any incoming calls.

"So how are things going with you, Polly?"

It was always difficult to begin—like wading into a cold lake, shocking and painful until her body adjusted to the water. Polly had learned the best thing to do was jump straight in.

"Not so good." She swallowed hard and admitted it. "Awful. Michael and I...we don't seem to be able to talk to each other anymore," she said slowly. "Not about stuff that matters. He's so distant. I know he's under a lot of pressure. He works more than ever these days. We're having some financial problems. We...we're going to have to sell our home."

"How do you feel about that?"

"Sad. Angry."

She bit her lip and then, in a rush of words, the rest of it poured out. "Bitter. And there's this kid I'm taking care of, Clover Fox." Polly explained about Jerome and the accident. "Frannie, this is so hard. I thought I was doing okay about Susannah, but this kid just brings up such horrible feelings in me.'' Shame washed over her, and she couldn't continue.

"What sort of feelings, Polly?"

"She...she annoys me." That was way too mild. She had to tell the truth, or how could Frannie help her?

She swallowed hard and forced it out. "I...I just don't like her. I *really* don't like her." Her voice was shaking as she tried to justify her attitude. "Kids are people. There're people I don't like, and Clover's one of them."

"What is it about her you don't like?"

"Oh, nothing in particular."

Frannie waited, silent.

"Everything, damn it," Polly blurted. "She bit me—hard. She defies me. She won't eat what I cook. She doesn't talk to me. She doesn't like me any more than I like her."

Even to her own ears, it all sounded so petty Polly felt mortified. "Frannie, I resent her so much, and it makes me ashamed of myself. She's only four—she's a child. I shouldn't feel this way about her. But...but I look at her and I think..." Polly trailed off and tears burned behind her eyelids, then began to trickle down her cheeks.

Frannie handed her the box of tissues that were always on the desk. "What do you think, Polly?" Her voice was gentle, encouraging.

The tears were scalding, like the pain in Polly's

stomach. "Oh, God. I...look at her and I think that my Susannah should have lived. Susannah *deserved* to live," she wailed.

"What is it in Clover that you resent?"

"She's...she's..." Polly struggled to put it into words. Finally, slowly, she said, "I guess she's the exact opposite of everything Susannah was. She's...she's bad-tempered and sullen, and...and unattractive. Susannah had so much to offer, and I see this kid and I wonder why she should be here and Susannah...not here."

"So she reminds you of Susannah."

"No." The denial was explosive. "Absolutely not. Why do people keep saying such a thing? My mother said that—that Clover reminds her of Susannah—and it's ridiculous. She's nothing like her."

"I meant that when you look at Clover, you think of Susannah."

With great reluctance, Polly nodded.

"And what else do you think of?"

"What else?" Polly considered the question, and the answer came. "I guess I think of Michael," she said slowly. "He doesn't have any problem with Clover. At first I wanted him around more to take care of her. And then when he was, I was..." She could barely whisper the truth. "I was jealous." She hastened to defend herself. "Not for me, but for Susannah. The attention he pays to Clover belongs to Susannah."

"But Susannah doesn't need it now," Frannie reminded her gently. "Who do you really have resentment for? For Clover or for Michael?"

With Frannie there was no avoiding the truth.

Polly's shoulders slumped. "Michael," she whispered. "It's Michael. He plays with her. He talks to her. He never talks to me about Susannah, but apparently he tells Clover stories about a girl he's named after our daughter. He buys Clover gifts. He laughs with her. He enjoys having her around. Yet he won't agree to having another baby so I could share those feelings with him."

"So when he doesn't talk to you, what do you believe about that?"

Unbearable pain seared through Polly. "He doesn't care about me." Her voice dropped to a whisper. "He doesn't love me anymore." Once the words were out, they took on a terrifying reality. She felt as if she couldn't breathe.

But Frannie shook her head. "You resent him and you've closed your heart to him, as much as you believe he's closed his heart to you. You've made this in your imagination, Polly. He's not here, so we can't ask him, but I want you to tell me honestly how you've guarded your heart from him."

Polly wanted to deny it. She'd tried to make him talk with her about Susannah, hadn't she? She'd begged him to come to counseling. She'd done everything in her power to make things better between them. How dared anyone insinuate the fault was hers?

She stared at Frannie, and slowly, unwillingly, the answer came. "Clover. He's tried to share his enjoyment of her with me, but I...I can't. I don't want to. How can he expect me to?"

"Why can't you, Polly?"

Relentless. Frannie was relentless, and for a moment, Polly hated her. This was too hard. Sobs built in her chest and she forced them down. She wrapped her arms around herself, holding in the pain.

"Because if I do...I...I'll do what he's doing. Don't you see that?" Her voice rose and panic filled her. "I'll betray my own child. I'll...I'll forget her. She'll be gone forever, along with the house and her room, her toys, all the memories..."

Again Frannie shook her head. "Your little one lives in your heart, Polly. She'll never go away. Think back now, and tell me what your greatest fear was after Susannah died."

That memory was a place Polly hated to go. She took a shuddering breath. "I thought my heart would literally break. I thought I would die of a broken heart."

"But you didn't die," Frannie told her gently. "Your heart broke, and you went on. You don't have to be afraid anymore. Sometimes hearts break to allow something new to be born, to force us to grow. And the love, the connectedness with your daughter, is a permanent thing. Nothing will ever alter it, because Susannah lives in your heart.''

Frannie reached over and took Polly's hand in hers.

"You're not lost in your sorrow anymore. You're not stuck there.'' Her voice was reassuring. "You've come so far, Polly—you know you have. Take a deep breath and check your heart right now for me. Close your eyes and feel how much you have there of the memory of Susannah.''

Polly did, and of course Susannah was there, unlimited and true and forever. And with a sense of wonder, Polly realized something else. Her heart was still sore, but it didn't feel broken any longer.

"You can allow yourself to love this child, Polly.'' Frannie's voice was soft. "Once hearts are open, their capacity for love is unlimited. As for Michael, we've talked before about how people grieve differently, on different time lines. My guess is he's doing it the only way he can, the only way possible for him. Give him space, Polly. Don't crowd him. Try to have faith that the universe will heal him just as it's healed you. Love him with all your heart and soul, but don't make him responsible for your happiness. Don't shut him out of what's happening with you. When the time is right, talk to him the way you have to me. You took a big step in coming here today. You can do the same with Michael.''

Could she?

Frannie gave her hand a squeeze and then released it, and Polly grabbed a handful of tissues and blew her nose.

"I'll try."

Frannie smiled, blue eyes alight with pride and compassion. "You'll succeed. I know you will. With Clover, and with Michael, too. You're very strong, Polly. It's a pleasure to know you."

BUT IN THE WEEK that followed, Polly didn't feel strong. She took Frannie's advice and tried to give Michael loving support without pressuring him in any way. He was sweet and passionate, but preoccupied. She didn't ask what about, and he didn't volunteer. He was busy, as always, but now so was she.

One of the first things she did was go to her G.P., Fred Hudson, for a prescription for birth control. Allowing Michael to take full responsibility for her physical safety was childish and unfair...and she understood fully that was what she'd been doing. Another pregnancy wasn't an option, and although it hurt to give up that dream, she knew it was necessary.

The days were suddenly filled with the immediate problem of getting the house in reasonable order for prospective buyers. There were dozens of chores, large and small, that she'd ignored during the past months. The garage desperately needed cleaning. The upstairs bathroom had to be repainted, and now that she'd let the cleaning service go, she had the day-to-day housekeeping to do. Not to mention that she and Norah had to begin the formidable task of sorting through Isabelle's possessions.

And there was Clover to care for. Jerome was now in Rehab, but it would still be several weeks at least before he could go home and take on the care of his daughter.

After the visit to Frannie, the relationship with Clover gradually and subtly improved. There were still times when Polly counted the hours until she could hand Clover back to Jerome, but she also began to see the girl as quirky and tough, instead of just obstinate and sullen.

With the shift in Polly's attitude, Clover bloomed like a cactus flower. She began to smile at Polly more than she scowled; she even agreed to taste certain foods she'd refused before. Like Polly, Clover loved to draw, and she also adored rock and roll. Sharing those interests formed a tenuous bond between them.

With Clover's eager but dubious assistance, Polly tackled some of the chores that needed doing. She cleaned the garage and chose bedding-out plants for the backyard. Clover loved digging in the dirt, and showed good color sense when it came to arranging the flowers. But one disastrous attempt at letting the girl help paint the bathroom was enough. After an hour scrubbing paint out of

Clover's hair and off ninety percent of her body, Polly finished the job while her helper napped.

Friday morning, Clover even agreed to let Polly trim her hair. It took some convincing, and Clover was adamant—*no scissors*—but finally she perched nervously on a kitchen stool, wrapped in a bath towel, and Polly wielded the electric clippers she generally used to tidy the hair on Michael's neck.

Polly was a bit nervous herself, but she knew that almost anything she did had to be an improvement; Clover's hair was appalling, thin and straggly and lank, her overgrown bangs hanging in her eyes. At least they could tidy it up a little, Polly assured herself. She'd just trim the ends.

"Here we go, kid." Mentally crossing her fingers, she switched on the clippers and gingerly tackled the straggly strands at the back.

"Don't cut my ear, okay?" Clover's eyes were screwed shut and her voice was quavery with fear.

"I never would—I promise. Did someone nick your ear before?"

Clover nodded vigorously, and a huge chunk of hair Polly hadn't planned on cutting fell away. She pursed her lips and felt sweat trickle down her back.

Like it or not, the little trim had just turned into a major haircut.

"Once my mommy's friend? She cut my ear with scissors. Blood came out all over me and it really, *really* hurt. I cried and cried."

No wonder the poor kid was terrified of scissors.

Polly concentrated hard, and when she finished, she could hardly believe how successful she'd been. She grinned at Clover and crowed, "Look in this mirror, kid. You're nothing short of gorgeous. I should have taken up hairstyling as a career, judging by you."

Clover looked, and her blue eyes widened. She tipped her head one way, then the other, and a hesitant smile appeared.

Under the straggle she had a well-shaped skull, and the drastically short cut with the gamin bangs accentuated the offbeat angles of her face, making her eyes look bigger.

"Just wait till your daddy sees you. He's gonna say, who's this beautiful girl?"

Clover giggled. "My daddy always says that." She tilted up her chin in a decidedly feminine gesture, intrigued by her reflection.

"Of course he does." Only daddies could give their daughters that special sort of confidence, the kind that came with unconditional love. Her own father had done that for her, Polly realized, just as Michael had for Susannah.

Because of Jerome's acceptance and love, Clover didn't feel the need to make everyone like her, Polly suddenly realized. Now that Polly understood her own complicated feelings a little better, she was beginning to appreciate Clover's uniqueness.

The child still irritated her, but she also made her smile.

CHAPTER TWENTY

VALERIE TAPPED on the door of the examining room and opened it a discreet three inches. "Doctor, the radiologist is on line three."

Michael had been anxiously waiting all morning for the call, and he apologized now to the patient he was with and hurried into his office, where Duncan's file sat open on his desk.

The results of the CAT scan he'd ordered for the boy lay on top. He'd received them yesterday, and they showed clearly that the tumor was still growing. Michael had immediately called Sophie, and she'd brought Duncan into the office late yesterday afternoon.

Michael had then done a complete physical on the boy, and this time he'd discovered a minute lump in Duncan's left testicle that hadn't been there before. He'd ordered an ultrasound, asking that the radiologist phone him immediately with the results.

He took a deep breath and picked up the phone. So much depended on this call.

"Dr. Forsythe here."

"I have the slides in front of me for the ultrasound you ordered for Duncan Hendricks. They indicate a definite mass in the left testicle. The right testicle is clear.'' The radiologist's voice was professional and impersonal.

Michael thanked her and hung up, his mind in a turmoil.

What was going on here? His heart hammered and sweat broke out on his forehead. An astrocytoma never metasticized. It was localized to the head. If the lump in the testicle was malignant, had Duncan developed a different kind of cancer, or had he been misdiagnosed?

Either way, there was no question about what needed to be done. Michael picked up the phone and called St. Joe's, arranging for a surgeon to perform an incision biopsy immediately. Then he called Sophie and explained what the ultrasound had revealed and what was necessary.

Sophie was obviously agitated, but there were no hysterics. ''I'll take Duncan straight to St. Joe's,'' she promised. ''I'll just call Dad first and tell him what's happening. I'd like him and Morgan to be there.''

''Of course. I'll meet you at the hospital within an hour,'' Michael assured her.

The day had become a pivotal one in the lives of everyone who knew and loved little Duncan Hendricks.

THAT SAME DAY, Polly began to use Clover as a model for her drawing. She'd been struggling to capture images of Susannah, but the results were consistently stiff and artificial. Polly had torn up all the sketches in disgust. They didn't do Susannah justice.

Clover loved Polly's cosmetics, and as the little girl preened in front of the mirror that morning, experimenting with blush and a pot of lip gloss, Polly found a charcoal and a sheet of paper and sketched rapidly, not giving herself time to be critical. She needed practice, and Clover was available, preoccupied enough to sit still for a moment.

The result was surprising and exciting; Polly had captured in the child the quintessential, self-absorbed look any female has adorning herself.

By lunchtime Polly had two more quick, rough sketches. In one Clover had her fists under her chin, as she stared with a wistful expression out the window at the pelting rain. In the second she was sitting on the floor with her face screwed into an exaggerated scowl of concentration and her tongue between her teeth while she tried to tie her shoelaces.

That afternoon, Polly ignored the jobs that needed doing and instead worked furiously on developing the sketches while Clover slept. She couldn't tell whether they were good. She knew only that they were very different from any of her other work, much less structured, less precise.

And more alive, in some undeniable sense. They

had a presence all their own, just as Clover did. They were raw, full of energy, and when Polly looked at them a satisfaction filled her. She thought of the artist from Saskatchewan and her flower paintings.

Michael was very late getting home. He explained that he'd been at St. Joe's because of some emergency, then had had to deal with an office overflowing with patients waiting to see him. He was in a strange mood, laughing at Clover one moment and lapsing into reflection the next.

It was almost midnight before Polly finally found the courage to lead him into the studio to show him the drawings. It had taken her all evening to work up to it because she still couldn't decide if they were good or just plain awful.

He studied them, looking at them so long that her stomach churned with nervousness, but when he turned to her, the glow of admiration and respect in his eyes told her what the verdict was before he said a word.

"These are marvelous, Pol. They're the finest you've ever done. You've captured not just Clover here but the essence of every little girl." He reached out and pulled her into his arms. "Congratulations, sweetheart."

His pride in her was evident in his voice, in the way he kissed her. Polly's love for him welled inside her. She adored this generous man.

"I kept trying to draw Susannah," she admitted,

"but I couldn't do it anymore." She added slowly, "I think I've figured out why, too. You know when you love somebody, how you assume you know what they look like?"

Michael thought it over and nodded.

"Well, you're not really seeing them. You're seeing a picture of them that you hold in your heart," Polly explained. "With Clover, I'm free to draw exactly what's there."

Michael narrowed his eyes and stared at her. He didn't reply, and Polly wondered if it was because she'd mentioned Susannah. He was suddenly distracted again, far away, and although it hurt her, she repeated Frannie's words like a mantra.

Give him space. Love him with all your heart...

Change the subject. "Have you thought about where we'll move to when the house sells, Michael?"

"It's up to you, sweetheart." With a visible effort, he shook off whatever it was that had absorbed him, as Polly turned out the light in the studio. "Do you want to move into your mother's house, Pol?"

The absolute utter horror she felt was mirrored on her face, and it made him laugh. "Okay, I won't suggest that one again."

She collapsed against him, pretending to faint with relief, and he slid an arm around her. They made their way up the stairs and into their bedroom, shoulder to shoulder.

"I've talked to the real estate agent. We can buy a home in New Westminster that would be comparable to this but much less expensive," Michael said. "Real estate is lower there. The area is beautiful, with lots of heritage homes. And the drive isn't bad—I could be at my office in twenty-five minutes. Would you like that?" He loosened his tie, unbuttoned his shirt.

She was stripping off her shirt and jeans. "I don't know. I've been too busy to think about it much."

"We could take a drive out there Sunday, maybe pack a picnic and find a park Clover would like."

Polly lifted a fresh nightshirt from her drawer. "I'd love that, but I can't. Norah and I agreed to start going through Mom's house Sunday." She pulled the shirt on over her head and then flashed him an appreciative glance.

He'd taken off his trousers. All he had on were white briefs, and his tall body was dark and powerful, familiar and alluring.

"Why not come and help, Doc? Sorting through all that valuable stuff is gonna be loads of fun. We can probably have a yard sale, or even five or six."

He gave her a pleading look. "How about if I take care of Clover, instead? I'll bring you and Norah lunch, then I'll take all of you out to dinner when you're done."

Polly put her arms around him. "Coward."

He held her close and grinned down at her. "I

admit I'd rather do anything than sort through Isabelle's house. What can I do to make it up to you?''

''Oh, I can think of a few things.'' She moved against him, blatantly sexual, and his hands caught the hem of her nightshirt and tugged it up and off. He stripped off his briefs.

''Let's lock this door.'' His voice was husky. He tumbled her down onto the bed and straddled her, holding her between his thighs. ''Now, exactly what penalty did you have in mind, Mrs. Forsythe?''

She giggled and reached down a hand, cupping him, teasing. He was already hard, and he moved against her and made a guttural sound.

''I can tell this is going to be painful.'' He took her head between his palms and held it, caressing her face with his eyes and his thumbs, as if he couldn't get enough of looking.

''My beautiful, talented woman.'' He lowered his mouth to hers, kissing her slowly and deeply, as if they had all the time in the world. He went on and on kissing her, until she squirmed beneath him, every inch of her wanting more contact.

''I love you, Polly. I love you so much.''

The whispered words went straight to her heart, and she pulled him down until his body rested lightly on hers, warm skin to skin.

He knew her so well. He touched mercilessly until she writhed, begging him to fill her.

Only then did he slide into her. Nearly senseless with craving, she grasped his shoulders and curled her legs around him, holding him tight and moving frantically against him, and almost instantly her insides convulsed. She arched up, riding the spasms that consumed her, crying out with the force of her pleasure, and suddenly his careful control was gone.

With a single deep groan, he buried himself once and then again, and she felt his powerful frame shudder as a wild cry escaped his throat and ecstasy claimed him.

For long moments they lay panting, sweat-soaked and glutted with the aftermath of joy. At last, he rolled carefully to the side, still joined and holding her close.

"Is that it for the punishment, or am I going to have to do this again and again?" His mock plaintiveness made her laugh, and he laughed, too. They were quiet for a time, and Polly began to doze.

"Pol?"

His teasing whisper right in her ear brought her out of the dream that was half beginning.

"Mmm?" She gave him a groggy smile.

"Why is it that women go straight to sleep after sex?"

"I suppose you want me to tell you how fantastic it was, and that I'll respect you in the morning." Her voice was lazy. Her head was pillowed on his shoulder, and she felt cherished and safe and happy.

"It was fantastic, Pol. It was like old times."

She smiled and nodded and waited. She knew there was something he very much needed to tell her; he'd never have awakened her otherwise.

"Something happened today."

He had a kind of hesitant wonder in his voice, and suddenly she wasn't sleepy anymore.

"There's this patient of mine—a five-year-old named Duncan. He was diagnosed with astrocytoma, exactly what Susannah had."

Apprehension and compassion filled her, for the child and his parents but most of all for Michael and his having to face this trauma a second time.

He told her who the child was, and a new wave of sympathy washed through her. She'd met Luke and Morgan Gilbert. She'd liked Luke and adored his quirky wife.

"Sophie and Jason are so young, and Duncan's this cheerful little kid, always smiling."

Polly could tell by Michael's voice that he loved the little boy, and her heart contracted. A doctor's job was fulfilling, but it was also heartbreaking at times.

He was still talking about Duncan. "Having to listen to him tell me all the time that he was getting better, when I knew it was impossible, was agony."

Michael explained about the radiation not showing any improvement. "What you said about your drawing, about not really seeing something because it's too familiar, and you see what you expect? Well, I almost fell into that trap."

He told her about the new tests he'd ordered, the lump he'd discovered and the biopsy that had shown the mass to be germ-cell carcinoma.

"It's totally curable, Pol. The surgeon removed the testicle. Everything points to its being the primary source of the cancer. It'll take a couple of weeks to tell for sure, but there's a good chance the tumor in Duncan's head will shrink and eventually disappear." Michael was jubilant. "He's going to get well, Polly—I know he is. Duncan's always insisted he'd get better, and now I believe it, too."

Polly hugged him hard, thinking about the little boy. "But what about his losing the testicle? Will he still be able to have a normal sex life? What about kids?"

"He'll be perfectly normal. Fortunately, nature gave us a backup system, a second testicle. He'll be able to have a dozen kids if he wants. The thing is, if all goes well, he's going to live to grow up."

Polly sighed. "It's a miracle, isn't it?"

"It is." He was silent a long time. "I didn't know whether to tell you about him. There wasn't any miracle for Susannah." His voice was infinitely sad.

"The miracle was having her with us for the

time we did.'' Polly spoke slowly, trying to verbalize what was in her heart. She lifted her hand and stroked his cheek. "I'm glad you told me about Duncan. I'm so happy for him and his family. I don't compare one child with another anymore. Frannie helped me figure out why I was doing it.''

She explained about her feelings for Clover. "I guess I was afraid that if I let myself love her, I'd somehow forget Susannah. That's partly why I've needed to talk to you about her, so I could keep those memories alive.''

"I let you down in that way, sweetheart, and I'm sorry." He was contrite. "It's hard to explain, but I felt a complete failure when we lost Susannah. I'm a doctor. I was her father. Somehow I should have been able to save her. I felt you blamed me for not being able to.''

"Oh, Michael." Polly was astounded. "How could you think that even for a moment? You were a wonderful father. You're a fantastic doctor. I would never, never think that. I love you totally.'' There was a catch in her voice. "My only fear is that you'll stop loving me.''

He hugged her so hard she could barely breathe, and it felt like heaven. "I'm yours forever, Pol.'' There was a telltale huskiness in his voice. "Remember 'till death do us part'? Well, add et ceteras.'' He sucked in a deep, shuddering breath. "The pain of losing our daughter was so bad, I felt so ashamed I couldn't bear to even mention her name. Then Clover forced me to.'' He explained about the goldfish and the stories. ''And now, because of Duncan, it's finally dawned on me that lives aren't mine to save or lose. There's a difference between medicine and miracles, Pol. I forgot that, but I'll try from now on to remember.''

What had happened here tonight was a miracle, Polly realized. He was sharing his thoughts with her again. They were in each other's arms, the chasm between them bridged by so many kinds of love.

And as she slipped into sleep, she imagined she heard Susannah singing.

CHAPTER TWENTY-ONE

EARLY SUNDAY MORNING, Polly and Norah tackled Isabelle's house. They worked methodically, throwing out bags of junk, picking out usable clothing for the Goodwill, packing the items their mother had insisted they send right away. Isabelle had called Norah three times the past week with an ever-increasing inventory of things she couldn't live without.

"If this keeps up, our new Daddy Sanderson had better think about buying a trailer to tow behind his trailer," Polly declared, rooting through the debris in the bottom of her mother's closet. "I ask you, why would anybody keep five grocery sacks of ruined panty hose?" She tossed them into the garbage. "And shoes. She's got shoes in here that I remember her wearing when we were little kids. They're antiques, for Pete's sake."

"Give 'em to Goodwill." Norah was sorting through the stack of cardboard boxes in the corner. "Teens are crazy for that retro stuff these days." She poked through a gigantic shopping bag. "Mom must have kept every greeting card anybody ever gave her. Here's a whole pile we made when we were in grade school." She held one up. In garish purple crayon and less-than-perfect printing, it said "To the Best Mother in the Unaverse, a Guluxy of Love from Polly."

Polly couldn't remember making it. "I never could spell. And obviously I had no basis for comparison as far as mothers went."

Norah gave her a reproving look. "She did the best she could, Pol. Think back on times in your life when you messed up. Wouldn't you have done it different if you'd known better?"

"I guess." Polly nodded. Of course she would have. "I hate it when you're right. How come you're so nice and I'm so nasty?"

"It's genetic," Norah said in a sugary tone. "You got the looks—I got the personality."

Polly pitched a red Cuban-heeled shoe at her sister. She missed and they giggled. "Neither of us could ever throw straight. You find that darned scrapbook she's having such a fit over?"

"Not yet." Norah blew a strand of hair back. The rain had stopped and it was hot and muggy in the bedroom. "Mom couldn't remember exactly where it was."

"Big surprise there—her filing system isn't exactly the best. She happen to say what's in it that's so valuable?"

"Nope, only that she wants it right away."

"That and fifty million other things. It's probably a record of her amorous adventures."

"Could well be." Norah got to her feet. "I'm gonna fix us some cold juice before we melt up here. Try the dresser. Maybe it's in there."

Norah left and Polly glanced through the dresser drawers. The two on top were stuffed to bursting with underwear and an assortment of scarves, gloves and more panty hose, but in the bottom drawer was the green scrapbook, buried underneath three lacy shawls and four heavy sweaters. The smell of mothballs wafted up and nearly choked Polly as she lifted out the book. Curious, she flopped down on the bed and opened it, and her breath caught.

It was an Isabelle-style record of Susannah's life. On the first page was a picture she'd taken of Polly, nine months pregnant. Next to it was Susannah's birth announcement, and beneath it was glued a crumpled paper napkin with a clumsy tracing of a tiny baby foot, made in what looked to be lipstick. Beside that was Susannah's hospital photo. Her enraged and slightly goofy expression had always made Polly smile. She stroked a finger across the photo and turned the page.

There were more photos—Isabelle holding Susannah at the christening, Polly bathing her tiny daughter, a treasured one that Michael had taken of Susannah's first smile.

Each page held some memory of Susannah's short life seen through Isabelle's eyes. There were scraps of paper on which Susannah had scribbled, childish drawings she'd made, a lock of fine baby hair, school photos, misspelled notes she'd printed. There were several dried-up dandelions carefully wrapped in plastic, even a baby tooth taped to one page.

Isabelle had written on several pages, recording events that Polly had half forgotten, most of them mischievous.

There was the summer Susannah was three and had insisted on taking her clothes off as fast as Polly put them on; the time she'd scribbled with indelible markers on the wall Polly had just painted; the day she'd cut her own hair within a half inch of her scalp. Polly noted that many of the words Isabelle had written were only half-legible because they were stained with tears.

The final entries were agonizing for Polly. The last photograph was of Susannah wearing one of the outrageous hats Isabelle had given her after the radiation, when she'd lost her hair. She looked pale and sick, but her smile was wide and she was holding up a Western novel.

Polly recalled being furious with Isabelle over those paperbacks. "I want her to start reading worthwhile books, and instead she's addicted to those trashy stories of yours," Polly had stormed.

"Rubbish," Isabelle had responded. "Susie loves them. There's no harm in them at all."

And there hadn't been, Polly realized now.

Norah came in and handed her a tall, frosty

glass. "So, you found the darned thing." Norah reached for the book. "What's in it, anyhow?"

Wordlessly, Polly handed it over. Norah sat beside her on the bed and opened it.

"I should have known," she said softly. "Remember the ones she made for us, with our report cards and stuff in them? I remember how mortified you were because she wrote down when you got your first period. I couldn't understand it. I was green with envy because I thought I'd never get mine."

Polly had forgotten.

"Look at this." Norah tapped a photo of Susannah dressed in Isabelle's clothing, sitting on a stool with a pair of high heels dangling from her crossed legs, a pretend cigarette held nonchalantly between her fingers.

"You're right, you know. Mom isn't the best example in the world for a kid. If…when…Jerome and I are together, I won't want her teaching Clover how to smoke."

"Too late. She already has." Polly gestured at the scrapbook, struggling with the feelings it aroused. "But Mom must have really loved her."

"Loved Susannah?" Norah looked surprised. "Of course she did. She was so proud of her. She'd call me and say, 'Guess what Susie did. Listen to what Susie said.'"

"I suppose I always wanted her to be a typical mom. Then I wanted her to be a typical grandma, the sort who wears an apron and bakes cookies. Because she wasn't, I figured she didn't care.''

"Well, she did. She does.''

Polly finally believed it, and with the recognition came an easing of the anger and resentment she'd always carried toward her mother. It was a peculiar feeling, a lightness where there'd been weight. It would take some getting used to.

"Mom's not perfect. She's just Mom.'' Norah set the album aside. "I've come to think of her as a force of nature.''

Polly giggled. "Funny, that's exactly how I view Clover. How are you and Jerome getting on?''

"Good.'' Norah closed the scrapbook and set it carefully aside, not looking at Polly.

Polly raised her eyebrows and waited.

Norah blushed. "Better than good, actually. I've asked him to move in with me when he gets out of the hospital. He can't possibly manage those stairs at his apartment or take care of Clover by himself. I've got two bedrooms, so Clover can have her own room.'' She realized what she was admitting and turned magenta. "Some of the nurses at work figure I'm nuts because he doesn't have a job or any money or a house or anything.'' She stole a glance at Polly. It was obvious that whatever her sister said would matter a whole lot.

"Do you love him?'' Polly considered the way she felt about Michael. She'd love him if he was penniless…and they'd come very close to that because of Raymond Stokes. Funny, there were moments now when she thought Raymond had done them a favor. He'd forced them to recognize what was really important.

"I love him with all my heart." No one could doubt the sincerity in Norah's voice.

"And he loves you?" At times she'd doubted Michael's love, but Polly knew she never would again. They'd come through the worst together.

He'd told her once that when a broken bone mended it actually became stronger than before.

Norah nodded. "I know he loves me." She said it without even a trace of hesitation.

"Then that's all that matters."

Life wasn't easy. Maybe it had never been intended that way. The thing was to put your energy into what was important, and let the rest go.

Polly knew she'd never forget what she'd lost. But she'd learned to value what she had, and what she had was love, Michael's love, and the love of Susannah, forever.

EPILOGUE

THE OCTOBER MORNING was sunny and glorious, the Vancouver streets paved with gold and crimson now that the late-autumn leaves had fallen.

Singing at the top of his lungs along with the tenor on the stereo, Michael wheeled into his driveway, past the Sold sign the real estate agent had recently placed there. He switched off the ignition and bounded into the house, dodging the packing boxes that littered the hallway.

"Polly?" He planned to celebrate, kidnap his wife and Clover and take them out for the rest of the day, buy them food and flowers, a new dress each, whatever their hearts desired. "Sweetheart, where are you?"

She came trotting down the stairs, her gaze anxious and questioning. She knew he'd gone to the office this morning expressly to examine Duncan Hendricks. Three months had elapsed since the child's surgery, and although Michael was confident the boy was cured, the test results and this morning's examination would be concrete proof.

One look at Michael's beaming face, and she knew.

"He's okay? Duncan's okay?"

"More than okay." The exultation he felt was there in his voice. "The CAT scan shows the tumor's completely gone. All the neurological symptoms have disappeared. The scrotal surgery has totally healed. His hair's grown back. He's in kindergarten—he brought in the class turtle to show me."

"Hooray!" She flew into his arms and he kissed her hard. When the kiss ended she stroked a finger down his cheek and gave him a quizzical look. "And how does it feel to walk away and leave David in charge of your office?"

In September, after a month of getting to know each other and assessing whether they could work together, Dr. David Crystal had bought half of Michael's practice.

"It feels like the smartest thing I've done recently." It had provided a sizable chunk of money that, along with the proceeds from the sale of the house, once again ensured he and Polly were secure financially. Even more important, it gave Michael the time he now longed for, precious time to spend with his wife.

"He doesn't realize it quite yet, but David's no more in charge of that office than I've ever been. Valerie's the one who runs the place."

"I knew you'd finally figure that out. So with all these hours on your hands you think you can stand three whole weeks with me in Hawaii,

Doc?'' They were leaving in fourteen days, right after the move to the waterfront condo Polly had found and fallen in love with.

It was time to simplify their life, she explained. A house took so much of her energy, and she wanted to spend it on her art. She'd gathered her courage and shown the Clover drawings to Jade Crampton, at Concepts. Jade had suggested a showing at the gallery as soon as Polly had a large enough body of work.

Michael loved the condo; it was minutes from his office, and he'd always wanted to learn to sail. They'd discussed it, and if they decided someday to adopt a child, they could always buy another house.

''Three weeks with you are a stretch,'' he teased her. ''But if you promise to wear the bikini I'm gonna buy you today, I'll try not to complain too much. I'm taking you and Clover out to celebrate.'' He slid his hands down her body. ''Although if we didn't have Clover in residence, I'd take you to bed, instead. Where is the demon child?''

''Upstairs. We're finishing packing up Susannah's room. I told Clover she could have whatever she wanted. She's busy loading a couple of packing boxes.''

''She in a better mood today?'' Clover was staying with them for four days while Jerome and Norah were off in Seattle on a short honeymoon.

When they returned, they'd be moving into Isa-belle's house.

"I just try my best not to cross her," Polly said, and they laughed ruefully.

Furious and insulted when it dawned on her that she wasn't going along on the honeymoon, Clover had tested everyone's patience in every conceivable way. She'd thrown a grand-scale temper tantrum at the reception, refused to kiss her father goodbye and declared in a loud voice that she didn't like Norah. She'd bitten poor Eric Sanderson on the thigh when he'd tried to console her and deliberately spilled a glass of orange soda on Isabelle's white dress. And in the two days since the wedding, she'd been as contrary with both Michael and Polly as she could possibly be.

"Only forty-eight more hours and we get to hand her back to her daddy and her new stepmom," Polly noted with gleeful satisfaction. "I'm counting the minutes. C'mon, I'll change these jeans for something more suitable if we're having a celebration." She linked her hand with Michael's and they walked up the stairs.

The door to Susannah's room was closed, and Polly frowned. "It's awfully quiet in there. What the heck is she up to now?"

Michael opened the door.

The room was filled with sunlight, and it was a disaster. Pieces of jigsaw puzzle, mounds of clothing and dozens of crayons littered the floor. The delicate roses on the wallpaper were scribbled over with magic markers in garish shades of purple and green, and a feather pillow had burst. Feathers were scattered everywhere, and in the midst of it all was Clover, curled into an innocent ball, sound asleep in the middle of the bed, her thumb in her mouth.

"Why, that sneaky little...I can't *believe* this," Polly gasped. "I was gone only ten minutes."

Michael pressed a gentle finger to her lips, silencing her. Pulling her into the curve of his arm, he led her back into the hallway and softly closed the door.

"Let sleeping demons sleep, Pol." He bent his head and kissed her lips, then pretended to frown at her. "You're obviously overwrought, Mrs. Forsythe. It just so happens I have the perfect prescription for total relaxation. Come with me into the treatment area."

"Really, Doctor?"

He leered down at her. "Trust me, my dear."

They were both laughing as he led her down the hall to their bedroom.

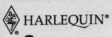
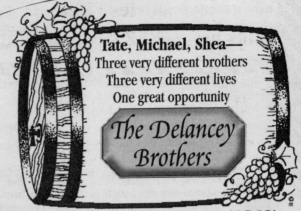

If you enjoyed what you just read,
then we've got an offer you can't resist!

Take 2 bestselling
love stories FREE!

Plus get a FREE surprise gift!

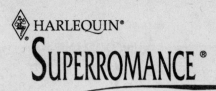

HARLEQUIN®
SUPERROMANCE®

From July to September 1999—three special
Superromance® novels about people whose
New Millennium resolution is

By the Year 2000: CELEBRATE!

JULY 1999—*A Cop's Good Name* by Linda Markowiak
Joe Latham's only hope of saving his badge and his reputation is
to persuade lawyer Maggie Hannan to take his case. Only Maggie—
his ex-wife—knows him well enough to believe him.

AUGUST 1999—*Mr. Miracle* by Carolyn McSparren
Scotsman Jamey McLachlan's come to Tennessee to keep the
promise he made to his stepfather. But Victoria Jamerson stands
between him and his goal, and hurting Vic is the last thing he wants
to do.

SEPTEMBER 1999—*Talk to Me* by Jan Freed
To save her grandmother's business, Kara Taylor has to co-host a
TV show with her ex about the differing points of view between men
and women. A topic Kara and Travis know plenty about.

By the end of the year,
everyone will have something to celebrate!

HARLEQUIN®
Makes any time special™

Super Summer Reading Blitz!

With the purchase of any three (3) Harlequin Superromance®
books, you can send in for a readingear™ Book Bag, retail
value $9.99 *or* with the purchase of any six (6) Harlequin
Superromance® books you can receive a readingear™ Sweatshirt,
retail value $25.00. Act now, quantities are limited.

Send in for your special gift today!

On the official proof-of-purchase coupon below, fill in your
name, address and zip or postal code and send it, plus $3.20
U.S./$4.50 CAN. postage and handling (check or money
order—please do not send cash) to Harlequin Superromance®
Summer Reading Blitz, to: In the U.S.:3010 Walden Avenue,
P.O. Box 9071, Buffalo, N.Y. 14269-9071; in Canada: P.O. Box
609, Fort Erie, Ontario L2A 5X3. Please allow 4-6 weeks for
delivery. Quantities are limited. The Super Summer Reading
Blitz offer expires August 31, 1999.

Harlequin Superromance® Summer Reading Blitz!
OFFICIAL PROOF OF PURCHASE

❏ Included are three (3) Harlequin Superromance® proofs-of-purchase
  Please send me a BOOK BAG   CSG3

❏ Included are six (6) Harlequin Superromance® proofs-of-purchase
  Please send me a SWEATSHIRT (one size)   CSG5

Name: _____

Address: _____

City: _____

State/Prov.: _____ Zip/Postal Code: _____

Account Number: _____

HARLEQUIN®
Makes any time special ™   097 KHJ